THE PRODIGAL SISTER

BOOKS BY G. WAYNE TILMAN

Ghost Posse

Zack Bodeway, Texas Ranger

The Legend of Bill Tilghman

Arizona Gunman

Six-Gun From Texas

The Blonde Murders

The Harani Trail (as AG Christian)

The MacLachlan Thrillers:

Honor Above All

Unsanctioned

Highlands Blood

Blood Sky

The Jack Landers Western Mystery Series:

Only the Blondes

Only the Vengeance

Only the Badge

Jack Landers, Sheriff

Heartland Deputy

Cinco Peso

Gun For Wells Fargo Series:

Gun for Wells Fargo

Wyoming Shootout

THE PRODIGAL SISTER

A NICK WOLF AND LOLA CALDWELL
MYSTERY
BOOK 3

G. WAYNE TILMAN

ROUGH
EDGES
PRESS

The Prodigal Sister
Paperback Edition
Copyright © 2023 G. Wayne Tilman

Rough Edges Press
An Imprint of Wolfpack Publishing
9850 S. Maryland Parkway, Suite A-5 #323
Las Vegas, Nevada 89183

roughedgespress.com

Paperback ISBN 978-1-68549-341-7
eBook ISBN 978-1-68549-340-0
LCCN 2023917211

THE PRODIGAL SISTER

1

Lola Caldwell stared at her partner, Nick Wolf. He was the kindest, deadliest man she had ever met, and she loved him with all her heart. He had just answered the phone in their business. Aaron and Ashley Investigations.

He had gone gray as the blood drained from his handsome tanned face. She saw tears welling up in his eyes. The eyes of a combat-hardened Army Ranger of the storied 75th Regiment. An awarded detective. And there he sat, speechless.

He fought to recover. Nick cleared his throat.

"*My* Angela Lynn?" His deep resonant voice a croak as he fought to control it.

"Your very own baby sister," came a female voice from the speaker to which he had switched the call. "From thirty-three years ago. When you, big brother, were not quite four, and I was one. When we were sent to different foster homes. I have looked for you for so long.

"Recently, you have gotten famous. So you hit the

Internet. Even the national news with your beautiful partner. So, my dream came true, and I found you.

"But my time may be running out fast. Unless you can help me. You are the only one I've got," she said.

"Angela Lynn...Angie...what do you go by as an adult?" he asked.

"Angie is fine."

"Angie, first off, exactly where are you?"

"I am in the south side of Chicago, not the safest of places."

"House? Hotel? Just a phone booth?"

"A hotel for now," Angie said, giving him the name, address and room number. Nick saw Lola writing it down.

"Are you safe there?" he asked.

"Maybe for now. I don't really know."

"Who is after you?"

"The mob. Which mob is the big question. Not the Mafia. More like a Russian mob. Somewhere in that part of the world. Bosnia."

"Why are these people after you, Angie?" he asked.

"It's a long story. Too long for right now. I need to get out of here before they find me. They would kill me, Nicholas. In a heartbeat."

"Are the police involved? This is Lola, Angie. I'm here to help."

"Hey, Lola. There may be some on the take with these guys, but no, they are not after me for any crime," Angie said.

"How much money do you have immediate access to?"

"About a hundred dollars cash and a credit card."

"Will the cash get you to O'Hare or Midway airports

okay from where you are? You should not use the credit card to avoid being tracked," Nick said.

"Yes. I can take the subway to either," Angie said.

"This is Nick's partner, Lola. Go to O'Hare and to the Western Union counter. Nick will wire you money to pick up there as long as you have a driver's license. As long as the DL is more than six months old, you can buy a plane ticket with cash, too," Lola said.

"How did you know all of this?" Angie asked.

"Internet. Just now. While you were talking."

"Okay. They may have a way to track your phone. What kind is it?" Nick asked.

"An old clunker flip phone. I have an iPhone, but it's turned off."

"Best yet. Harder to track. Will you be safe between the hotel and the subway?" Lola asked.

"The station is adjacent to the hotel. I guess so."

"Go, now, Angie. Pick up the money at O'Hare's Western Union counter. I will have it wired before you get off the subway. Are you still Angela Lynn Wolf?" Nick asked.

"Well it's arguable, but that's what it says on my license."

"Go now. Watch for tails. Report them to transit police if you see one. Can you send a text with your current phone?"

"Yes."

"Send me a text to the number I am getting ready to give you. It's my cell. That way, I will have your number. Once you get a flight to Tampa, Florida, or the quickest airport in the region to use, text me your flight number, airport, and arrival time. I will text you Lola's number, too.

"We will be waiting at reception at whichever airport."

"Nick?" she asked.

"What do you look like?"

"Let me tell you," Lola said.

"He's six feet, one hundred eighty pounds, light-brown short hair, killer blue eyes, and he is drop-dead gorgeous."

"I figured he had to be. He always was in my dreams. I am five-eight, long light-brown hair, average build, probably the same eyes. I will be wearing a light gray business suit with a matching skirt.

"I will text as soon as plans are set.

"Nicky? I think I may have called you that as a toddler, you know,"

"What, Angie?"

"I love you. I have wanted to say that for over thirty years."

"I love you, too, baby sister. I have looked and looked for you. Yet, you found me. But now, just go. The sooner you leave, the sooner we will see and protect you."

They could hear her sob over the speaker, joined by the tough former trooper leaning over Nick's desk.

"Bye!" and she was gone.

Nick's iPhone beeped in a minute. It was the text from Angie. He finally had a contact number for the name which had always been in his contacts. He put the two together and saved.

"What amount should we send her?" Lola asked, never anything less than half the equation which was Nick Wolf.

"I was thinking twenty-five hundred to get her here and have some pocket money."

Lola nodded and said, "Where should we put girl three in this sorority house?"

"I hadn't thought of that. Can we get another roll-away bed for the gym and she can bunk with Maria? Maria should be going away to the brief academy for officers from other agencies joining TPD soon. Once she has a job, she will be getting an apartment," Nick said.

"Oh, you so don't understand women. Which doesn't matter, except for me of course. As soon as Lottie and Carly move to the Keys, she is already thinking their room. I don't think she wants to leave us."

"Because she is new to this country and our law enforcement and we are her support group?" Nick asked.

"That, too. I think her interest may be more physical. I think Lottie has put some exploratory ideas in her head and she likes them," Lola said, amused.

"Exploratory? I don't understand."

"Here's a clue, detective. The operative word is 'three.'"

It hit Nick after a second. Lola did not need him to say anything. His face gave away nothing, his eyes were a full deposition on the matter to his partner.

"We need to convince her to get an apartment. I am going to Publix or Walgreens or somewhere to send Angie the money and separate myself from this disturbing conversation."

Lola leaned down and gave him a long kiss. "That's my boy," she said.

Lola knew she would have to control the three frisky young women staying with them for a while. But that did not mean she could not have fun watching the situation unfold. It would be a hoot to see.

Nick drove to the nearest Publix supermarket. The Western Union area was part of Customer Service. He sent the twenty-five hundred to his long-lost sister. *What a suck term! She had not been lost. She just was at a place or places unknown to him. In reality though, she had been lost to him for over three decades. Years where they could have enjoyed the simplest of things. Where he could have protected her from danger, like whatever she is now facing. He was a protector by nature. A sheepdog who protected the mass population of sheep from the wolves circling. Whether wearing a helmet or a badge, he was a protector. A protector who could not protect his own baby sister. Until now. Woe unto whoever was after her. Whatever he had to do to take them down, he would do it. With a great deal of malice of forethought. Just like he did to every single person who had tried to hurt his Lola.*

Angie texted her airline and flight number and thanked him for the money. She said she would pay him back. He did not respond. There was no way he would accept money from her.

"Honey," Nick said to Lola after wiring the money and a few minutes at his desk. "Look at this on my screen for a minute."

She walked over and saw a bid for his Jeep from a national car dealer known for its clean, no-hassle sales of late models only.

"Wow. Who would have thought Ruby would be so valuable?" she asked.

"I know. We've been talking about me getting a car like yours which we can actually use on the highway. I have been doing some comparisons when I was flying. This same dealer has a two-year-old model of what I think would be a good solution. It's a BMW 330i. If they stick with the bid, and they almost always do, I think I could write a check out of my personal checking for about what I sent Angie and drive home with the Beemer today."

"We have time. Let's go test drive it. Lottie and Carly will be back shortly. Let's go when they get back," Lola said, always excited about driving something new.

Nick went to the gun vault and removed the title for the paid-for Jeep Rubicon and slipped it in a thin leather case with his checkbook. He knew, by trading, the tax would be on the difference and much less in the long run than selling the Jeep and buying something else.

It took them forty minutes to get to the dealership after the two house guests arrived. The salesperson took the keys and printed bid and delivered them to their appraiser so he could examine the off-road champ.

As they knew from the ad for the BMW they printed off the dealer's site, it was maroon with saddle leather. It was Teutonically plain but had a classic look for a mid-size sedan. Nick asked Lola to test drive so he could observe and "feel" the way it handled and rode. Mainly, he knew she was itching to drive it.

Out of sight of the dealer, she saw a break in traffic, pulled over, stopped, then accelerated. A bit over five seconds to sixty.

"Good enough for government work," Nick said as he looked over at her instead of the dial of his Luminox SEAL dive watch.

She drove it for fifteen minutes or so in mixed traffic. Other than handling and acceleration, her favorite thing was the blind spot monitor. The vans had it, but their personal cars were before the safety feature became available.

"What's the top speed in your research?" she asked.

"North of one-fifty governed."

"Okay. Let's get it. I like it already," Lola said. "I may have to drive it a lot," she said, as a reality and not something she was questioning.

"What's mine is yours," he said.

They returned to the dealership and found the bid on the Jeep had not changed. The sales associate wrote up the deal and got it approved with Nick's local check without any back and forth with a sales manager.

Nick had the license tags registered in both names, unlike how their two vehicles were currently. The plates were installed. Lola noted the fact and did not say anything. She did smile, however.

He patted Ruby on the hood a bit sadly as they walked over to the low mileage two-year-old BMW, key fobs in both of their hands.

"Maybe you should test drive it home, huh?" Lola asked.

"Ya think?" he said as he was already heading for the driver's side.

Lola did not bother to ask if the vehicle change had anything to do with the arrival of his sister later tonight. She knew it didn't. It was just not the way her Nick operated.

"How much do you like driving my GTI?" Lola asked.

"As much as I dislike driving a van," he said.

"Good." She stretched her long form and wiggled her butt on the caramel-colored leather seat.

"You remind me of the way Finn rubs his face against things to claim them," Nick observed.

She purred. Rather seductively. She said nothing else and began to set the instruments on the dash monitor and pair their phones into the system.

"You know, this car and paying off the house and office. You have passed some major life milestones. You have an almost-wife, three daughters, a successful business."

"Yep! Terrifying isn't it?" he said.

"Bull! The only thing which terrifies you is when I am in dire danger...and now when your sister is."

"Don't forget global warming," he said, unable to resist it.

"Of course. And global warming. World peace. All that stuff.

"But seriously. These are major things you have accomplished in...well, the last week."

"None was part of any master plan. Opportunities for things we talked about just fell into place. I didn't just grow up on you. I am still your boy toy."

"Thank the good Lord, you are still my boy toy. I don't have the time with our schedule. keeping the three house guests and keeping my mother from snatching you to break in another boy toy. Besides, nobody could top the one I have," she said, her jests turning serious at the end.

"You are right. I really have a lot on my plate. Much of which is pretty delectable."

"Thin ice, Wolf."

He drove on, enjoying the car and, for once, almost ignoring his partner. Almost, but not quite.

———

They arrived at Tampa International early and went to the cell phone area. Large electronic billboards showed flight statuses.

"We sat closer in the Jeep," Nick noticed.

"We also got bugs in our teeth."

"Part of the Jeep experience. Nobody in a Jeep will do the Jeep wave to us in this. I bet BMW drivers don't wave at each other," Nick said.

"In patrolling the highways for a decade, I admit I never saw BMW drivers wave at each other. I seemed to have written speeding tickets for a larger proportion of them than other drivers. VWs, too.

"Think it's a German car thing? Or just an 'I'm going to drive this until I can afford a Beemer' thing?" Nick asked.

"No clue. Probably not worth worrying about solving. Now I drive a VW and you drive a BMW. We both drive fast. Because we were cops. In our cases, it has nothing to do with the car brand."

"I wonder how we will hit it off?" Nick mused aloud.

"You and Angie?"

He nodded.

"Like you saw each other yesterday. Like the separation at your parent's death never happened. You watch!" Lola said.

"I hope so, Lola. I sure as hell hope so."

They watched the flight number on the board change to landed. She might still be twenty minutes from the curb, depending on how far back she was seated, restroom needs, or whether she had to claim luggage.

She called fifteen minutes later with her arrival door under the airline's name.

"Lola and I will be there in maybe five minutes. We will be in a maroon BMW."

"I can't wait, Nick. I don't think I have ever been so excited," Angie said.

They drove over and stopped at the door. In the

crowd was a beautiful woman who absolutely had to be Angie. She was a female version of her brother. The resemblance took Lola's breath away.

"If the brunette is not your sister, we will take her anyway. She would be so easy to pass off as your twin," Lola said.

The brunette spotted the maroon car, broke into a tearful smile and ran towards the man who limped as fast as he possibly could around the hood of the car to embrace her. They just stood there, in a strong embrace. Lola had to intercede with the airport parking guy and explain why they were delaying getting in. He nodded, smiled and walked over to move another parker along.

Nick walked her back to the car and Lola embraced her almost as long as Nick put her carry-on in the trunk he had never opened. It was a good trunk, he thought. Today. This moment. This place. Any trunk would be a good trunk.

The two women got in, Lola opting for the rear.

"I would have recognized my Nicky anywhere!" Angie told Lola.

"I told you he was gorgeous, didn't I? But it seems to me it's kind of like looking in a mirror. You are gorgeous, too. In all the same ways Nick is."

"We have to get the hell out of here. Three of the Bekrić crew got on my plane. If they saw me, they did not make eye contact. I got on first and was seated in the rear. They were late and separated in the front. But they are here. That's for damn sure."

"Okay. Let's get out of Dodge right now. They have to get a rental, which will put them walking across this roadway to the rental counters.

"Let us tell you about what you are heading into. Angie, we have our office in the downstairs of an old St.

Pete two story. The living quarters are upstairs, along with one very busy bathroom.

"Lola, why don't you tell Angie about the bunch of sisters, or nieces or whatever, she is getting ready to inherit?" Nick said.

Lola did and did not hesitate to mention how they were all hitting on her brother constantly.

"And you put up with it?" Angie asked.

"You will too, it's so hilarious to watch!" Lola laughed.

"I'll get a hotel. There has to be one close by."

"Of course you won't. For one thing, we have thirty-some years to catch up on. And we both will defend you against anyone who wishes you harm," Nick said.

"Even the Bosnian mob?" Angie asked seriously.

There was dead silence for a moment.

"We have a bit of experience with the Bosnian mob. I was trying to negotiate with a Bosnian in Honduras a few days ago as he pointed a submachine gun at me from a few feet away," Lola said.

Stunned more by the mob familiarity even than Lola's precarious competition situation, Angie asked "What happened?"

Lola looked at Nick's face in the rearview mirror. He looked back at her and nodded.

"Nick is a former sniper. He shot him between the eyes with a high-powered rifle from a distance away."

Angie did not say anything. Finally, she took a deep breath to speak.

"We have to talk."

"We will, dear sister. First, we will watch our sixes, get you home, figure out the sleeping arrangements, and introduce you to the ladies. Two exotic dancers and one detective."

Angie tightened and released. Lola from the driver's side of the back seat only saw the reaction because it was so much like one Nick would do.

One of the career descriptions had struck a responsive chord with her. Lola wondered whether it was the dancers. Or worse, the police detective.

She suspected the imminent meeting with Maria, Lottie, and Carly would suggest the answer.

"Do you have boarders in a big house?" Angie asked.

"Not really. We have hopefully temporary guests. All are related to a big case we just did in Roatan, Honduras. We helped bring down a resort which catered to high-dollar pedophiles. One dancer was there, the other was her college and dance roommate in a club south of DC," Lola said. There was the faint reaction again, Lola noted.

"The detective is a friend we met on Roatan. Things could be getting dicey down there with an upcoming election and she wanted to come here for a job. So, Nick introduced her to some key people and one, in Tampa, hired her. She's just waiting for a transitional training course and to begin before finding an apartment. We hope!"

No reaction. Interesting, Lola thought.

"And they are all in love with my brother?"

Lola laughed.

"More like there's a lot of estrogen in the air!" Lola said.

"It's all just Lola's perception. It's really because I am a father figure and a really nice guy," Nick said.

"Yeah, right!" his partner murmured loud enough for the other two to hear clearly.

"And it doesn't make you jealous, Lola?" Angie asked again.

"Not in the least. If they think they are competition, they are sadly mistaken."

"Finally something I can agree with," Nick said, this time seriously.

"Nicholas, I will make up my own mind on the matter after close observation," his sister said.

"When do you want to give us an executive summary, or even the eventual detailed summary on your threat situation? We want to be prepared for us, our office manager who is Lola's mom, and our guests to repel boarders if necessary," Nick said.

"I may have foisted a load of hurt on you. I am so sorry."

"You came to the only place you could. It also happens to be the best place. We will protect you," Lola observed.

"Okay. Quick version. Longer one later. At two, I was adopted out of foster care. My new family, the Sinclairs, moved from Florida to Kentucky for job reasons. I had a good life with them. They were kind, loving people. I started college at the University of Kentucky in Lexington, where we lived. My stepfather got into financial difficulties and couldn't pay off a loan shark. Both were killed in an auto accident. I have always thought the accident was a mob hit. Déjà vu our parents. At nineteen, I had to leave the UK and find work. This is going to make you think less of me, but I became an exotic dancer. I made a lot of money. Most was tax-free.

"I did it for years and socked away the money with an investment adviser. The Bosnians owned the club chain. I progressed to be a headliner at their signature club in Chicago. I was already thirty-one, but I was still able to draw them in.

"The assistant manager was a hunk. Muscular, bald,

short beard. He was funny and sweet to me. I married him and he had me named "talent" manager and made me stop dancing. All of a sudden, he did not want anyone to see me but him.

"His boss, his uncle, who was named Ibro Bekrić, didn't like me not pulling in the money. They quarreled, and it led to a fight. Bekrić won easily, which surprised me. I had to take my husband, Adin Dedić, to the hospital. He had three broken ribs and a broken cheekbone. He went back, and I was forced back to totally nude dancing. I was startled Ibro was so harsh on his own nephew. It was as if he did not like his nephew.

"Nick, are you ashamed of me now and wish I'd never shown up?" she asked shakily.

"Not in the least. I am in love with someone sitting in the car who has a long tenure in nude pole dancing."

Angie looked back and over to Lola, who smiled and said nothing. *Long tenure, my ass,* she thought without verbalizing it. *But it might become long tenure, given half a chance,* she thought.

"Go ahead, honey," Lola prompted.

"Okay. Over the last year or so, things got very tense at the club. The Bekrić's older brother was the owner of a bunch of clubs back east and somewhere in the Caribbean. He tried to put a lot of pressure on him as revenues declined. The lead club was in a dangerous part of Chicago, as if the whole place wasn't dangerous enough. I saw my husband work over several people for just touching a dancer instead of just tucking a twenty in her G-string. Most recently, I saw him beat a man to death in the alley behind the club.

"Others from his little group stood around smiling. Just before it was over Ibro Bekrić came out the door and saw the man was dead. Bekrić said 'get a car, put him in the trunk and take him to the usual place. Make sure you are not seen.'

"That night I told my husband I could not live in these conditions. He was a murderer and apparently others at the club were, too. I said I was leaving.

"He looked me in the eye with a look which chilled me to the bones.

"You leave me, and we will track you down and kill you a little bit at a time, bitch. You are my wife and my property. Leave, and you will regret it until your last screaming sound.

"I don't know if nonconsensual rough sex is rape under the law when you are married, but it's what I got. He had been drinking and passed out afterwards.

"I sneaked out a few days later and did what I had been planning since I located you on the Internet a week before. I checked into a hotel and called you."

Nick and Lola thought for a second, both the same thoughts but soundlessly.

"Angie, we know the name Bekrić. You reacted when we talked about the Bosnian mob a few minutes ago.

"A man named Luka Bekrić ran the operation including Lottie and Carly's club south of DC and a pedophile place on the Honduras island, Roatan. We suspect he is under federal investigation now. His men, one of whom I shot to death, were behind several murders under investigation by Honduran authorities. One was the murder for hire of a US Congressman. I suspect this family criminal enterprise is farther flung than you realized.

"It's a strange coincidence you came here now. If I was not so certain you really are the sister I have yearned to see for so many years, all sorts of red flags would be up with both Lola and me," Nick said.

"I should never have put you in the middle of this. They may come to your house. I am so sorry, Nick. And Lola too! And Luka is the brother I just referred to. They are close and the businesses are all interrelated."

"We were already in the middle of it. So is each of the young women at the house. If they come, we will be ready. I will also warn a friend of mine with the state's investigative agency.

"I think it's important to keep your married name out of this for now. From the driver's license you used to claim the Western Union funds, I take it you never used it legally?" Nick asked.

"No, I didn't. The marriage was only mildly abusive until a few days ago, but I never was comfortable with the situation, so I kept my name. Adin never knew the difference," Angie said.

"Angie, we are almost home. Since they all have a history with some faction of this bunch, especially Luka Bekrić in Virginia, south of DC. I think it would be only right for you to share your story with our house guests, don't you, Nick?" Lola said.

"I'm big on keeping things on a pure need-to-know basis. I think, however, the ladies have a valid need to know why we are hardening the house and so forth. They may elect to move out earlier. We may want to set up a remote workstation at your mother's also, Lola.

"Angie, are you good with sharing all of this with the 'girls,' as Lola's mother, Erica, refers to them?" Nick asked.

"I don't see why not. I brought all of this on top of them."

"You need to forget the guilt, honey. They were already involved and so were Lola and me. We have spoken several times about potential retribution by Bekrić.

"Just out of curiosity, can you shoot?" Nick asked.

"I have never even held a gun."

"Excellent!"

She looked at her brother as if he was crazy.

"Which means you don't have any bad habits. I have an instructor friend who is excellent. Legal ramifications of deadly force, how to hold, trigger press, sight picture, and most importantly the Four Rules of Safety."

"Can't you teach me? And what are the four rules?" Angie asked.

"It's always better to have a professional instructor than a family member. The rules are keep the gun pointed in a safe direction, treat all guns as if they are loaded, keep your finger off the trigger until your sights are on the target, and be sure of your target and what's behind it."

"Logical. Are all the girls armed? I suspect Lola is. How about the detective?" Angie asked.

"Probably not," Lola said. They wouldn't have let her bring a gun in from Honduras and she has not been issued one yet at Tampa Police Department."

"Do we have enough guns to protect the place?" Angie asked, sounding more and more like Nick's sister.

"We probably do. We are short our two main ones. Lola and I each shot someone in Boca Raton the other day, so our primary sidearms are at the Florida Department of Law Enforcement, or FDLE, Forensics. They may be in Boca or maybe in Tallahassee. Maybe I should call our main man there and see if he can speed up the process," Nick said.

They came in, the PIs escorting Angie as bodyguards might, covering her with their bodies, ready to shoot at the first sign of a threat.

They saw Erica's car, so they knew the tribe had assembled

All of the guests were gathered when they arrived home. Erica had driven over from her beach condo out of curiosity. Lola had already told her the story about how Nick and his toddler sister had been separated years ago.

Angie got a warm greeting. Erica already had coffee and a variety of alcoholic and non-alcoholic cold drinks set out with snacks.

The two could have been twins when they walked through the door. Even Erica was awed, though Lola had forewarned her by text.

"Have I got a dance career for you!" Carly exclaimed when she saw the tall, statuesque Angie.

"Have I got a dance story for you," Angie replied and began to relate her life in quick time from when she and Nick were separated thru adoption, moving to Kentucky, losing another set of parents and becoming an exotic dancer from age nineteen to thirty-two.

"So you were an exotic dancer at a Bekrić club for thirteen years? Lottie and I began dancing at the Bekrić club in Northern Virginia about seven years! We did dance, strip, and pole. What did you do?" Carly asked.

"The same. Then, I saw my husband commit a murder in the alley behind the club. It was the most unnecessarily violent thing I could ever imagine. He was cheered on by his fellow Bosnians.

"I complained and told him I could not live with a murderer. He told me if I left, he or the group of them would track me down and murder me by rape and torture.

"I found Nick, then Lola on the Internet. They had, in the last year or so, become so famous the Internet had page after page on them. They helped me to leave.

"They don't know this yet, but as I slipped into the subway station, I saw a carload of them screech up and run into the hotel. The hotel nobody was supposed to know I was staying. Somebody, probably a crooked cop on their payroll, told them I used my credit card to check in. I don't think they would have the ability to monitor credit cards.

"I took the Blue Line train to O'Hare, picked up the money Nick sent me at Western Union, bought a train ticket and here I am. I always used my maiden name. Adin and I had some sort of wacky Eastern European wedding without an Illinois marriage license, so I figured I was not legally married anyway.

"I also had three of them on the plane with me. They are following me somehow."

Her audience sat, absorbing the tale she spun. Lola sought inconsistencies and found none. She felt her kind of sister-in-law was telling the truth.

"Okay, ladies. We are hardening up. I don't know how long each of you is planning to stay. You are welcome to stay until you have a safe place to go. An apartment in Tampa." Nick looked at Maria. "A house in Key West," looking at Lottie and Carly.

"Erica, I want you to stay here with us until we assess the threat is over, then we will help Angie start a new life."

"You have a pretty full house, Nick. Where are you going to squeeze another person?" she said.

"I don't know Erica. What I do know is we will adapt and overcome. It may be blankets on a sofa or sleeping bags on the floor. We can do this. If an attack comes

Lola and Maria and I want to know where everybody is," Nick said.

"Everything I am going to say and all we are going to do on an immediate basis is to lead us to a more permanent plan. This is all interim. Quite frankly, Lola and I don't know what the final plan is going to look like. Maybe we stay here, maybe we all go into seclusion for a while," Nick said, with his partner nodding supportively.

"Does this mean we have to hunker down until this is over? No restaurants, no clubs, no runs?" Lottie asked.

"No," Lola responded. "It means early teen rules. Mommy, Daddy and big sister," she said nodding to Maria, "will take you and pick you up everywhere. You want to go for a run? We will take you across town to the Pinellas Trail or somewhere."

"Maria, I take it you did not bring any guns from Honduras?" Nick asked.

"No, I could not transport any in."

"Okay. Let Lola and me do an out loud inventory of weapons. We both have our primary handguns in a forensic unit, probably in Tallahassee."

"Why?" Carly asked.

"Because we both shot people in Boca Raton when two hitmen descended on Lottie's house there," Lola answered.

"You shoulda seen Lola clock the guy who came inside. She popped him in the chest twice and then between his eyes!" Lottie said with enthusiasm.

"Anyway. You shoot somebody, the police have to analyze your gun to make sure it was what was used. Kind of unnecessary in both cases in Boca, but still procedure," Nick said.

"Okay. We have two Sig 9mm's. Great guns, not my

first choice in this kind of close quarters battle or CQB. Right caliber, but their small size makes them harder to shoot than a service-size pistol.

"We have one Glock 19, which fits the bill. We have one .357 Magnum revolver. Great stopping power but only six cartridges. We have one five-shot snub nose. Close and dirty, but not CQB material.

"We have two short pump shotguns. Devastating but hard to shoot in a multiple adversary gunfight. We have two rifles. A semiautomatic Ruger carbine and a bolt action in .308. It's a battle worthy caliber in a good but slow-firing and limited-capacity rifle.

"Everything I have mentioned is fine for general PI use. Holding off multiple attackers...not so much."

"What do you think we really need, honey?" Lola asked.

"At least three more long guns in semiauto. Either M-16's or AK-47's. I lean towards the latter.

"You find 'em and I will write the check," Lottie offered.

"Thanks. I think we can find them, hopefully at the same place. If we buy them under the PI firm banner, we won't send up red wacko flags. Let me poke around tomorrow.

"I had a great detective sergeant with St. Pete Police who was one of my human trafficking task force guys. He hates traffickers. His name is Joe Horner. I will try to meet with him tomorrow ASAP and fill him in. I am not sure I want patrolmen increasing their patrols here. They are good guys, but not for machine gun-armed gangsters. If they had subguns in Roatan, they might have tanks here. Who knows what they checked in their luggage on the plane. I will talk with him and maybe he will run it up the ladder. This is their jurisdiction and we owe it to them to be aware.

"The big thing, the uppermost thing when we gun-up this house is rule 4 for gun safety Nick said earlier to Angie. Always be sure of your target and what or who is behind it," Lola said. "We don't want to shoot each other by mistake or shoot through a wall and kill one of us on the other side. Got it? Also, I will make sure by this time tomorrow everyone will have a high-power small flashlight to keep with them at all times. It's indispensable at night and a good defensive weapon to hit with anytime."

All nodded. Whether they would remember everything when the shit hit the fan might be another thing.

"For now, I am going to give Maria the Glock 19. She is familiar with it and trained with one very similar. Over the next day or so, I will try to take you others to the range and do a familiarization short course with whichever gun you are assigned.

"Lola, who was a ten-year state trooper, or I will be at the house at virtually all times. If we are not, Detective Maria will be in charge. One of us will escort you for groceries, running, whatever. You are not being treated like juveniles. You are being treated like VIP protectees, okay?" Nick said.

"I want to be downstairs as first level of security. SWAT or military operators might come in through an upstairs window. These guys seem to be mainly knee breakers from our experience with them so far. They will bust in through a door. I want to be there if they do.

"The most firepower we have currently is the Ruger Mini-14 with thirty-round mags. Which is what I want on door duty.

"Another thing. I'd like us to keep the alarms on 'Stay'

even during the day when we are in the house. It's just extra protection, pain in the butt or not. We have not installed perimeter cameras here yet, and I am kicking myself for it.

"Angie, I have a Faraday bag in the van. I am going to get it. Do you know how to check your iPhone to see if your Find My Phone is activated?" Nick said.

"Not really."

"Lola, would you show Angie how to do it? I'm not sure, but the feature may work when the phone is off."

Nick found the bag which blocked radio waves and precluded anyone tracking a phone by Find My, or any other conveyances.

"Nick, her husband is listed in Family in the Find My page," Lola said.

"Alright. Cancel him and turn the phone off. Angie, put the phone in this bag, which will prevent tracking. Keep it there until the Bosnian threat has subsided.

"We will get you a clean burner phone with an area code from nowhere near here or Chicago," Nick said, adding, "Throw away your flip phone." One source of future tracking was eliminated. It had been enough to get them here. He would do a deeper dive for more trackers later.

"Other sleeping arrangements. Erica, please sleep with your daughter in our bed. The rest of you stay where you are. Angie, we have a pretty comfortable cot in the van. I will bring it in and bunk you with Maria in our workout room where she is now.

"As a primary target, Maria provides you the protection of a trained police officer with good experience in violent situations. I might add, she saved my life on a beach in Roatan from a corrupt cop who murdered a US Congressman and his bodyguard in front of us and was getting ready to take me out. She will forever be my hero," a pronouncement which made the detective swell with love and pride and no embarrassment whatsoever.

"Lola, anything you want to add?" he said.

"No. Obviously, this will be an evolving situation, but I think this is a great start. Maria, how about you?" Lola asked.

"It's good. We are blessed with being with the two best people I can imagine for something like this."

"Okay. Let's rock and roll. New sheets for our bed, and Maria—how about you take the Mini-14 and watch my back while I bring the cot in from the surveillance van for Angie?" Nick asked.

Shortly after, sleeping arrangements were set and occupied. Though the old locks were weak, they provided some noise security since someone breaking in had to burst them. Bedroom doors were closed and locked.

The house resumed its usual late-night solitude. Nick and Lola had left the glass front door in place. It enabled them to see clients and deliverymen approaching from their desks.

As he laid there in his boxers on the too-short sofa in the former living room, now office, he regretted the decision. A heavy hurricane front door with three dead-bolts would be much more difficult to breach.

He heard one of the old floorboards creak on the stairs. Nick switched from shooting pioneer Jeff Cooper's Condition Yellow to Red. He slowly picked up the short rifle resting on the floor beside him.

"Nick?" he heard a whisper. Female, but not Lola.

"Over here," he said softly.

Maria appeared, Glock in a safe position. She wore nothing but a short tee shirt. Short in that it only came to her navel.

"I just wanted to say there's no place I'd rather be than here with you."

"Lola and I are glad too, honey. But go back to bed and get some rest in case everything gets real busy."

She leaned over and kissed him and quickly stood back up before he could stop her.

She turned and padded to the stairs and disappeared upwards into the darkness as silently as she had come.

We need to get her settled in her new job and a new apartment he thought. As pretty and sexy as she was, he did not need this. Not at all.

The night passed quietly but only too quickly. Nick pulled on jeans and a shirt and appeared in a kitchen already filled with too many chefs. Erica was in her glory, fixing a breakfast worthy of a church social. Finally, she shooed the tee shirt-only crowd upstairs to await her call.

Nick was glad to see his night visitor had changed shirts. He could tell because her whole bottom and front side were hidden, unlike six hours earlier when they were intentionally exposed for the world, or rather him, to see.

He still had St. Petersburg Detective Joe Horner's mobile number in his contacts on the phone.

Joe must have had his, too, because he answered with "Damn, Nick. A bear? From a foot away? Did the news get it wrong?"

"They did, Joe! I stuck the barrel in his mouth. Much closer than a foot. He had bad bear breath so close, too!

"How are you?" Nick asked.

"Fine! What can I do for you?"

"I wanted to give SPPD a heads-up on something. And I always consider you to be my contact there."

"What's up?"

"Did you happen to see about the pedophile case in Honduras and the murder of a congressman?"

"I did on the news. I guess there is some sort of Bosnian connection?" Joe Horner asked.

"Exactly. Which is why I was calling. You know how we talked over lunch in the task force days about no such thing as a coincidence? Well, I have a really big one.

"Lola and I were there in Honduras after someone who ended up being an undercover at the pedo resort. We had tracked her down from one of the Bosnian clubs in Northern Virginia. I had to kill one of the Bosnian hitmen who arranged the congressman's death. They are not too happy with Lola and me, I suspect. They are after the undercover, who is here staying with us on Central Avenue for now. cops.

"I'm going to drop back thirty-plus years for a minute. Our parents were killed in a car crash in Tampa. I was almost four and my sister was one. We have been looking for each other unsuccessfully ever since.

"Because of my recent fame or infamy, she found me two days ago and begged for help.

"Here comes the impossible coincidence, Joe. She was employed at one of the Bosnian's clubs in Chicago and married to a relative of Bekrić, the owner. Same family which is after the undercover and us from the Honduras case. My sister witnessed a murder and wanted out. Her husband said he would personally kill her. She called me and ran. As she left, a carload got out and entered her hotel. We thought the only way was tracking her credit card. Now we know her phone was tracked, too. She suspects police corruption in the

Windy City and saw it firsthand at the club. They were on her plane. It is unclear whether they saw her."

"Yeah. Among the few left after police defunding in a murder capital..." Joe interjected, then more to the point said, "So it's definite they are here."

"Yes. The other person here at our house on Central Avenue is a former detective from the Honduran National Police Major Crimes Unit. She is switching over to TPD. The big case she worked on was, you guessed it, the pedo resort owned by the Bekrić crime family," Nick finished.

"Let me see if I have the bottom line. You think, with cause, some Bosnian organized crime hitmen have come to St. Pete. Their five targets, including you and your partner, are all at your place on Central Avenue. Is that about the sum of it?"

"Pretty much, Joe."

"Would you like increased neighborhood patrols, Nick?"

"No. These guys had submachine guns on the resort island of Roatan. Imagine what they would bring down from Virginia. I don't want to see a patrol officer alone in a solo cruiser and armed with a handgun take on a bunch of these thugs. He or she wouldn't have a chance. Risking increased patrol is not worth the probable outcome."

"I could instruct 9ll for any shots fired in your neighborhood to send our and Pinellas County's SWAT for response and put patrol units on standby," Joe said, thinking out loud.

"Seems reasonable. My fear, other than getting machine-gunned, is if it goes up the ladder at SPPD, some administrator will overreact and get a shitload of people killed. Probably needlessly.

"I am working on some alternative plans, hopefully to take the threats out of the area.

"I know you or anyone else there at SPPD who is aware is obligated to push it up to the chief's office.

"Which makes me regret putting you on notice, my friend. Give me a couple hours to formalize a plan other than hardening our house before you mention it. I think I know a way to get you off the hook I put you on. Sit on it for two or three hours, okay?" Nick asked.

"Done. Call me on this number by eleven this morning?"

"I will," Nick said, hanging up and wishing he had never made the call. He was torn between his duty to cooperate and his fear of departmental overreaction. Maybe he was not being fair to a really good police department. It was a conundrum for sure.

He would not call Rob Gadsden at FDLE yet. He needed to harden up and think.

His next call was to a regional gun dealer. He asked for their commercial sales rep.

"Hi, this is Nick Wolf with Aaron & Ashley Investigations. We are getting ready to offer a patrol carbine course. I need to pick up maybe five trainer ARs or AKs today. Do you have sufficient stock to accommodate me?"

"I doubt it on the AKs. Probably on the ARs. Let me check." Nick was put on hold.

"I checked our warehouse and some nearby store inventories online, and I was wrong. I have three AKs, American made in South Carolina, in Tampa. Because of some political statements out of the White House, there's been a run on ARs. More so than the Kalashnikovs. I can't explain it, it's just the way it is," the man said.

"How much are the AKs in Tampa? And do you have any ammunition?"

"They are about nine hundred each with fixed polymer stocks. The Tampa store should have some soft point tactical loads and some kinda dirty Russian target loads. The latter is available in bulk for your class if you need it."

"Will you hold the three AKs in Tampa for me? I will give you a credit card deposit right now if needed," Nick said.

"Give me five hundred on your card and I will make sure Tampa holds them and gives you five hundred bucks credit." He did and broke the connection.

"Hey, Lola and Maria. Quick near-cop and ex-cop meeting?"

"How about pole dancers? Are we excluded?" his sister asked.

Nick laughed.

"No. Pole dancers and mothers and sisters of ex-cops are cordially invited, too."

"I have located three semi-automatic versions of AK-47's in Tampa and ammo for them, so I am going to run over there. I wanted Maria to be aware since if you have to go to TPD for any reason, this would be a good chance."

"Actually, Nick, I do have to sign a waiver for the short academy for Florida accreditation," Maria said. "With last night's excitement, I lost track."

"Lola, do you feel comfortable holding the fort for a couple hours?" Nick asked.

"Sure. It's daylight on a busy street. I think we have night and dawn to fear. I hope these guys would not be stupid enough to attack us on a bright, busy day like today," she responded. "I'll keep the carbine close by," she said, meaning the Mini-14 in 5.6 NATO. Nick nodded.

"I'll have my revolver and a pocketful of speed strip reloads," Erica added.

"Alright then, let's head across the Howard Frankland Bridge to Tampa in ten minutes."

They met in the backyard at the maroon BMW, a surprise to Maria, and went down Central to Martin Luther King, hung a left and ultimately merged onto I-275 and the bridge over to Tampa.

Maria looked like she wanted to say something and did not for the first fifteen minutes. She cleared her throat and spoke.

"Is everything okay with us after last night?" she asked.

"Everything is fine. I am flattered. But you are a very beautiful friend. Lola is a very beautiful partner and we are in a committed relationship, Maria."

"Couldn't you be committed to both of us?"

"I am committed to both of you. But, in different ways. As long as there is a Lola and a Nick, our status won't change. Even if it's another fifty years."

She ruminated on his words as they crossed the long bridge.

"Your and my relationship is important to me. You are all I've got, Nick. You and Lola."

"As you noticed, neither of us have a very big circle. Lola has her mom and me. I had the two of them, then added you. Now, a sister from the past. Still only four people though.

"You know what, Maria? Four is the biggest family I ever had. Ever. I'll take it and kill anyone who attempts to harm any of the four of you."

Maria reached over and squeezed his hand. She

seemed satisfied with his response. It was surely sincere and from the heart. It would have to suffice. For now.

Nick waited outside TPD headquarters as Maria ran into human resources and signed her paperwork.

"I'm done," she said, getting back into the Beemer. "They say another state-approved transitional academy will start in a couple days.

"Isn't it amazing Lottie, Carly, and your sister were all exotic dancers?"

Nick thought *Oh-oh* to himself, then responded, "It is. Certainly a small world, Maria."

"Do you think I would be a good one? Dancer that is?" she asked.

"I think you would excel at anything you undertook to do. You are fit and move like a panther. However, I also think your new police department would take a very dim view of exotic dancing as a side hustle."

"You are probably right. But a girl can fantasize," she said.

Nick focused on traffic, though a small part of his brain flashed on a dance vision he quickly dismissed.

They bought the three American-made Kalashnikovs with an electronic background check and Nick's driver's and concealed weapons licenses. He picked up ten fifty-round boxes of Norma Tactical cartridges in 7.62x39, some Russian steel-cased practice loads, extra thirty-round magazines, and five small high lumen tactical flashlights.

After the large purchase, the range fee was waived and they loaded several mags each with the Russian rounds, borrowed ear and eye protection and took some targets into the longer portion of the indoor range.

Though the Honduran National Police had the Israeli Galil version of the AK, Nick gave Maria a refresher on the iconic rifle's simple manual of arms. The three short rifles were semiautomatic only. One trigger press, one shot.

Maria seemed to be a good shot with anything she picked up. Just like Lola was. Lola, the former Ranger thought, might even be able to outshoot him. His greater strength was vastly more combat experience.

The probability she may be able to outshoot him did not impact his male ego whatsoever. On the contrary, it made him proud. As did the proficiency of his petite protégé sitting beside him in the car.

He told her so and she beamed.

The simple rifles performed perfectly with the one hundred-twenty test rounds they fired among the three. Nick would not carry a handgun he had not tested with carry ammo and a variety of other bullet designs and weights at least two hundred times.

He was confident with this Kalashnikov test, short as it was. He had experience with the gun and trusted it totally. Like a Glock, you loaded it and it went bang until the cows came home.

They packed their purchases and drove home. One AK was loaded with the good Norma rounds in the back floorboard of the sedan. Just in case. Nick knew Maria could wield it while he was doing evasive driving.

He and Lola had been taught pursuit driving as law enforcement officers. Before, he had been taught evasive and convoy driving for the unfriendly places he was destined to go. He became proficient at it. As if his very life depended upon this skill. Which it most certainly did.

Nick called his St. Pete detective friend.

"Joe, I have almost worked out a solution. Can you

give me another hour?" Detective Joe Horner did, wanting, understandably, to pass off the responsibility.

His next call over the audio system in the car was to Rob Gadsden at FDLE.

"Rob. I have a potential issue with the Bekrić crime family."

He proceeded to explain it.

"Let me do some thinking on what we can do. I'd say excuse the locals. You are right about upping patrols. It could end very badly. Have you considered moving venue? Going to ground a while? Give it some thought. I will too on my end and I'll call you back."

While Nick was not sure where they might go. I was surely an option he had been thinking about. He called Detective Joe Horner back.

"Joe, thanks for extending. I have explored options and decided for the household to leave town. Go somewhere untraceable and hunker down for a while. It's best for all concerned."

"It makes good sense, Nick. I will hold the threat to myself. If anything comes up in my jurisdiction, let me know," he said, with relief in his voice obvious.

"I will, buddy. Thanks for letting me vent and think. It's good to know you are there."

At home, he gathered what he had begun to think of as his Amazon warrior team and they watched him field strip the rifles and clean all three. He got them to participate by helping load the tactical cartridges into all of their magazines.

One AK went out of sight under his desk across from the front door. The Mini-14 went near the inner door to the kitchen, which housed the house's other outside portal. The second AK went upstairs on the floor beside Lola's side of the bed. The third went with

Maria in the former workout room she shared with Angie.

He did a quick manual of arms on the Mossberg Shockwave short pump shotguns. The twenty gauge, with its lesser recoil and lower penetration shells, went into Lottie and Carly's room. Erica got the twelve gauge but loaded with short 1 ¾" shells for less recoil and more capacity.

He took Lola aside and told her Rob agreed with the idea about going to ground. She liked it but asked "Where on earth can we find a place we can get for a few weeks overnight?"

"I don't know. But I may know somebody who does. Lee Strang was my deputy commander at the task force. He just retired from the Polk County Sheriff's Office. He knows everybody and everything in rural Polk County. I thought I'd give him a call."

"Go for it. Mom should be able to go to the condo with Finn. She still has it for a couple of weeks. I cannot imagine they would connect her to us if we do this quickly, can you?"

"No, I really can't. Tell her what we are contemplating. See if she agrees."

Nick walked out in the fenced and gated rear yard. He got in the larger surveillance van and made the call to Lee, who had been a friend well before the task force days.

"Damn, boy. You just can't stay off the news. I thought you'd cease to be a thing after the task force, but no!" Lee answered.

"How's retirement?"

"My PI business is not flourishing like yours, but it keeps me from chasing old ladies at the bingo parlor. Which keeps my wife happy."

"I bet. Listen, Lee. Once again, I need your guidance," Nick said.

"Speak to me, my son."

"Lola and I are protecting both ourselves and a couple of witnesses from elements of a Bosnian mob. I am looking for a rural retreat ASAP for maybe a couple weeks, maybe less. Can you think of any place in the far reaches of Polk County we could rent for a few weeks? Not fancy, but a couple bedrooms."

"I have a couple ideas. Give me the rest of the day to check out availability and I'll call you back," the older retired lawman said.

"You are the best!" Nick said.

"Please call my wife and tell it to her, too. I'll be back as soon as humanly possible."

"Luck?" Lola asked as he came in.

"Maybe. Lee is going to check something out and call me back. In the meantime, we stay firm and resolved here."

"I told Maria what we are doing too. She thinks she will be starting the transitionary academy in a couple days. She will need a car. How can we help her?"

"I don't know. Loan her one of the vans for a couple of weeks? They will just be sitting here most of the time. We won't be working cases."

"Then let's go with my smaller one for her," Lola said. "It has good locks and alarms for wherever she has to park it."

"If you don't mind," Nick said.

"Mom's car is here. Do you think one of us should escort her and Finn back to St. Pete Beach and her condo?" Lola asked.

"How about if I tail her back in the van in a manner neither she nor any Bosnian tail would know?

I could pick up on whether somebody is following her."

"I would really like it if you would," Lola replied and reached over and gave him a kiss.

Erica came out with Finn in a carrier and got in her red Jetta after a full round of hugs. She left. Three minutes later, the van pulled out and the electronic rear gate closed.

"How long will Nick be gone?" Lottie asked.

"Maybe twenty minutes. We could delay him! Anybody need feminine products? Not just for now, but over the next few months," Lola asked with an evil smile.

She waited another five minutes and texted a fairly comprehensive list of needs, or made up needs, to Nick. She wished she could see his reaction.

"Done! Got the tools out? Ready to install it?" The group ran off giggling like pre-teens at a pajama party.

Nick knew where Erica was going and the route she took. Watching for tails was made easier by not trying to predict Erica's next turn.

He spotted a full-size sedan with four very large mouth breathers. It was just too damn obvious to not be the Bosnians. He knew the Bekrić family members were both bright and well-educated from Lottie's observations. Their muscle was clearly neither, just effective in a brutish manner. Which was probably in their job description.

He called Erica's cell phone.

"Did I forget something, honey?" she answered.

"No, I am following you in a protective capacity. I want you to make four right turns, starting at the next right you can make. The traffic signal coming up is a perfect place to start."

"Why"

"I want to see if a sedan behind you follows your four turns. If it does, it's a pretty sure indication it's following you."

"Okay."

She made the turns. The not-so-proficient guys did also.

"Okay, Erica. They are on your tail. Here's what I want you to do. Go well past your condo building. Find another one and pull in. I will take it from there," Nick said.

"This would be fun if I was not terrified," she said.

She pulled into a different condo complex. It had a larger parking lot than hers did. The rental car, a dark gray Charger, pulled into the entrance and stopped, idling.

Nick saw a spot he liked and pulled over and parked. He stepped out, leaving the AK in the front floorboard. He took a position behind a plumber's van. Nobody was around. The Charger, four guys inside waiting, was less than one hundred feet away.

Nick did a three-sixty scan. Nobody. He drew the pocket-sized Sig 9mm, and fired the shots as fast as he could at the glass and tires of the Charger. He saw holes appear in the glass and one tire collapse. In panic, the driver spun his tires, including the one going flat, and took off. Nick was unsure if he had hit anybody. He smiled as the car picked up speed with a right rear tire almost flat. He pocketed the Sig and did another three-sixty scan. Still nobody looking at him. He got in his own ubiquitous van and followed them, calling Erica.

"Erica, they are taking off. Pull out and hotfoot it back to your condo. Try to park way down from your door to not give away your location.

"Call me when you and Finn are safely in."

He followed the Charger as it sped bumpety bump down the road. They were going to have a lot of explaining to do at the rental counter. Or, if they got pulled by the police, which he actually hoped for the officer's sake, they did not get stopped.

"Erica? I have rethought this! I cannot leave you alone there. You and Finn watch for the van and run out and get in it. Screw any luggage. We will replace anything you need. I'll be there in two minutes. We have to get out of here," Nick said.

He picked up speed to a mile per hour or so above the limit, but no more. As an official gangbanger now, he did not want to be stopped either.

The future mother-in-law and the yellow cat got in and Nick took them back to Central Avenue. He went direct, knowing he could get there while the guys in the Charger were regrouping. If he took a circuitous route, they may get there and be waiting.

"Lola, we are coming in hot. You and Maria wait out back, each with an AK. The Bosnians picked up your mom on our street. I delayed them, but we are heading back now. Expect us in ten minutes max, okay?"

"Bad news, honey! Everybody okay?"

"I'll let Erica tell you, but yes. I need to watch for these guys." Nick said as he nodded for Erica to continue the call via the van's audio system.

Once she got the lowdown from her mother, Lola called Maria downstairs with her rifle and they set up stations in the back. Maria was behind a lawn equipment shed and Lola behind her van. They heard a vehicle coming down the alley and went to full alert. Then, the power gate opened and the three creatures

Lola loved more than anything else in the whole wide world slid in and stopped.

Nick powered the gate shut from inside the van and exited. He ran around to the passenger side, AK at low ready, shielding Erica and Finn as they exited and he and the two others wielding AKs clustered around them and went in the back door.

Once inside, Nick called everyone downstairs and had a confab.

"Listen. These guys managed to track Angie to the airport. Now, they have come here and tailed a vehicle from here. There is only one answer. They have tagged Angie with a locator. We know about the finder on Angie's phone. We have to make sure there's nothing else.

"Angie, please bring me your purse and carry-on downstairs to search. Lola, please go through the bags while I watch out of the windows for a shot-to-hell Charger.

"Angie, you need to be thoroughly searched. A strip search. Lottie and Carly, please go through Angie's winter coat. Feel the lining, the pockets, under the fur collar.

"Maria? Please do the best strip search you ever did, okay? Angie, sorry but it has to be done," Nick said.

"I don't have a problem. If I am bugged with something, nobody wants it found more than I do!"

She walked over into a corner, waving Maria and the other two to follow. Lola and Erica started on the purse and carry-on, Maria performed the search with Carly watching, and Lottie searched the heavy winter coat. Finn, now out of his carrier, supervised.

Nick patrolled from window to window, the shades almost fully drawn and blinds almost closed. Since it was daylight, he was not backlit by lamps or the chandelier. Living room, to dining room/conference room, to kitchen and pantry. Nothing yet.

His cell phone rang.

"Lee, what's the news? Good! The enemy is at the gates. They know where we are.

"Can we head up there tonight? Okay, great! I owe you so much, my friend.

"Text the address near Bartow. We will get underway from here in fifteen minutes or less. Thank you so much!" Nick said.

Everyone had stopped and was listening with rapt attention.

"My friend Lee has a hideaway for us. We have to leave right away. Grab your assigned weapons and ammo. The flashlights are paramount. Take basic clothes like running clothes, jeans and jackets, tee shirts and toiletries. We need to move out.

"Any luck on bugs?"

"Yep!" Lottie yelled. I got this thing in her coat." She held up something Nick recognized as an Apple Air Tag. It allowed someone with it set up on an iPhone to track the small disc.

"I have one, too!" Lola said from where she was searching Angie's small suitcase.

"Give those to me. Lola, will you pack something for both of us? Also, food for Finn. I will patrol around down here.

"Angie, you better put some clothes on so you can leave with the rest of us. Okay, sis?"

Ten minutes later, Lola was at the wheel of the Mercedes, with Lottie beside her and Erica, Carly and Maria in the rear. Maria had an AK along with the Glock.

Nick was in the larger van, which held all of the provisions, extra ammo and baggage. Angie was beside him. An AK and the Ruger carbine were between them. Finn, already tired of being in his carrier, was sitting in Angie's lap purring.

A few minutes after they left, Nick called and had the Mercedes pull in behind him at a convenience store at Fifth and 34th Street North.

2

Finn went back into the carrier under protest as brother and sister went into the store. Per plan, Angie put the Air Tag tracker behind the toilet in the ladies room while Nick bought a small carton of chocolate milk. He drank it on the way out the door. Nick walked over to a trash can by a gas pump. He tossed the empty carton in and deposited his Air Tag tracker in the bag the milk had come in. Nick covertly dropped it into the open trailer of a lawn service guy fueling his truck. It landed under some mowers and would not blow out once underway.

"Maybe this will confuse them and buy us some time," he said to his prodigal sister.

They got in and pulled out onto 34th Street North, which is also US 19. Angie programmed the address of the farm Lee had located in Polk County into the Nav system and they headed for their new temporary home.

"Sorry I flashed you, brother."

Nick shrugged, then grinned.

"After this week, I am used to it. At least you are

family in your home and not guests who are virtual strangers," he said.

"There is that," she agreed.

"I can see what Lola was talking about. Those three girls adore you. The roomie dancers are more in a seductive vein. The young Latina detective is just simply in love with you."

Nick let out a long sigh.

"I have the world's best partner. Love and business. She's all I want. I wish these three would cool their jets."

"And of course, there's always the hot mother. She really is one hot proposition if you haven't noticed."

"How could anyone with a pulse not notice the West Virginia school teacher who was married to an accountant. I wonder whether she always looked and dressed the way she does now?" he wondered aloud. "Hell, if I take you, Lola, and Erica out on the boat, I will have to throw the horny little dockhand in the water."

"Boat? You have a boat? Like a cruiser or big sailboat?" Angie's attention switched to a new subject to Nick's relief.

He told her about the boat and the fun they have with it in the mouth of Tampa Bay and the Gulf of Mexico.

"What's the ETA on the Nav?" Nick asked.

"Six forty-eight p.m."

"We should have time to get the house squared away and move in before dark. I wonder if there's a barn in which we could hide the cars?"

"What's the deal on this place?"

"It's an estate property. The last grandparent died and the beneficiaries don't yet know what they want to do with it. My friend found it through a realtor who told the grandchildren who inherited it they should lease it to us for a while. It would be 'found money' for them. I don't know what the condition or furniture or anything is like. Lee says it has working bathrooms, water and electricity. It's fully furnished. Which is all I know.

"I need to make a call about thwarting the attempt on Erica," he said and pressed re-dial for his FDLE friend.

"Rob, it's Nick. I have to advise you of an action."

"Will I need a medical examiner?" his FDLE friend asked.

"I don't believe so. The adversaries had bugged my sister with Apple Air Tags. Seam of winter coat and lining of her carry-on suitcase. They found us.

"We were unaware. I sent Lola's mother home, thinking it would be safe. I followed looking for tails. Saw four big bruisers in a rental Charger. Had her go to a different condo complex. They followed. I canceled their grab with about fifteen 9mms to their car and one tire.

"I didn't and don't want the locals involved for reasons we already discussed. They will have to ditch the Charger, so watch for it or you may have to call St. Pete Beach PD.

"We are changing venue to a farm in rural Polk County and I will send you location once we arrive and assess it," Nick said.

"Yeah, like we talked about, finding an alternate location is smart. What happened to the bugs?" Rob asked.

"One is behind the commode in the ladies room of a convenience store at Fifth Avenue North and US 19 in St. Pete. The other is in a lawn service trailer some-where. I doubt they'd stop the guy once they see what it is and have found the stationary one.

"Hopefully, they are disrupted, and we bought ourselves some time to get away."

"I take it y'all are fully equipped to stand off a concerted attack?" Rob asked.

"I don't know about what kind of barriers the farmhouse has. Weapon-wise, three AKs, one Mini-14, a .308, two Shockwave shotguns and some pistols.

"If your forensics is finished with Lola's and my Shadow Systems CR-920s from the Boca Raton fight, we sure could use them now," Nick said.

"I will have them expedited to our Tampa office. Stay safe and let me know the safe house's location and any events, okay?"

"Will do, Rob. Thanks," Nick said finishing the call.

Angie waited a minute, then spoke.

"You heard my story, Nicholas. Tell me yours. I gather you were kind of permanently fostered by a nice Cuban couple and Spanish is close to a first language for you. I bet Maria likes that!" He frowned and his sister broke out in peals of laughter.

"We lost three very important decades, big brother. We have a helluva lot of catching up to do!"

He told her about the Rangers and most of the places he went. Some, he omitted. He spoke very seriously about what he did, saw, and felt. About how he started a criminal justice degree at night while he was a CID special agent and finished it while a deputy sheriff, then detective.

"Tell me about the limp. Is it permanent? How did you get it."

He told her about the human trafficking ring and about going to free a young girl who had been bought as a sex toy.

About the hostage situation and him drawing his

pistol and shooting the man in the head. And, the rare instance where the bullet did not penetrate, but followed his scalp outside of his skull allowing him to shoot Nick twice with a .45. One destroyed his left femur the other clipped his femoral artery. How it was touch and go...tourniquet applied by SWAT...his then-partner on the job taking out the shooter with a shotgun...not remembering the helicopter medevac to a trauma center...surgeries, rehab. This story was one he had only detailed to Lola. No one else knew the whole set of tribulations he went through.

"It's called an antalgic gait type limp. It's permanent, though I exercise in a way which seems like it helps reduce it."

It felt good sharing with his sister. Hell, it felt good just sitting. Feeling her there after too many years without her. He was driving with one hand. Angie had taken his free hand and held it, tears running slowly down her cheeks as he related the story about being shot. She realized how very close he had come to dying. This time he was shot. Not the other bullet holes or times he had been hit by mortar and IED shrapnel. Not the knife wound from a hand-to-hand fight to the death with a mujahideen sapper. Knives and fists. Yet here he sat.

She would see those scars when he had his swimsuit on in the boat. Stories for another time. Maybe. Stories he glossed over to keep them buried deeply. To keep him focused. Sane.

He did not get into the medals. He would give her the photo taken of him in his Class A uniform with ribbons and medals and his tan beret. The 75th Ranger Regiment. The real deal. He thought she might like it. He had no idea how much she would cherish it and would keep it framed next to her bed until she was an old, old woman.

As dusk approached, they got nearer and the view outside the vehicle windows got more and more rural.

Nick thought it was interesting how much this part of Florida with its slight hills and sand reminded him of out west. No cacti. Same damn rattlesnakes though.

They pulled into the entrance to the farm. One dirt road in, but anything from a crossover all-wheel drive up could drive anywhere on the twenty-acre property.

The lights were on. Nick saw a big imposing man standing next to an F-150.

He got out of the van, hands empty, and embraced his old friend Lee Strang, the recently retired Polk County Detective Sergeant and one of Nick's two Deputy Commanders in the I-66 Corridor Task Force West.

The two had worked on cases since Nick's early days as a detective and though from another jurisdiction, Lee had liked the young deputy and mentored him throughout.

"Let's get you all into the place," Lee said, shaking a ring with a couple of keys on it.

"Then, when the coffee's on, you can update me and see if I need to share anything with the sheriff," Lee said.

"Deal! We will move in quickly, then see about hiding the two vehicles in the barn. After, I will introduce my partner, my sister, and the rest of the ladies."

He saw Lee's eyebrows elevate as Lola and Maria dismounted their vehicle, AKs at low ready, Erica Caldwell, .357 in hand scanning her area, then shifting to a hundred-yard stare. Angie was at the passenger door of the van, holding Nick's Kalashnikov. Lottie and Carly were behind Maria, loosely holding the short Shock-wave scatterguns.

Lee studied the scene and chuckled to himself.

"Only you, my young friend! An all-female A-team. All you need is Ms.T!"

"Every one of them has experience with the Bosnian Bekrić crime family. In Chicago, Northern Virginia, Florida, Honduras, and even a North Carolina rest area. And each is a target.

"My sister is running from one who's her husband. They want me for killing one of them. It's a long story, Lee."

"Whew! Well, okay. Let's get everybody checked into the Strang Hotel. I already checked the house and outbuildings and walked the perimeter. I take it you didn't see any tails?"

"I didn't. We found two bugs and deployed them. One is making the rounds with a lawn service, the other in a ladies' room. About the best we could do on the run.

"For a bunch of no-neck thugs, I have to admit these guys are better than I originally thought. I am hoping it's not because a Bekrić is here supervising," Nick said.

"Say, Nick? Didn't you mention you had a missing sister you had not seen since you were a kid?" Lee said softly.

"I did."

"And this 'sister' showing up at this time doesn't hoist a bunch of red flags?" Lee asked.

"It would. I will stand beside her during the introductions in the house with the lights on. You tell me!" His friend nodded, looking forward to being convinced.

"Okay ladies, toss your belongings into this bedroom for now," Nick said, pointing to a room. Bathroom break while the coffee is brewing, then I want to introduce one of the very most important persons in my life to each of you."

There was a race and subsequent line at the bathroom door after guns and bags were tucked away. Nick brought in the one cot they had and two sleeping bags from the van, as well as the foodstuffs Erica had selected for the getaway.

Five minutes later, a relieved group was gathered and coffee was poured from the pot of an old and well-used coffeemaker.

"Gather around. I want everyone to meet my friend and longtime mentor, retired Detective Sergeant Lee Strang. Lee made this place possible for us on no notice. He makes things happen.

"Lee, the tall one with the green eyes beside me is my partner in all things, Lola Caldwell. She partnered with me after a decade with the FHP."

Lee nodded.

"The woman over there who looks like her sister is Erica. Believe it or not, Erica is her mother." He watched his friend's normally stone face change in amazement.

"The young lady still holding her rifle is former Honduran National Police Major Crimes Unit Detective Sergeant Sosa. Maria saved my life in Roatan on the big pedophile trafficking of young girls case where the congressman was murdered."

Lee nodded acknowledging, like almost everyone in America, he was familiar with the general case, though much was still withheld.

The two young dancers are Lottie and her lifetime best friend, Carly. Lottie was an undercover in the Honduras case.

Lastly, the woman standing on the other side of

me is my long-lost sister, Angie. She came to me for help to get away from her employer and his henchmen, the Bekrić crime family. You taught me there is no coincidence in law enforcement. You were right. You still are. Except for when Angie and I were reunited.

"I have to say, Angie could be your identical twin, but aren't you older?" Lee asked.

"I am, Lee. By about three years."

"Amazing. Congratulations to you two. And congratulations to all of you for finding yourself under the protective arm of the toughest, most caring cop I ever knew. You could not have done better for a partner, brother, or protector.

"I am going to head back for a late dinner my wife is holding for me. But I am going to put my Ford truck in four-wheel drive and leave, lights off, avoiding the path in from the county road. I'm gonna sit somewhere private for a few minutes and watch.

"Nick, I will call you when I am leaving for home and knowing there are no hostiles in the area," Lee said.

"See where I learned this stuff?" Nick asked the distaff audience.

Lee gave him a cop hug, which Lola and Maria stepped in line for. Angie hugged him and said, "Thanks for always being there for my big brother!" Lee nodded.

"Be safe!" he told them all, as he had told subordinates for decades before. Nick slipped out the door ahead of him with his rifle ready and Lola and Maria followed Lee the same way.

Lee turned and smiled at them.

"God, I feel safe!" Lee said, looking at the group. He saluted and swung long legs and cowboy boots into the cab of the late model F-150. He started and the twin turbo V6 rumbled.

Flowmasters Nick thought as soon as he heard the burble of exhaust. Lee inched it forward and energized the four-wheel drive system. He circled the house, lights off and disappeared around back. Soon they heard him proceed hundreds of yards away to the county road and take up a surveillance position. The sound ceased as the career lawman watched for bogies in the darkness.

They stood and watched. After a while and with only rare traffic passing, Lee turned on his headlights and turned left, passing the front of the house. Ever conscious of operational security, he did not honk, blink or wave. He went on like the cowboy at the end of a classic Western, never turning to look back.

———

When the three walked back in, they found Erica had somewhat arranged things.

"We have two double beds. Sheets are in the washer now. There's a sofa which could be slept on, and the cot from the van. I am guessing, from the prior arrangement in St. Pete, Lola and I are in one bedroom, Lottie and Carly and a cot in the other. I assume Nick will be out watching the doors. Which leaves Maria and Angie. It's a shame the sofa is not convertible, but it's not. Which means two on the floor. None of the beds are anything but regulars, so tripling up is out of the question.

"Ideas?"

"How about Angie on the sofa, and Nick and me with rifles across the front and rear doors?" Maria suggested. Lola wondered about an underlying motive, but under the circumstances she felt it was the best and most logical arrangement until more cots could be obtained.

Besides, Angie will be right there. I have a feeling she'd be like a mama bear looking after her big brother. She grinned inwardly and shook her head in support of Maria's suggestion.

"I wanted to do earlier today what I am going to talk about now. But we had to run. These guys showed familiarity with trackers. I want to get under the van and the Mercedes tomorrow with a flashlight and search for more devices. I have a bug detector in my kit with me. It's better than the naked eye. But the search is best done in daylight.

"So, tonight is suspect and high alert. Hopefully, tomorrow on, this will be a true sanctuary. We will get more cots and blankets and any food specialty requests. I fear this stay will not be a five-star holiday. I just want it to be a safe one.

"Maria, what is the latest on your start date at the transitionary academy? You said a couple days, I think, yesterday," Nick asked.

"It's tomorrow. I was thinking of calling in sick."

"No, they don't have these things but every so often. I believe you should go ahead as planned. Lola, what do you think?"

"Maria, as your new family, I agree with Nick. Get started, ace it and get the gold badge. And the salary. Your offer was great. Take advantage of it and start your new life!"

"How will I get there?" Maria asked.

"We planned on you using the small surveillance van for the duration of the academy. Unfortunately, the fast run here last night changed the plan.

"The only thing I can come up with is taking you to the house early in the morning, scouting the area and picking up the van and I will follow you to Tampa or wherever the academy is to make sure you are not being followed. We can run the device I used in Roatan on it. I will have to run it under and in the two vehicles we have here in the dawn before we go," Nick said.

"I have to be at the academy offsite at eight in the morning," Maria said and told Nick and the others the address. Lola recognized it and said it was not bad and easier to get to during Tampa Bay rush hour than the police headquarters was. It was close to their St. Petersburg home and office.

"I need to be under the two vehicles here by four a.m., and we need to leave by five," Nick said. "Since you have to be up early and showered and dressed, why don't you shower while Lola and I am doing the TSCM on the van and Benz?"

"Okay."

"Maria, go ahead and settle by the back door, rifle at ready. Lola and I will do one sweep outside and come back in to get some rest. Everyone else, it's been a helluva day. Try to get some early shuteye, okay?"

Lola went into the second bedroom and got the Ruger Mini-14 carbine.

"I am more familiar with this than the Kalashnikovs," she said, and Nick nodded his agreement.

They slipped out the back door, telling Maria they would do the Bob White quail whistle before coming back. She was unfamiliar and Nick whistled it, sounding just like the name "Bob White," as the real bird did.

They patrolled without their tactical flashlights

energized. Both knew soft words were harder for a listener to perceive than whispers, so they spoke softly.

"I am worried about tomorrow, honey. Two-thirds of the trained shooters will be gone for almost half a day. Maria is out of the picture for about as long as we are here, since she will be boarding near Tampa. You have the whole thing on your very lovely shoulders until I get back," Nick said.

"Not a problem. At least not a problem unless you find car bugs in the morning," she said.

"For them to plant bugs, someone would have had to scale the back gate or fence. They did not know which to bug and I doubt they had enough devices for two vans, our two cars, Erica's, and the Lottie's Mercedes. And, just walking once they got over the fence would have set off the motion detector flood lights. I did not see them come on. I think I would have," Nick said.

"Good points," Lola said. "I suspect you will not find any bugs on the van or Mercedes tomorrow either. Our cars at home might be by now, though."

"I will check on the small van once we get there. I doubt we'll have time for the rest. Oh! Do you have the van keys in your purse? You do? Good. Then, we don't have to go in in the morning. I will also tell Maria to lock the Glock in the safe in the van. I never asked whether she was going to be loaned a gun or expected to use her own. Either way, she will be covered."

"Let's get this thing closed soon. I love my mother, but I miss you next to me at night," Lola said.

"Me, too. More than you know. I am hoping Maria will settle into the mode of being a little sister to both of us. And be kept really busy in her new job."

"I will miss the humor watching them all over you!"

Lola laughed. "Mom and I think it's hilarious."

"Aren't you jealous?" Nick asked.

"Should I be?"

Did I just get set up and walk right into it? Nick wondered for a second and dismissed it. Lola is one of the most straight-forward, self-confident people he had ever met.

"Of course you should be! Look at your fiancé! A marathoner, sprinter and all-around stud muffin. The only reason all of these hundreds of women are after me, is they know I can't run after them," he took a chance responding.

"Did you just say fiancé?" she asked.

"Of course I did."

"Did you ask and I missed it?" she asked seriously.

"No, I've been trying to figure out how to get down on one knee without falling on my ass like in Boca Raton."

"On your ass or not, you saved my ass!" Lola said.

"Is that a yes?"

"Yes."

"Then kiss me and seal the deal before you change your mind," he said.

"I made up my mind a long time ago."

"Okay. Kiss me anyway." So she did.

"Ring or new pistol?" he asked.

"How about we swap cars?" she asked.

"Okay. It's a deal."

"You realize this is the weirdest proposal in history?"

"And, with the weirdest response?"

"Could be."

"Good by me," he said.

"Good by me, too, husband-to-be."

They finished their walkabout and headed in,

holding hands. Each with a rifle in the other hand.

Nick was up at dawn. Angie rolled over on the sofa but did not awaken. He saw Maria get up and stretch, probably almost as stiff from sleeping on the floor as he was. He waved and she returned the wave. She pulled off her tee shirt and walked into the bathroom to shower. He walked out of the door and scouted the area. All clear, for now at least.

Nick aimed the light under both vehicles and slid under, conducting the TSCM with his detector. It did not sound an alarm under either vehicle or inside. So far, so good. He would check the small surveillance van with Maria guarding at the house before turning it over to her for a week or two.

She came out with one of the AKs, dressed in the fatigues and golf shirt used for the academy. She was ready for her first day at the 57-hour equivalency training. It was her first academy in years. Lola followed in one of Nick's tee shirts and barefooted.

Nick brushed himself off as best he could.

"Ready to go to school?" he asked Maria.

"Yes and no," she said. "I hate to leave you with just one person having the training needed to hold off an attack."

"You concentrate on learning the Florida code and refreshing your skills, we'll guard the fort while you are away," Lola told her and gave her a hug. Maria got into the van and put her AK in the footwell accessible to both of them. Nick kissed Lola and got in and they left.

They arrived back at the house and circled the block before entering the alley and powering the gate open. Maria raised the rifle and both put their windows down for shooting mobility.

"I will check just the small van you are going to use.

I will do the bugging check and check for possible explosives as well as I can," he said.

He did both and nothing was apparent.

"Go over behind the shed until I get it started," he said. Her face reflected the terror she felt.

The van started without exploding, which both considered a very good thing. It had three-quarters of a tank, which gave a lot of miles endurance with the four-cylinder engine.

"Do you have sufficient cash?" Nick asked.

"Yes, Dad."

"Dad, your ass." He smirked, then grinned at her.

"If you don't end up needing the Glock, lock it in the safe in the van," he said, pointing out the right key.

She gave him a big hug and slid behind the wheel.

"Know how to get there?" he asked.

"Kinda."

"Doesn't matter, I was going to tail you and watch your six anyway. Now, I'll lead and you watch mine."

She smiled and nodded.

It took them ten minutes to get to her destination. There were already instructors present, so she went in. He waited for a minute, then saw her come back out and handed Nick the Glock.

"I won't be needing it." She waved and sprinted in like a happy kid.

Happy kid. Just the way Nick thought of her, adding "who saved my life in Roatan" to the happy kid moniker.

He noticed a Walmart was open on US 19 near the school. Not much of a shopper, he had no idea many opened at six a.m.

He stopped in and bought three heavy duty folding cots, a couple of sleeping bags, six blankets and some more towels and fresh pillow and cases. And, guy he was, bought beer, colas, pretzels and snacks. He would have bought more ammo, but though previously one of the largest ammunition dealers in America, they stopped selling it for political reasons. Something he did not appreciate. But, who else had what he needed at six in the morning?

The trip back was uneventful. Just the type he relished. He returned to find the hot water heater needed a long time to recover from so many morning showers.

Nick explored the barn. It had a stout hasp for a lock. Just no lock. He would remedy the absence later and store the vehicles out of sight and protected inside when they did not contemplate immediate use.

He sat down for coffee. He had missed his normal early breakfast time and did not wish to throw his meal schedule off-kilter.

"Did our little detective matriculate?" Erica asked.

"She did. And freed up a fighting pistol," Nick said, handing the Glock to Lola.

"But how about you? Shouldn't you take it?" Lola asked.

"Nope. You carried one like it for a decade. I spent a lot of time undercover with a subcompact semiauto or snub nose revolver hidden. I have long familiarity with the little guys! Also, Rob is going to get our Shadow Systems pistols back from forensics ASAP. I'm good until then," Nick said.

"Let me fix you some toast or something," Erica offered.

"No thanks. Since the water in the shower would freeze the antlers off a brass buck after all these long girly showers, I am going to go all Nordic on you and go outside and take a cold shower with the water hose!"

"That'll be a sight!" Carly piped in.

"One you should avoid," he said. She merely wrinkled her nose at him as noncommittally as she could. Erica rolled her eyes and Lola shook her head, though neither was mad. They were amused at Nick's obvious chagrin.

Angie was already setting up two of the new cots, one for herself, one for her brother.

"I like the idea of sleeping bags for the cots instead of trying to make a too-bit sheet fit and having a blanket drape down on the floor, Nick," she said.

He nodded and took the AK and a bath towel and headed out the door.

Minutes later, he gasped aloud at how damn cold the water was. So much for Nordic ice bathing. He liked the concept, but this was torture. Maybe if he got used to it...

Once toweled and dressed, he picked up the rifle and walked around the farmhouse. The walls of the house were frames with light sheathing underneath and siding which had been added later. Almost any centerfire round, even from a pistol, would penetrate it. The .308 would go into a side wall and through the one on the other side of the house. Though people think of refrigerators and furniture as barriers, they were not. Not by a long shot.

Bottom line. The walls would keep rain and mosquitos out. Not gunfire. There was no way he could put up barriers.

He told Lola he would be back in half an hour. There was a farm store and he bet it would have something he needed.

They did. He bought five infrared wireless game cameras. He found an old rickety ladder and installed one on a fence post several down from the gate to the trail down to the farm. Nick thought it was far enough out of line of sight to keep someone at the gate from focusing on it. The other four were wide angle view and he would put them in the center of the four walls of the house. He downloaded the program to monitor them on the laptop via the hot spot in the van.

He could at least see them coming with the audible alarms catching the house occupants' attention. Then, perhaps given the lack of barrier protection of the house, he could take the fight outside to them. Away from his loved ones.

Four against one? He did it in Afghanistan and prevailed.

Now, of course, offensive action was down to Lola and him with the other trained fighter off getting retrained. He would want Lola inside, close to the others. In case the perps got past him. Plan for the worst, fight for the better.

Now, to harden up. To arrange a safe room. There was only one whose setup might work. The bathroom.

The bathroom was surprisingly large. He and Lola discussed a crazy idea and decided it was not as crazy as first thought. Thirty sandbags the size of big grain sacks could turn the bathroom into a bunker. The small window would require some thought.

He left again, this time to the nearest home improvement store. Which was not really near. He bought as many large bags of playground sand as the van would hold. Nick loved that the female part of his A-team was Lola and three fit dancers. They were strong women physically and in their constitutions. Right now, the physical part topped his agenda.

He included Erica as a supervisor, as she held Finn,

and the remainder as a bucket line to pass in heavy bags of beach sand. Once stacked outside the bathroom, they began to fortify the bathroom into a bunker. When finished, it was not pretty. It was a decent saferoom however. With a bonus toilet and sink. A line of bags grew from floor to window and past, closing off the one remaining unprotected area.

The plan was whenever the computer audibly reported a cam recording something which broke its beam, Nick and Lola would gun up heavily and Nick would leave by the door opposite from where the cam was reading. Lola would be primary security in-house. Angie would take the "eye" and relay positions, number of combatants, and category of weapons (handguns, long guns, rockets) to Nick by cell phone. If anyone but Nick came in a door or window. Lola would kill them.

It was a simple plan. Simple plans were often the best...until brother Murphy stepped in and everything went all to hell.

"We could use some real food, now the beer and pretzels are covered," Erica announced, her tongue firmly planted in her cheek.

"Do I detect mild sarcasm there?"

"No, dear. Boys will be boys," she responded to the one she secretly knew had committed to son-in-law status.

"Make a list and I will take Lottie and Carly shopping. Otherwise they will get cabin fever," her daughter suggested.

"If you do, you might want to take the van. I think the S-Class might be too memorable. I think I scanned them both pretty well, but I was not using world class equipment, so I'm not real comfortable about either."

They compiled a list and left, Lola driving, Lottie

riding shotgun in the most literal sense, and Carly in one of the counter chairs in the van's back compartment.

They arrived at a supermarket about ten miles away and Lola stayed in the van, using its 360-degree cameras to watch for threats. Lottie and Carly got a cartful of groceries and returned even more animated than usual.

Nick sat down finally. Erica and Angie joined him.

"What's your read on our situation, Commander," Erica used the title he held at the task force, though she had not known him then.

"Hard to tell. I have a nagging worry there's a Bekrić or two down here running things. Everyone else I have seen in either branch of the crime family has just been muscle. While they are using basic trackers, the fact they are using them at all suggests to me there is more than the thugs. I don't think any I met would be that sophisticated.

"Angie, honey, you lived with and worked with them for some time. How far down into the ranks does the brain power sink?"

"Not very. Your call on them as being thugs is correct. Even my family member husband, though good looking, was barely above knee breaker level. The top guys, like Ibro Bekrić at the top of the Midwest branch and his brother Luka in the east, are smart. They are also as cunning and savage as their underlings. They manage by intimidation and making examples of people who do what they consider to be wrong. Family is everything. Which is why they want to kill me. I betrayed one of them and brought a loss of face to the family.

"Nick, they *will* hunt me down until there is not a Bekrić left standing," Angie said.

"I will be happy to accommodate the last man standing aspect. We have senior people at the Florida Department of Law Enforcement, St. Petersburg PD, and the Polk County Sheriff's Office aware they are after us. I will give Detective John Ross's name to Maria. If he's not at the academy, she can look him up later. We worked together on the task force. He's a good man and a good cop. So, key law enforcement people around the area should be aware of the Bekrićs. Depending on where we are, one call should bring help."

"With what you called both a bunker and a safe room around the bathroom. I have never felt so safe sitting on the toilet," Angie said. "But what about the rest of the house?" she asked.

"I think the bunker is fairly safe from small arms fire. I think you could shoot straight through the house walls with a .22 rifle. Which is why when the game cameras alarm, I am out the door or a window, everybody goes into the bunker and Lola stays inside the bunker door ready to repel boarders. I will have to kill them before they think of fire. This place would go up fast if torched."

"Aren't you signing a death warrant going outside?" Erica asked.

"I don't think so. It's the last thing they would expect. I suspect it will be dark. Other than beatings in dark alleys, these guys have not trained in and experienced night fighting. I have and it gives me an advantage over them. At least over the ones I have met or interacted with. Erica, you might be half Mattaponi Indian, so you'll understand I fight like a Native American. I think these guys won't know what hit them.

"How did you become so tough, Nick?" his sister asked.

"My foster father fought Castro and then contracted with American intelligence. He pushed me to be tough. The Army picked up from there and then the Rangers took the ball and ran with it. I don't think of myself as tough, Angie. Perhaps more as being careful and resolute.

"I define tough as fighting smart. Not giving up. I doubt the Bekrićs think like I do. They define it as fists and brawn. And it will be their undoing.

"Angie, talk about your Bekrić to me. I need to recognize him and know what to expect," Nick said.

"The older Bekrić, Ibro, is in his late forties. He has the bulky build and shaved head of the guys who followed me on the plane. I'd say six-two, two fifty or sixty for weight. Don't underestimate him. He's smart. Real smart. And, he has a presence about him. Charismatic until you cross him. Then, he would devote his entire being to destroy you in the most violent, public way possible."

"Facial hair?" Nick asked.

"Yes. A light-brown mustache and goatee. Not heavy. Almost a shadow growth for both. The so-called husband looks the same but fifteen years younger and not as bright."

"Perhaps we will meet. If they come after you, we will," Nick promised.

Maria called Lola about four.

"I missed something pretty big. This course for the remaining seven days or so is at a school. A school without residences.

"I have to either find a hotel room or drive home tonight. Quite frankly, for tonight, I would rather come home to you and Nick. I'm embarrassed to admit it—after all, I'm an experienced police detective. But this

new country, and new traffic laws, and new training...
well, on top of the Bosnian threat, it's all overwhelming
me!" Maria said. Lola knew from her voice she was close
to breaking into tears.

"I understand, honey. This whole thing has been a
lot. Let me get the address for the farm and tell you how
to program it into the van's CarPlay system. Hold tight
one minute."

She obtained the address. Nick had it in his phone,
so he did not have to get it from the Nav system on the
larger van outside. He walked over to Lola as she was
finishing and motioned he wanted to speak with her.

"Maria? I want to meet you part way. I don't think it
is safe for you to come straight to the house. They'll
know where it is. So start this way. I will pick you up as
you pull into Bartow. Go to the McDonald's, It will be on
your right. Go through the drive-in and buy something.
I will be parked nearby and watch to see if you have a
tail. If you do, I want you to look for Eighty Foot Road
and turn onto it. It's the opposite direction from the
farm. We'll be talking handsfree CarPlay phone system
in the vans. I will tell you where to turn."

"Isn't eighty feet very short for a road?" she asked.

"It's much longer. I know it because the great sheriff
up here has a Jeep off-road event yearly and I used to
come up to it. Eighty Foot Road leads to the place it is
held. There has to be a story about the odd name. I just
don't know what it is.

"Watch your rearview mirrors for any vehicles
tailing you. It's hard to tell at night, but will be harder
for them to not be obvious on the more deserted roads.

"Call along the way, okay? My cell is programmed
into the CarPlay. Just plug your phone in and watch for
the App to come up, then tap it. On the left side, you

will see a phone icon. Just press it. I wish we had left the Glock in the van's safe so you'd have it close. I am going to leave shortly and will see you at McDonald's. Obviously don't wave or acknowledge me except over the phone." Nick handed the phone back to Lola, who turned the call off.

"I wish I could go and ride shotgun," she said.

"We need you and your rifle and shotgun right here," Nick said.

"How about me coming? I brought all of this on you," Angie said. "I could hold the rifle and short shotgun out of sight for when you need it."

Lola, feeling how much the sister wanted to contribute, did one of her extra sensory perception looks at Nick.

"Okay, sis. It could be violent," he said.

"I've seen those bastards give violence. I'd like to see them get some!"

"We are closer to Bartow than she is. I think we should leave now and head towards her. I know her route and will verify it by phone.

"By doing it this way, we can see if there's a tail. Either way, we can slip in behind her and follow her to the McDonald's. If there's a tail, we can chance going ahead since they won't attack in a well-lit, populous place. We will pull over on a dark part of Eighty Foot Road and set up an ambush. I can't legally justify shooting to kill, but I will disable their car and shake 'em up a bit," Nick said.

Angie and Lola smiled.

Both had on dark clothes. Lola gave Angie a dark ball cap to wear pulled down over her eyes when needed to hide her face from people who knew her.

Half an hour later, Nick called Maria.

"See any tails?" he asked.

"I don't, but there's enough traffic they could be cruising four cars back," she said.

He asked her location and she gave him a fairly accurate best guess.

"Okay. You have not passed us. You are maybe ten minutes away. When you pass, Angie and I are going to see if we recognize anybody behind you. Yes or no, we will slip in behind. Continue towards the McDonald's drive-in lane as planned. If someone is tailing, we will speed off and set up a little surprise for them."

"Sounds good, Nick," Maria replied.

Nick later pulled in across the street from the McDonald's in Bartow. Both surveillance vans had really dark windows as approved for police vehicles and PIs. He retrieved some Steiner binoculars from the safe in the back of the van and Angie watched with them.

Coordinating on the handsfree phones, they knew when Maria was approaching in Lola's surveillance van.

They watched as she pulled into the fast-food lot and the drive through lane.

A silver full-size Buick sedan signaled, then turned into McDonald's. It had four big guys. Their shaven heads were clear in Angie's binoculars.

"It's my damn husband driving and three who I recognize as enforcers. Can I just shoot him?" she said.

"Nope. We will move on and speed ahead for an ambush," Nick said.

"Maria, you cannot see us from the drive-through lane. You have a big silver Buick. Angie has identified the four as being from the Bekrić mob, including her husband. We are pulling out and speeding ahead. Stall as much as you can while we find an ambush spot. Don't give away knowing they are back there. I will warn you when you are approaching the ambush. I will want you to slow down until I give the signal.

"Call me as soon as you are back on the main road you came into. I will give you directions to Eighty Foot Road," Nick said.

"Got it. Getting ready to order dinner now."

Nick pulled out, unnoticed by the people in the Buick. A white work van with a ladder on top did not jump out as odd to anyone in Florida, even Bosnian tourist assassins.

Once around the corner, he accelerated and got onto Eighty Foot Road and accelerated more until he spotted a place where he could turn off and get out. He drove the van a hundred yards down a dirt track and got out, AK in one hand and shotgun in the other. He slipped his Kevlar tactical vest on with two 30-round mags in the front pockets and sprinted as fast as his limp would allow to a bush beside the road.

Angie had gotten behind the wheel and was watching, motor running, for Maria to come by.

"Okay, Maria! You just passed Nick," she said into the handsfree system.

"I didn't see him."

"Good! Neither will my so-called husband and his thug boys. Now, slow down to about twenty per Nick."

She did, and the Buick did the same, maintaining the same quarter of a mile tail distance behind her.

As the Buick passed, Nick put a load of nine double-ought buckshot into the right front tire. It obliterated the tire, and the Buick was on the steel rim a second later.

Nick dropped the shotgun and aimed the AK at the engine compartment and opened up. He was not sure he could crack the engine block, but he was damn sure he could take out necessary engine parts like radiator, battery, fuel injection system and more.

Thirty rounds of 7.62x39 Russian did the trick and he changed mags and put a couple rounds into the top edge of the rear window. He aimed to not hit anyone, but to scare the living hell out of them in the car, which had now rolled to a final stop fifty yards ahead.

He saw Angie coming hard, lights off and held up a hand to stop her where she was. He opened the door and she slid over, taking the AK and short shotgun.

Lights still off, he powered away, the twin turbos in the van screaming. Several men stumbled out of the destroyed Buick, disoriented.

"I've totally destroyed two full-size rental cars for these jerks in a couple days. They are going to find it difficult to rent cars soon," Nick said to his sister, whose only regret was her husband still able to breathe and take sustenance. Maybe not too much longer, she hoped.

Nick spoke into the still active call with Maria.

"We stopped them. All they know is what county we are in. And it's a large one with one of the best sheriff's offices in America. Their car is destroyed and there is no way they are going to call the sheriff and report it. They have a long walk back to town and have to secure transportation. I just hope they don't carjack somebody.

"Take your next left. Your Nav system will reorient and direct you to the farm ten miles away. We might see each other. Either way, call Lola and tell her when you are approaching," Nick said.

"What would I do without you?" she said.

"Probably lead a safer, quieter life."

He killed the call and concentrated on driving. No need to watch his mirror.

He called Lee Strang.

"Hey, it's Nick. There are four armed Bosnians stranded on Eighty Foot Road. Their rental car is seriously and permanently disabled. They tried to stop and kidnap the female you saw who is transferring from being a Honduran detective sergeant to Tampa PD as a detective. Nobody is hurt on either side.

"If the sheriff wants to send deputies to check on them to prevent another carjacking, maybe SWAT would be the best choice to send. No matter what these bozos say, they were trying to stop and kidnap a police officer and had followed her from the transitional academy in St. Pete."

"And you didn't kill them?" Lee asked.

"Ugh, it was more a case of kidnaptus interruptus. I wanted to avoid a firefight. Just save the young detective."

"I will make a call. I know just who would like to chat with these foreign interveners," Lee said, his voice signaling a great deal of relish.

"They might say they were tourists out for a tour along a rural road in the dark when they were ambushed by criminals. I doubt anyone would buy such a story, given the weapons they either have or have just tossed into the bushes," Nick suggested.

"I'm sure you are right. Let me hang up and dial someone real high in the structure. Bye!" Lee said.

Nick grinned at his sister.

"You are a piece of work, brother," she said proudly. "No wonder your tribe of women all love you!"

"Don't remind me. All I want is Lola and you to. Maybe my future mother-in-law. The rest? 'Like' would be just fine."

3

Maria called Lola and advised she was coming in and not being followed.

"How do you know? Is Nick behind you?" Lola asked.

"Nick worked his magic and destroyed another rental car full of the bad guys. Nobody was hurt, but they will have a lot of explaining to do to the rental company!" Maria laughed.

"Oh! Nick and Angie are not far behind me. The Nav says I am a mile away," Maria said.

"Okay. I will open the garage. Pull far enough in for Nick to put the big van in. You will need to get out in the morning, so leave space. There is probably room for twenty cars in there, so it shouldn't be a problem," Lola said.

She picked up the Mini-14 and went out to the barn. The whole cadre heard the conversation so there was no reason to say where she was going.

Maria came down the dirt track, spun around at the barn door and backed in like any cop would do. As she was hugging Lola, Nick and his sister arrived and also backed in.

Nick walked into the farmhouse, and having two more loaded ones, immediately field stripped the rifle and reloaded the empty magazine. He angled the bottom forward and rocked the loaded mag back into the Kalashnikov, and racked it. No cruiser ready empty chamber and rack it now. Things were ratcheting up too fast.

"Hi, darling! The rental car companies are going to hate you," Lola greeted him.

"Who me? I don't exist to them. I bet they will be leery of anybody signing in with an asterisk over the last letter in their name though." He grinned at his new fiancée.

"I got to see our boy in action! He's pretty impressive destroying cars! Missed killing my husband, despite my begging though!" Angie told Lola, arm around her brother.

The phone rang. It was Lee Strang.

"Just wanted you to know, SWAT got to the car formerly known as Buick. Nobody to be seen. We have not had any reports of car thefts or carjacking. Maybe they were laying down in a field.

"While the boys in tactical gear are still in the neighborhood, we are scrambling a helicopter with FLIR (Forward Looking Imaging Radar) to look for heat signatures of four humans in the area. I'll let you know.

"You did a righteous job on the Buick. We found the thirty empty AK shells. No shotgun one which was apparently used on the right front tire. Must not have pumped it, huh?

Also, there were no traces of blood inside the car. They are using Luminol on it now to make sure we just aren't seeing blood because it's dark in the car. I'm predicting urine and fecal stains on the seats. Those old boys were probably soiling themselves being caught inside a target without notice like that!" He laughed.

"Thanks, Lee. The toughest part was disabling the car without hurting anyone. God in Heaven knows what they would have done to the lovely young female detective they were trying to carjack and kidnap," Nick said.

"You and she might have to sign statements to the effect it was an attempted kidnap. Thirty-one rounds is a lot of lead to throw downrange," Lee said.

"I'd sure like for us to stay out of the limelight until this thing is finished," Nick said.

"May be difficult. We'll see, Nick," Lee said and said he would call back with anything new which came up.

Maria, back to the rest but facing Nick, mouthed "lovely?" and blew a silent kiss. He smiled at her but did not respond.

"There is something we need to figure out. How did they know to pick up Maria on the way here? Have they been surveilling her? Did they follow her from the house this morning? Is there a tracker I missed on the small van?

"I'd like to answer these questions right now. But we cannot. I must have missed something in the dark. Lola, have you seen the interior of the barn lit?" Nick asked.

"No, but judging from the decrepit nature of the barn, I cannot imagine it has sufficient light for you to search the vehicles for bugs tonight," she said.

"Okay. We will stand close watch tonight in case they have secured another vehicle, which I doubt. Then I will search all three vehicles here in bright sunlight."

Maria had eaten what she bought at McDonald's for dinner. Nick and his sister put together some sandwiches and a beer apiece. It had been a long day and most were ready to turn in early. Though Lottie and Carly had not done much, what they did was a lot of exercise in the barn.

Lee called Nick about six the next morning.

"I might have a small problem solved for you. Did you do any planning in the St. Pete house? Calling me? Figuring out a game plan? About the young Honduran going to a transitional officer academy?" Lee asked.

"We did, but only inside the house. Why?" Nick asked.

"Because our forensic guys towed the shot up rental car in and took a good look at it. Luminol did not find any blood traces inside, for one thing. Three different brands of cigarette butts were collected and sent for DNA.

"Ready for the biggie? They found a large cone-type audio amplifier with earmuffs like we use shooting wired into the unit. They told me it was good enough to listen through windows from fifty feet or more away.

"*That*, my friend, is how they knew you were escorting the Honduran young lady to the academy. A little research would tell them how long it lasted. So, they would arrive an hour or so early and just smoke cigarettes and watch for her to come out. They already knew what vehicle she had.

"Sometimes, the old way is the best way. No black bag job with hidden mics and cameras. Just hunker down in the bushes and listen," Lee said.

"Well, I'll be damned!" For one thing, you just saved me from laying on my butt and searching for trackers under one car and two vans first thing in the morning. I was on the way out just when you called.

"Thanks, Lee! You are not only the best, you always

have been!" Nick said to his longtime friend and mentor.

"I'm guessing you have picked up patrols near Bartow last night and this morning since there are probably four armed guys walking around looking for a place to stay and to get some transportation."

"We absolutely have. And the deputies know they are tough customers who just attempted a kidnap. If anybody on patrol sees something which seems related, they will hold back and call in the cavalry. Haha. You know how effective our 'cavalry' is.

"I don't have anything more yet. Maybe with some DNA hits off the cigarette butts, we can see if any of these mokes have outstanding warrants anywhere and pick them up," Lee Strang said.

"I think the whole world knows how effective your cavalry is, buddy. Thanks for everything. If there's a way to keep us on the down low, don't hesitate, okay?"

"I will try, but I suspect the best I can do is delay the signed statements. I don't foresee anything negative about using firepower to stop a kidnapping in progress. I wasn't there, but you could probably have justified shooting them and not just the car.

"Anyway, I'll be in touch," and Strang hung up.

Nick related his relief about the hearing device the Bosnians had used.

"It gives me pause to think what else they might have heard which they could leverage against us. At least we can have some comfort the three vehicles here are most likely tracker-free.

"The small van is known to them. Maybe the big one is and maybe they spotted the Mercedes parked in the back in St. Pete.

"Maria, for the rest of this week's commute to the

academy and a motel or here, we need to get you a rental car. Based on recent experience, we should probably take full insurance on it, too," Nick said.

She and Lola both agreed the small van was compromised, and since the house in St. Petersburg had been under surveillance, the rest of the vehicles probably were known to the bad guys, too. It was Maria who was going to do the most driving, so at the very least, she needed a new "clean" car.

Lola, who had been looking at something on her smartphone, said, "There is one major rental company over in Bartow and several local ones.

"How about Lottie, Carly, and I take her over in the Mercedes. I will stand guard outside and they can go in with her?"

Since the two dancers had developed cabin fever already, they jumped at the chance.

An hour later, Lottie was calling Lola, who was outside the rental company watching for tails.

"We got her a cute one! Just for grins, I put all of us on it as drivers!" Lottie exclaimed as she put her credit card and driver's license in her wallet, then fought to replace it in jeans which looked like they were painted on.

A red Mustang came roaring around the building with Carly at the wheel and Maria grinning broadly. *This is like looking after three teenage boys,* Lola thought.

They turned towards the farm and Lola followed watching for tails. She did not see any. *But damn! I am an ex-trooper, not a trained intelligence or surveillance operative. I have not been taught how to do this. However, I'm all they have...*

She pulled the Mercedes out and followed. There did not seem to be anybody following the red pony car.

She called Nick as they neared the farm.

"Darling, we are coming in now. The lead car would not be my optimal choice for a subtle car nobody would notice. It's a bright red Mustang."

"You are kidding? Kids! Wait. Did I just sound like an old fart?"

Lola giggled at the prospect and ran with it.

"Omigosh! You did! Like Dennis the Menace's next-door neighbor," she said.

"Just call me George Wilson," Nick said.

"You even knew his name! Have you been studying him so you could grow old just like him?"

"No, my dearest, only since we met."

"The BMW looks like it won't be enough then. You are going to have to spring for a big rock."

"Rock, your perfect butt! Hey, you have to go and open the barn door for me."

"Anytime," she replied, ending the call and mentally declaring herself the victor in their little repartee exchange.

It was a perhaps silly thing they did. Something which includes making up funny songs about the most pedestrian of things. They agreed it kept them sharp. On their toes.

Feeling too frisky for a trooper, Lola watched the Mustang slide into the dirt track leading to the farmhouse and speed up. She did a controlled drift with the powerful German car and punched it, passing the three twenty-somethings handily. She was far enough ahead when she approached the garage she threw it into a one-eighty and backed in without slowing down.

Even after a year, Nick still marveled at how good a driver his fiancée was. A good everything, he concluded.

Somewhat outdone by Lola, Lottie brought the standard engine Mustang to a stop in a more normal fashion, did a raw and slightly jerky Y turn, and backed in.

Angie and Erica watched with mixed amusement and disapproval. Both chalked it up to a very talented adult showing three kids how an expert does something.

Lola walked past Nick, stuck her tongue out at him and patted him on the butt on the way by. The other three omitted sticking out their tongues but followed her example with pats on his butt.

He just shook his head in resignation, turned and walked to the house, his sister and Erica giving him identical bemused looks. He just shrugged and went in.

Later, he picked up the AK and did a walkabout around the farm. He was not looking for adversaries as his primary goal. Rather, he wanted to see where future adversaries could set up sniper nests. Upon arrival, he had thought the farm would be sacrosanct. But he was kicking himself for underestimating these guys. They just seemed to pop up. The handheld cone with the sound amplification was an example. Lee was right. Sometimes, the old ways worked better. They did not have to do a black bag job and bug his house. They just had to hunker down in a neighbor's yard in the dark, aim the device at a window, and start listening. They could only hear half of a phone conversation, he knew, thinking of his with Lee about a getaway. However, it was enough to add to the intel over Maria starting the academy, and their familiarity with the vehicles in the rear of the house to start piecing things together. Just as Nick and Lola would have done had they been in the Bosnian's places.

Nick focused on two areas. The first was near the gate, for want of a better name. It separated the main county road from the dirt track into the farm proper and was simply a cattle gate. No big arch announcing you were entering King Ranch or North Fork or somewhere.

Nick looked appraisingly at a copse of trees across the county road. He wondered how savvy these particular men were in the outdoors.

The copse looks pretty snaky to me. Not a place I would want to lumber into with a rifle and squat down for a stay. There was another clump of trees a hundred fifty yards down the county road from the gate. The trees were set farther apart, but it still could accommodate a vehicle to put a bag or rolled up jacket on to support a rifle. A good sniper nest, Nick. Not good at all for us.

I could use the drone to check it out prior to leaving, night or day. Ditto the gate, with the nearby night penetrating animal cam helping at ground level.

What about relocating to Lottie's Boca mansion. It was like a fortress. The problem was close quarters and no place to run if it all hit the fan.

How about separating the targets? No! What's the old expression? Divide and conquer. Lola and I can protect them better when we know where the elusive heiress and her girlfriend are. After three decades apart, there is no way in hell, I'm gonna let Angie get out of my sight. The others interrupted Bekrić business. Angie violated Bekrić family honor. Probably worse!

None of his thoughts gave him much of a plan or sense of direction. It was not time for a "family" meeting to discuss options. He had to be the strong one. To act and not show hesitation. He had to keep everybody alive.

He went back in. Nick watched from the kitchen. Everyone was in the living room. He had not been noticed yet.

His sister, Lottie, and Carly were in sports bras and some sort of shorts and were teaching exercises to Maria. Lola and Erica were watching with rapt attention.

"Okay, this stretch strengthens you for doing splits, either on the floor or the pole. Yoga is a great thing to keep you in shape for working the pole. When all is said and done, though, having a pole is essential. They are cheap and easy to install," Angie said.

"Oh, we know all about buying and installing poles," Carly said and there were giggles around the room.

"You three have done this for years. How will I ever be able to catch up? And how will I be able to dance with the public job I have?" Maria asked.

"You could dance some in Orlando on weekends," Lottie suggested.

"I just want to see Lola follow through on a club down here," Carly said. "I had her on the floor and at the pole titillating the audience like you couldn't believe. Then, the lights went out and the whole place went crazy! Lottie or Lola, is that where and when the two guys Lottie was working with got their nicknames?"

"It was. Sore nuts and Headache. Sorry, Lottie, but they deserved it. They were lucky Nick was in a good mood or he would have crushed a windpipe and twisted a neck unnaturally and they would have flown home zippered in black bags," Lota said.

"You got that right!" Nick said, entering the room holding directions from the game cameras.

"I just finished installing a game camera near the front gate. Now, I am hoping there's a tall ladder in the barn and it isn't rotten so I can put four more, one on each side of the house.

"We will have a grid of five screens on the laptop when I am finished. The computer will beep when something taller than a squirrel trips lens of a camera. Now, except for the one down by the county road, a beep on any of the other four will mean they are really close.

"So, when the call for 'battle quarters' rings out at three a.m., go to the bathroom, okay," Nick said.

"Not to worry, when I hear it, I will go to the bathroom right where I am lying," Carly said.

"You better not! I am bunking with you, remember?" Lottie added indignantly knowing Carly was probably serious.

"Expect to hear shooting not long after the computer beeps. I would crawl on my belly to the bathroom bunker. These walls won't stop squat, so stay low!" Nick said.

"Angie, Finn has been sleeping with you on the sofa. Try to grab him and take him to the bunker with you. The shots and our alarm will terrify the little guy and he will run off to an unprotected place for sure," Lola said.

"Will do. He's the only nephew I have. So far...and we seem to have bonded," Angie said.

"Back to the cameras, Lola, want to grab the rifle and come with me to the garage? I may need someone to hold the ladder even if we find a decent one.

"We could all come watch. And maybe jog around the barn for some aerobic exercise Carly suggested."

They found a ladder which was tall enough, but kind of shaky. He used it while Erica and Angie held each side and Lola stood guard.

It did not take him long to install the remaining four cameras. Lola stayed on-station as his ladder guards joined him on a walk around the farm.

"Do you think they will come for us here?" Angie asked.

"I think the only way they could would be to tail Maria or plant a bug in the van while she's in class. Which could happen. They have proven far more adept than I originally gave them credit to be."

"Which means Ibro is here with them or brought along someone else. My so-called husband is not smart enough to do these spy things."

"Him having a technical surveillance guy is a scary thought, Angie," Nick said.

"Well, Nick, we don't know who he brought in from Chicago. It may not have been just the three on the plane and Adin later. He may have come with others who are specialists," Angie said.

"Which gives me an idea. I am going to call a friend," Nick said, excusing himself from the group, but motioning her to follow to the quieter kitchen.

"Rob, it's Nick. I have an idea. A very obvious one I should have shared with you earlier. Want to find out how many Bosnians came down from Chicago? Look at the flight manifest from O'Hare and Midway to Tampa for the last four days.

"Virtually all Bosnian surnames end with an accent over the last letter. Which makes them easy to pick off a list."

"It sure would! I had no idea."

"Furthermore, my sister worked with them at *Bekrić's lead club in Chicago. She was married to one. She could probably verify if you gave her a list from the recent flight manifests.*"

"I will put somebody on it and get back to you. Okay to just text you a list of names with no further explanation?" Rob said.

"It would be fine. Thanks, buddy!"

Angie winked at him and held up crossed fingers.

The next call was from Maria, saying she was approaching. Nick and Lola reached for their rifles and headed for the door.

While Nick opened the barn door, Lola greeted Maria and ushered her in.

"All clear behind you?" Maria asked.

"As far as I can tell. I have been watching, but nobody seemed to be too interested in me. A couple of teenage boys waved at the Mustang."

"Don't kid yourself, honey. They were waving at you, not the car. Look in a mirror when you go into the house. Even with your hair in a cop bun and a golf shirt on, you are a hot proposition."

"I always thought my lips were too full and my butt was too big," Maria said.

"I believe tastes may have swung in your favor, girl."

"All good behind you?" Nick asked as he walked in from securing the barn.

"Apparently so!" Maria said with a big smile.

"Good!" Nick said, baffled. Lola, the *agent provocateur,* said nothing.

"While Maria is here with us, there is an idea I have been tossing around," Lola said.

"What is it?" Nick asked.

"There are seven of us at night. If the game cams alarm and we think an attack is imminent, you go out and take the offensive. I guard the rest from the bunker. It's a damn small room. A bathroom. What if Maria, with a light, pistol, and rifle goes out with you? Maybe she takes a position in a dark corner and watches the house while you seek out the attackers? I think two of us shooting is too much for the small room. Our plan is great for times she's at the academy, but..." Lola trailed off.

"She's right, Nick. I have been on raids, taken watch positions to eliminate criminals sneaking up from behind. I have the experience. Two high power rifles going off in the bathroom would be deafening and dangerous in such small quarters," Maria said.

"You both make sense. Maria, remember, I will go out a door or window *opposite* where the camera shows the threat to be. So, be sure to follow me out the door. Don't use another way out or you may run smack dab into a hostile."

"I have it Nick, I will be covering your six," she said.

"Ladies, if we keep this up, we are going to refine this thing into a real plan," Nick said. "I think tomorrow, they will determine what car you are driving and begin to follow you. And remember, they know the general direction you will take home. They know we are somewhere near Bartow.

"By the way, if you were as stiff as I was last night from the floor, you'll be happy to note a new cot by your door position. It is complete with a sheet but no pillow. There's a new sleeping bag if you think you may get a little chilly," Nick said.

"Thanks, I will take both. I won't zip in though, because it might hamper getting out fast."

They walked into where the rest of the group was gathered.

"Angie, do you want a cot and sleeping bag instead of the sofa and a sheet?" Lola asked.

"No thanks! I'm good with what I've got."

After light conversation, the line for the bathroom formed. Tee shirted women holding toothbrushes anxiously shifted weight from foot to foot.

Nick slipped out the door in his boxers and with flashlight and AK. While performing one last security check he avoided getting in line.

By the time he came back in, the house was dark. Lola was there to kiss him goodnight and made it a memorable event before quietly walking into her bedroom.

Angie was on her sofa half awake.

Nick bent over her and kissed her on her forehead. "I thank God every day we are back together. I love you, baby sister."

"I love you too, Nick. Thanks for everything you are doing to keep me safe," Angie said.

"I always will. Get some sleep," he said, squeezing the hand she had put on his cheek.

She rolled over to face the backrest of the sofa and sleep. Nick adjusted the sheet and stood up.

Maria was standing at her new cot, in a more normal-length tee shirt. She turned and blew a kiss to him. He smiled and waved and mouthed, "Good night."

He kicked off his boat shoes and positioned them for quick access in the dark. He padded over to the computer, draped to not emit a light signature visible from outside.

Nothing seemed to be going on. He returned to his new cot and laid on it, rifle and Sig 365 on the floor in instant reach.

His mind was spinning with ideas, worries, plans and a myriad of unrelated thoughts.

Sleep seemed like a long ways off. Sleep tricked him

and gathered him in quickly. Ten minutes later, he was sound asleep.

Four hours later, Nick was awakened by game camera two on the rear of the house alerting.

"Everybody on the floor and to the bunker, now!" he said in a soft conversational tone. His voice reached the entire small farmhouse. He heard sleep partners awaken the other and roll from bed or cot onto the floor and begin crawling to the bathroom bunker.

He caught Maria's attention and nodded to follow him out the front door. She had slip-on shoes on her feet, her tee shirt and an AK.

They went out the door after Nick peeked and exited. A kind of reverse PIE maneuver.

"The alert was the cam on the back of the house. I will go around the left. You take a rear-facing position on the right corner. I will whistle a signal before coming around so you will know not to shoot," he said.

They were both crouching. He had an arm around her shoulders and pulled her in closely to speak in her ear. Both knew a soft voice did not travel as far as a whispered sentence. She nodded understanding and looked up at him with her big brown eyes. He patted her and turned to move in the other direction.

He sliced the pie going around the front corner. Nothing on the side. At least not this second. Nick moved at a crouch, rifle at high ready.

He sliced the pie. The rear looked clear. He edged his way along the back of the house. Nick squatted at the back door, just below the camera.

He laid the AK down and shielded his tactical flashlight, looking at the prints around the door. Most were his. There were also large dog prints. Probably a coyote had passed through.

He'd take a coyote any day over a big, bald guy with a machine gun. He'd already killed one of those this month. His big bald guy bag limit was full, as far as he was concerned.

He whistled low at the far corner. Maria whistled back and he eased around, saw her smiling and walked quickly to her. She moved in close, questioning look on her face.

"Coyote as near as I can tell from tracks. All clear." They went to the front door, and he whistled the Bob White call Lola knew. She returned it from inside.

They went in and the women in the bathroom bunker came out, and he said, "Coyote, or maybe big stray dog. Everything else seems clear out there. Sweet dreams."

Lola and Angie came up to the two.

"Looks like the procedure worked well," she said.

"I guess. It would be a helluva lot more hectic if it was a real attack. But everyone got the basics right," Nick said and smiled and left before a group hug was initiated, though he loved all three.

He got back on his cot by the front door and went back to sleep. He was awakened at five-thirty by the creak as Maria got off her cot across the room. She put the day's golf shirt, fatigue pants, socks and running shoes on the cot. Took off her tee shirt and stood silhouetted for a moment, then walked through the dark to the bathroom for a shower. Fifteen minutes later and fully dressed for her day at the academy, she walked over and tapped Nick lightly on the shoulder.

"Will you go and take care of the barn door so I can leave for the academy?" she asked. He nodded and checked the computer for game cam action. There being none, he put his shoes on and picked up his rifle and they walked out of the door.

He checked the area again anyway and opened the barn door. She got in the Mustang and stared at him a minute, smiled and started the car and pulled out of the garage.

Nick closed the door behind and returned the wave she extended out of the window as the car powered off.

Her drive was still a bit unfamiliar and took her two hours. She pulled into the parking lot for the fun day at the academy. The driving course day. She had already checked available vehicles. The classic academy fleets of retired Crown Vics had long gone to the elephant graveyard. The new retired vehicles were an assortment of Explorers, Chevys, and Chargers.

Since the SUVs and Dodges had basic engines, versus the larger respective twin turbos or Hemis, the Chevys were the fastest. She got in line for one of them.

Maria had only briefly been on a driving course in Honduras. This one had an hour or so classroom and most of the day driving. She loved it and excelled at it.

It is easier to maintain breakfast where it is digesting instead of on your lap if you are driving. However, each instructor took a team of three student riders through the course several times at speed.

One of the male students lost breakfast in the back seat. Luckily for Maria, it was not one of the Chevys.

She spent a half hour with an instructor telling her how to carve the corners, when to accelerate instead of braking, and how to recover from a skid. She excelled in the driving course, setting driving as capably as Lola as her unadmitted goal. While good, she did not have the decade as a state trooper in her toolbox.

Tomorrow was going to be on the range, where she

expected to excel again. The issue firearm would be ubiquitous. A Glock 17. Probably the gun in more police holsters worldwide than any other. Even countries like Great Britain, which did not issue firearms to police officers or detectives, had many thousands of the G17. She would be surprised upon her arrival at TPD by being issued a Sig 320 pistol.

Maria was surprised how tired she was. The driving course had been stressful, every second on the track with its twists and turns requiring total focus and physical concentration.

She only wished Lola and Nick could have watched her. Especially Nick. Being like a little sister had benefits, though less so since beautiful Angie had appeared as his real little sister. Being a lot more was what she really wanted. She just did not see a way to get there. Who could compete with Lola. Lola, who was drop-dead gorgeous, could shoot, drive, and was one of the nicest and kindest people she had ever met.

Maria was thinking about these things as she walked off the track and around the building to the parking lot where the red rental Mustang sat.

She saw a nice-looking guy in a dark collared pullover shirt like hers and tan slacks. She thought he might be an instructor with his ball cap and sunglasses.

He looked up from his car next to hers. It was a gray Charger. Certainly looked like an unmarked police car.

As she approached, he called out, "Hey, Maria!" and waved in a manner which suggested they knew each other.

Maria waved back and smiled, her mind running at top speed to place him.

"Maria, my name is Adin Dedić, I believe you know

my wife, Angie. Before you do something stupid look at the car beside you."

She saw a larger Toyota. She did not know the model. She did know the man in it was pointing a pistol at her.

Dedić approached her and escorted her to the Toyota, opened the door and said in a much less friendly tone, "Get in, bitch!"

A couple of her fellow students were walking towards them, still a hundred feet away. One waved at Maria, who just looked at him as she got in the car.

Dedić walked around the car and got in the backseat from the other side while Maria was still considering whether to bail out and run.

The car sped off before the Bosnian could even fasten his seatbelt.

"Did you see that?" one of the students, all of whom had been cops with other agencies like Maria, said.

"That was really odd. Maria is friendly and didn't even acknowledge us. It's like she was taken or something. Let's go get one of the active-duty cop instructors and report this. It stinks to high heaven," he told his companions.

They all agreed.

One, a transferring detective from outside Florida like Maria, noted the license plate number of the Toyota.

St. Pete dispatch got the snatch immediately. It was labeled "officer involved".

Detective Joe Horner was in the area when the call went out. He marked responding and called his friend he had just spoken with a few days ago. Nick Wolf.

"Just now? Descriptions and car tag? Okay, stand by for possible location!" Nick said.

He turned to Lola.

"Honey, pull up the Find My Phone for Maria, she has just been taken at the academy parking lot." She quickly did and gave the location in St. Petersburg to Nick who relayed it to Joe.

"This could be where she was when they turned the phone off. But it's a ways from the academy, so it could be real time. The description sounds like our boys, Joe. Lola and I are on the way."

Lola turned to Nick.

"You go. I will pull it up on your phone so you can track it until they toss the phone or turn it off. Now, go!"

Lottie tossed the Mercedes fob to Nick.

"It's faster than the van. Take it!"

He adjusted the seats rearward in the big sedan and pulled out of the garage.

The S-Class jumped ahead as he poured on the power.

Lola called her best friend at the FHP and explained an officer had been taken in St. Pete and Nick was en route in a Mercedes and gave the color and plate from the registration Lottie handed her. She gave Nick's route away from the farm. Listening for a few seconds, she began to smile and thanked the senior state trooper.

"Nick, there will be a trooper waiting on the outskirts of Bartow. It's a friend sent by another friend. Let her get in front and follow. You just got a Code-3 escort."

"You are the best fiancé I ever had!"

"Aren't I the only fiancé you ever had?" she asked.

"Yes, but irrelevant. Thanks! I will be in Bartow in seven or eight minutes. Be careful in case this is a diversion."

"I thought about that. I will arm up the ladies and

we'll watch the cams. Nick? Be safe and bring our little friend back safely, okay?"

"Both are my objectives. I am about ready to look for the trooper."

The marked Tahoe was sitting on the far edge of town. Nick blinked the lights of the Mercedes and the Tahoe instantly lit up. He let the SUV pull off and accelerate and floored the Mercedes to get in behind and stay there.

Nick's cell phone rang. It was an unknown number. And his phone had not been paired to the Mercedes, so he held it in his hand and answered.

"Nick Wolf."

"Nick, this is Trooper Amy Gray. Look at the Tahoe."

He did and saw her wave. He waved back.

"So. You are Lola's boyfriend?" Amy asked.

"Now, I'm her fiancé," he responded.

"And you headed the trafficking task force?"

"I did."

"So as a cop and in the Teutonic hot rod you are driving, you should be able to keep up?" Amy asked.

"Since I suspect you drive like Lola and I had a pursuit certified Tahoe as my last official vehicle, it's gonna be close. But I'll give it my damnedest, Amy!"

"Great! I'm fixin' to rock and roll!" And she did.

He called Lola.

"I am trying to keep up with Trooper Amy Gray. She seems to know you."

"Amy? Oh, yeah. Don't believe anything she tells you about my wild early days."

"Sounds worth looking into. Anyway, why don't you feed the phone tracker info to Joe Horner and me. I am working hard to keep up right now." He recited Joe's number.

She called Joe.

"Joe, this is Lola Caldwell. I'm Nick's partner and the kidnapped detective's friend. Nick has an FHP escort and is busy keeping up. I will keep you advised of Maria Sosa's Find My Phone locator."

"Thanks, Lola. Pass me what you have. We are saturating the area Nick first gave us. It's northwesterly from the academy site," he said.

"Still is. Vicinity of Central Avenue and Forty-Ninth Street North right now."

"Thanks, Lola. Let me broadcast the update now," and he switched from phone to his Motorola police radio.

Nick was nearing St. Petersburg and was coming south on 49th while the police units were still on Central. He knew the reported description of the car was a "larger Toyota sedan with dark windows." He did not have the color.

"Nick and Joe, it looks like they have stopped at around 39th Avenue North and 49th Street North. The car is moving off-road, maybe hiding around back," Lola reported to both.

"Okay, I am ringing off now, Lola. We have arrived and setting up a perimeter. SWAT will be on scene soon. It's a two-story house. We have them contained. Thanks!"

And Detective Joe Horner was off the phone. Since it was not a conference call, Lola advised Nick.

"I am coming in from the other direction and slowing way down. I won't get in the middle of a police operation and lose my license because of it. I will just hang back," Nick said.

One of the things a wise older Ranger told him about responding to a violent situation is to slow down and watch. Your tangos may think it's too hot and make some stupid errors. Watch oncoming traffic. Ya never know what ya might see." The young Ranger took it to heart and used it rounding up high value targets in hot zones, as a CID special agent, and as a deputy sheriff. He would continue to use it today.

As Joe Horner and five marked units came around the corner to the position Lola had given where the tracker stopped, a small sedan left the premises by the alley in back. It circuituitously made its way back to 40th Street North and proceeded away from the developing scene.

"It's my wife I want to kill. My cousin in Virginia wants you and the small group who brought his business to a screeching halt.

"I have not had any action for a while since my damned wife freaked out. Now I have you, pretty little thing. And you are going to be my action until I trade you for my wife. Or maybe I'll just forget the bitch and keep you. You aren't as pretty and not quite as much a hardbody. You are cute and soft. I already noticed how soft. We are going to have fun! Even if you don't, I will. You can bet on it," Adin said.

Nick saw a car coming towards him faster than traffic. The driver's face was clear. *Bald, light color mustache and goatee. Younger than me. One of the bad guys? Maybe. Maybe not. Hard to tell. There's something in the back seat. A lump. Like a rolled up sleeping bag sitting upright on the seat. Could it be a small person with a bag over his or her head?*

Nick pulled over and ran hard down a side street, then one parallel to 49th. He hung a right and got back on 49th.

Where was the yellow Mazda? His stomach was

churning. He was heading away from the action. Did he misread the car? The churning gut said no. He started searching the area. No need to notify Joe Horner yet. Joe had his hands full setting up a perimeter and awaiting the arrival of the SWAT team and maybe a negotiator. Nick doubted these guys would give up without a fight. Fighting was inbred to them.

The Mazda turned and pulled into an alley and drove slowly down it. The driver, Adin Dedić, saw the type retreat he sought and pulled in behind a large 1930s house. He got out of the car and walked around to the rear door on the passenger side. He opened it and dragged Maria up close to him. A large, hard fist punched her on the jaw. The blow was not lessened at all by the pillowcase over her head. She collapsed into as prone a position as a seat belted, duct taped person could on the seat. She was out and would be for several minutes. Adin knew. He was good at this sort of thing.

Hoping the driver in the yellow Mazda had not circled back, Nick began a systematic block and alley search of the area. It was the proverbial needle in a haystack.

It was also the only damn thing he could do. He was well aware of his lack of options. High tech was gone. Tire rubber and shoe leather had taken over.

Impatient, he drove on.

Nick's more or less brother-in-law, Adin Dedić, walked confidently to the rear door and knocked.

An old man came to the door, surprised someone would knock there instead of the front.

Having a Bersa .380 pocket pistol pointed at his face from several feet away surprised him more.

Adin jerked the screen door open and stepped in,

virtually on top of the man, his bulk sending him crashing to the floor.

His fist to the jaw had worked so well on the Latina cop, he did it again. No pillowcase, a bigger wind up and the man was out. Which was just a temporary convenience to Adin who rather enjoyed hurting people.

The only people in his entire life he had not hurt had been his older cousin Ibro and Angie. He had tried to hurt Ibro, but had the hell beat out of him for the effort.

Angie? Well, all that was in the wind. He would hurt her. A lot. Then kill the ungrateful bitch for betraying him. Mainly for embarrassing him and the family.

Adin knelt with one knee on the floor. All was still quiet in the house.

He put very large, very strong hands around the unconscious old man's neck and began to squeeze. It didn't take long.

For not having a fence, the rear yard facing the alley was fairly private. It is the sole reason Adin had chosen this house. He left the old man lying on the floor and searched the house. *He must be a widower. Or old bachelor. There is no sign of a woman around, or anyone else. Good!*

Adin went back downstairs.

He removed the old man's wallet and read the name on the credit cards and driver's license. Robert Dolan. He memorized the name. "Uncle Bob" if any nosey neighbors came around. Forty-eight dollars in cash. Adin added it to the man's credit card and put all in his own pocket.

He lifted the old man and slung him over his shoulder like an old rolled run he was going to put in the trash.

Which was exactly what was going to happen. He walked out the door and immediately dropped the body with a sodden thud as he saw Maria getting out of his rental car.

She still had the bag over her head and her hands and feet bound with duct tape. She had gotten the rear door open and was in the process of falling on her back with a pained groan as he reached her.

Adin dragged her to her feet and gave her an open-handed slap across the right side of her face. He released her and she crumpled down to the sparse grass.

May as well bruise both sides consistently. Symmetry is everything, he grinned.

He left her laying there and returned to the dead man. He picked him up again without any effort and took him to the large rubber municipal trash can. It was the kind a truck lifted and dumped instead of a human. Adin wondered when trash pickup was, then discarded the thought as being superfluous. He dumped the body in and saw a cinder block in the yard. He placed it on top to help keep raccoons and other creatures out until trash day.

He put Maria over his shoulder and went into the house and up the steps. One bedroom was much larger than the other.

He reached down, still holding Maria, and ripped the bedspread and top sheet off and onto the floor.

Adin threw the still-unconscious Maria onto the bed. It was a four-poster. The room was fairly neat for an old codger living alone. And dying alone.

Adin knew what he wanted and found it in the closet. Four silk neckties.

He ripped the clothes off the woman. Every stitch of them. With more anger and violence than lust.

Using the neckties to bind her, he tied each hand and each ankle to bedposts. He had to get two more ties and lengthen the bindings for the ankles.

Adin stopped and smiled at his work. She was spread-eagled on the bed and could not move. *She looks good. Real good.*

He pulled the pillowcase off her head and rearranged her black hair on the pillow.

Adin walked around the bed, admiring his handiwork. He paused longer at the foot of the bed, looking at her and anticipating the things he would enjoy doing to her.

The concept of *with* her totally eluded him. *To* her was operative.

Before going downstairs, he checked the duct tape over her mouth. It was still tight. He checked the bindings. All four tight.

Adin sure hoped the old fool drank. He needed a drink. Or five. To help him shake the stress of a kidnapping and running from the cops.

He smiled again. The cops. He would get back at them by enjoying one of their own.

Back downstairs, he looked out of the door. The Mazda was bright, but it did not matter. He had rented it with a set of very expensive forged ID and reloadable credit card. It was not known by any cop or other adversary. It was fine just where it was.

He opened the refrigerator. A partial six pack of Bud Lite. Not much kick. But cold and the five would help take the edge off. Along with the white powder he carried in a travel size foot powder tin.

Nick was twenty minutes into his methodical search. He stopped the car and paired his phone.

He called Lola successfully on the Mercedes's audio system.

"Anything from Joe Horner?" he asked.

"No. But we are all watching Tampa Bay news on the television. There is video of a hostage situation in mid-St. Petersburg. SWAT is there. A negotiator.

"Where are you?" she asked.

"Following up on a gut feeling about three miles away. I met a yellow Mazda coming towards me as I was driving to the scene. It looked exactly like Angie's description of her husband driving. There was a shadow in the back seat. It may have been Maria.

"There's nothing I can do at the scene. So, I'm following up on this."

"Just be careful and keep me in the loop," Lola said, and they broke the connection.

———

Adin Dedić finished his third Lite beer and belched loudly. He went out to the Mazda and recovered the carry-on bag he had placed in the trunk several days earlier.

He took it in and removed the fake foot powder can. He took one of Robert Dolan's crisp one-dollar bills from his pocket and folded it just right.

He poured a healthy amount of the white powder on the kitchen table and, using the bill, snorted it.

The beer and the cocaine made him feel better. It was time to go upstairs and enjoy hurting, but not killing, the hottie tied to the bed. She may have barter value to get Angie, so he knew he had to be careful to keep her alive. He had lost a couple in his day.

He went upstairs eagerly anticipating the next ten minutes or so. He knew it was about all she could handle before losing any trade value.

Adin went over to Maria and ripped the duct tape of her mouth, causing her to scream out in pain. He took his shirt off with as much theatrical drama as he could under the influence of beer and coke. Flexing his pecs, he expected her to be impressed. She was not. *Bitch!*

He dropped his trousers and kicked them away and his shoes the same.

Standing there in tight turquoise briefs, he knew she would be impressed. At least in his altered mental state he did.

"You can scowl at me all you want, you piece of trash. But, I'm going to have my way with you and thoroughly enjoy it! Then, I am going to make you feel pain. A lot of delicious pain! You may not enjoy the pain so much. I will though.

"Then I am going to slowly kill you. You will be aware of dying each second of the way to hell. Afterwards, I am going to kill my deceitful wife. The same exact way!"

"You may kill me, but my Nick will track you down and kill you for it. You better get on your bony knees and pray to Jesus. Because Nick will come for you and kill you," Maria said in such a strong convincing voice it even surprised her.

"I have watched your Nick limp around. Like I said, I am going to kill you and then his sister! Ha!"

"You are not going to kill anyone. Instead you will die. Right here in your girlish little panties," said a strong, serious voice behind him.

Adin Dedić turned in shock and looked into the barrel of Nick's old backup, a S&W 442 snub nose. He could see the hollow point bullets facing him in the front of the cylinder.

Nick knew the man was between him and Maria. There was no way he could shoot. Rule number four. He pocketed the small revolver and gave a confident smile to his brother-in-law.

He looked the man in the eyes, then glanced downwards.

"I don't see anything impressive, *little* man. Give it your best!"

Dedić charged him like a bull. Just as Nick expected. And, dreaded. He was only so mobile nowadays and the room did not give much space.

Nick stepped aside and two hundred fifty pounds slammed into him and pinned him to the wall. Which Nick thought was far preferable to be knocked through the door and down the stairs on his ass.

Dedić did the next expected thing for a brawler. He put both massive hands around Nick's neck with full intentions of choking the ex-Ranger to death. Right there in front of Maria.

Being pinned actually gave Nick more stability than standing on two feet.

Nick raised his left arm and dipped his hand as far as his arm could reach into the space between Dedić's chest and his and against his own chest. He grabbed the Bosnian's right hand and dropped down as he spun towards the wall.

The leverage induced on his foe's arm dislocated Dedić's right shoulder with a loud *pop* and accompanying scream, worthy of a prepubescent girl.

Both hands free, Nick elbowed the man's chin upwards and slammed a knife edge hand into his throat.

Dedić's eyes bulged and looked as if they might pop out onto the floor. For good measure, Nick hit him in the throat again with as much malice aforethought as he could muster. The gurgling for air was obvious.

It might be possible to reach the throat with a grasp by one hand and relieve the trauma somehow. Nick had heard of such things working.

Nick dismissed the idea of first aid. This man was going to rape and kill his real and his adopted little sisters. Not the hell now, he wasn't.

Nick watched him die. It did not take long at all.

He walked over to Maria, searching every inch of her only to ascertain wounds. She was smiling and sobbing at the same time.

He took his automatic knife out and cut the ties from her wrists first, then ankles.

She immediately threw herself in his arms, now sobbing uncontrollably.

He held her and patted her back, unsure of the best thing to do. After a while, he brushed her tears away.

"We need to get you decent and get my friend Detective Horner over here. I just killed someone and you are a witness."

"I think he must have killed the owner of the house. I heard him knock on the back door and talk to a man. Then, later as I was getting out of the car blindfolded and with hand and foot restraints. He dropped something big to come get me. After, he walked nearby and put something heavy in a trash can.

"Can't you just hold me longer?" she said.

"Crime scene, Detective. We have to report and

protect it until the right people get here. Then be questioned.

"It looks like your clothes are totally destroyed. Even your panties. Your trainers and socks may be okay.

"Let's rummage around here. Maybe the victim has something you can use to cover up."

There was nothing. She put on the shoes and socks while he went out to the Mercedes and rummaged in his Bug-out bag knapsack. He came back in with a clean tee shirt and some running shorts.

Nick got Maria to turn around and he twisted the elastic waistband and knotted it.

"I'd keep my hands near the waistband to catch it in case the knot lets go. You don't want to begin a tradition of Tampa detectives flashing St. Pete detectives, do you?"

She smiled with a slight quiver to her lips and tears still flowing and shook her head.

He awkwardly patted her on the shoulder.

"Okay let's report one murder, one kidnapping, one attempted sexual battery, and one death justified by self-defense." He called Joe Horner.

"Hey, Nick. Same status here. Our negotiator is still trying to get them to surrender. At least to send your Tampa detective friend out as a token of cooperation."

"Joe, they cannot produce Detective Maria Sosa," Nick said.

"Why the hell not?"

"Because she is right here with me, very relieved. You might want to drive over. I will look up the street intersection in a minute. Call for the ME also. We have one probable body, the owner of the house. The other is not so probable. He's just flat out dead. I had to kill him in an unarmed fight to save Maria. She witnessed the whole thing."

"Nick, have you verified the owner is dead?" Joe asked.

"Not really. I was fighting for my life. Maria's too, just a minute or so ago."

"How about the other one? The bad guy?" Joe asked.

"His name is Adin Dedić. He is one of the upper management guys in the crime family. Cousin to the two big guys.

"By the way, in the interest of full disclosure, he was also my brother-in-law," Nick added.

"Are you sure he's dead?"

"Pretty much. His eyes are locked open and he does not have any pulse. Just a big Bosnian in his undershorts."

"Nick, you know this gets weirder and weirder as you relate it, right?"

"Yeah, Joe. It sure sounds weird to me also. Maria, do you think it's all weird? Yep, she agrees, Joe."

"Don't go anywhere for a sec, Nick." Nick heard Joe tell the on-scene commander, SWAT commander and negotiator the people in the house did not have Detective Sosa.

"Nick, this all changes the paradigm here. I suspect after one more negotiator warning, they are going to pop a bunch of teargas in the house. Hang tight there. Don't agree on a version of what happened, okay? I will be there as soon as possible. The ME may arrive first. I will take the report and do any interviews. Nobody else."

"Roger all," Nick said and hung up.

"Come with me. Call Lola and get Angie on the phone. Tell them we are okay. It's my responsibility to tell my sister I just killed her husband."

Maria nodded, took his phone and hit Lola on the favorites.

Nick opened the trash can. The urine and fecal smell suggested death. He reached a wrist. No pulse.

"Lola! It's Maria. Yes, I am okay. I am with Nick who saved me. SWAT still has the house with the Chicago guys surrounded. They were bargaining me for their deal. I was several miles away.

"Yes, your Nick and my big brother hero is fine. He wants you to put Angie on the phone please." Maria handed the phone to Nick.

"Nick! Are you okay?" Angie almost screamed into the phone.

"Maria is fine and I am fine, honey," Nick said.

"Did you see the no-good bastard I was married to? More or less married."

"I did."

"Did you kill him?" she asked in all seriousness.

"I did."

"You really did?" Angie asked almost incredulously.

"I really did."

The line was silent for a moment. Grief? Probably not. Relief? Most likely.

"Did you shoot him?"

"No."

"Then how did you kill him, Nick?" Angie asked.

"The old-fashioned way. We went at each other bare-handed. He lost, I won."

"Wow," was all his sister could say as she absorbed the information.

"Keep dinner in the oven. Maria and I are in for hours of questioning before starting home. No, scratch that. We will be back closer to breakfast. Or Maria may just go straight to class."

"I'll tell Lola you love her," Angie said, recovered and very serious.

"Tell yourself the same thing," he said and hung up.

A car with two detectives pulled in.

"Mr. Wolf? Detective Sosa? We are here to secure the scene. The captain wants Joe Horner to handle the interviews, though one of us will probably sit in, too."

They introduced themselves and Nick showed them the two bodies.

It did not take the investigative prowess these two obviously had to notice Nick limping, particularly going upstairs.

They looked at the very large pro-NFL-sized guy lying dead in his briefs then at the very muscular Nick who was considerably outweighed and had a mobility challenge.

"Were you armed?"

"Yes, but when I came in the door, he was between Detective Sosa and me, so I could not use my firearm.

"It immediately became a grapple fest," Nick said, liking the martial term he had just invented.

"And you outfought this giant in his little panties, bare-handed?" the shorter detective asked.

"I did. He had more strength than style." Nick said.

"Not part of your interview, just curiosity. What killed him?

"I dislocated his shoulder as he was choking me, then a couple straight fingers to the throat."

"So you probably crushed his windpipe or larynx or something?"

"I believe I must have. I used something similar as a Ranger in Afghanistan fighting a mujahideen sapper.

"Listen, I need a favor and you are encouraged to call Joe Horner to get it cleared," Nick began.

"Go ahead," the older of the two detectives said.

"We need to go to a local shopping center and get some clothes for Detective Sosa. She and I are going to be questioned about all of this for hours. When I got here, the deceased bad guy had tied her to the bed and ripped every stitch of clothes off her. They were torn beyond repair or even temporary use.

"It will take ten minutes to get her something to appear decent in. One of you can accompany us if you want."

"Having witnesses or victims, and she's both, leave a scene before questioning it not good procedure. In this case, it seems like a reasonable accommodation for a fellow officer. Especially if one of us rides along.

"I will approve that. We can take my car over to Tyrone Square Mall. Are you familiar with it?"

"I am," Nick replied. "One of Joe's and my victims in the trafficking task force days was taken from the theater there and we got some clues leading to her recovery and that of fifty more teens."

"Let's go now, then," the detective, whose name was Larry Wilton, said.

"I've got a light nylon Columbia windbreaker in the car. Let's also grab it for her on the way to your car," Nick said. Maria looked up and smiled. She was not shy, but a man's size 34 shorts and nothing else but a thin white undershirt was not how to meet people she might be working joint cases with for the rest of her career.

A few minutes later, she was picking out undergarments, slacks and another dark collared pullover shirt. As she had no idea where her ID and purse was, Nick paid for the items and they returned to the house off 49th Street North.

The ME and a crime scene team were there. Joe

Horner had called and updated Detective Larry Wilton about the scene a few miles down the street.

The barricaded subjects had not been responsive. Knowing their alleged hostage was safe, St. Petersburg SWAT had deployed heavy teargas and made a dynamic entry.

Three men who looked amazingly alike were taken into custody with no shots fired. Their eyes were relieved by bottled water and their clothes were aired out before they were transported.

Detective Joe Horner slipped over to the house off 49th to walk the scene and take photos and notes. He had officers do a house-to-house and try to ascertain facts about the homeowner victim and any next of kin.

"We are going to need your sister to come down and identify this Adin Dedić person's body at the morgue."

"I will bring her down, Joe. The only issue I see is you don't know if you got the other most dangerous one yet, the Chicagoland boss, Ibro Bekrić. He has every reason to want to kill her. I believe, but cannot yet prove, he was here running this operation you just broke up. He is a definite threat to her life until he is put behind bars. And maybe afterwards," Nick said.

"I understand. We'll know who we scooped up soon enough. Thank Lola by the way. She led us right there."

"Detective Horner, I know you might need my phone for evidence, but could you release my purse, IDs, credit card, and money? I have to be back at the transitional academy for the shooting segment at eight a.m. tomorrow."

"I don't see why we can't oblige you there," Joe Horner said, adding, "I will do my best to break you two loose by ten or so tonight. This is a pretty straight forward kidnap, attempted sexual battery, self-defense by Nick and witnessed by you, and murder of the old gent who was in the recycle bin. The bald bruisers will take longer."

"Just remember, Joe, Ibro Bekrić is the big boss and the key to this whole thing. I shudder to think of my sister, Angie, having to go back up into the quagmire up there to testify."

"There's always the witness protection program," Joe Horner said.

"I lost my sister when she was a toddler. We have just reunited. *I will be her only witness protection program.* With Lola."

"And me!" Maria chimed in.

"Nick, Lola, and Angie are my only family now. I would do anything to protect each of them!" she said.

"Joe, Maria saved my life. She took down the man who shot the congressman and his bodyguard in Honduras, where she was a detective sergeant. I was unarmed and the shooter turned his gun on me. I would do anything to protect her."

"And he just did! He took on a much larger man who was going to rape and kill me. Took him on with his bare hands. I have never seen anything like it, Detective Horner!" Maria exclaimed.

"Okay, you two. Save this for the interview room please," the detective ordered.

Horner and Detective Larry Wilton interviewed Maria first. It took two hours. Nick sat in a break area and drank too much coffee. He called Lola and spoke, in turn to Angie, Lottie, Carly, and Erica. What a family he had amassed in just weeks. Of course Erica had counted for longer, he thought to himself.

He finished several well-worn gun magazines, a couple of police magazines, and even one Better Homes and Gardens. He was a homeowner and destined to be a husband. He figured he needed to know that sort of thing.

Retrospectively, dismissed the décor and planting stuff. Let the ladies handle the first and a guy like the one into whose lawn service rig he ditched the tracker handle the other.

Joe and Maria walked back. Both were tired looking, but otherwise smiling and happy.

"I wish we had snagged this one instead of Tampa getting her," Joe said.

"She's a catch for any agency." Back to Horner, she silently mouthed "Or for you!" and smiled. Nick knew her well enough by now to even read the exclamation point.

"Your turn, my friend. I'll make it quick and pain-less. Anything you need first? Restroom break?" Joe Horner asked.

"After most of SPPDs supply of coffee, yes. Speaking of pain, do you think anyone here would have an Advil? I forgot I have a bum leg while running up the stairs and fighting a giant guy today. My leg is reminding me big time."

"You hit the head, and I will see what I can scrounge up."

Nick said "Thanks," and turned to visit the facility with which he was now well-acquainted.

Nick had seen Horner in action during one of the more perplexing cases while running the task force. He knew he was thorough and the consummate professional.

Detectives Joe Horner and Larry Wilton proved it in the next two hours. Shortly after the interview was finished, Wilton gave him a statement to review and sign.

Nick had a couple of small changes mainly to emphasize points he thought should be brought out stronger. Wilton made the changes quickly as Nick waited due to automated policing and signed the statement.

He was left sitting in the interview room for ten minutes. Then, a woman in a conservative suit walked in.

"Mr. Wolf, I am Assistant State's Attorney, Laura Belk. I have just gone over your statement with the boss. We both agree it was a clean, if not amazing, kill you did today. I just dropped in to advise you no charges will be coming as a result of your action. We see it as what it was, defense of your life as well as of Detective Sosa's. It met all the tenants of Florida laws regarding self-defense."

"Thank you, Ms. Belk, for your courtesy. I really appreciate it. It, as you might imagine, has been a very long day. Stiff and very sore, he struggled to his feet using the table for support and proffered his hand. They shook and she nodded and walked out of the door."

Detective Larry Wilton walked in. He had been standing in the hall outside the interview room.

"Larry, any word on whether Ibro Bekrić is in the group you rounded up today?" Nick asked moments later as they walked down the hall to be greeted by Maria.

"I don't know with absolute certainty, but I think the answer is 'no,'" he said.

"Not good. He's dangerous to all of the folks under my protection. I am certain he is here somewhere."

"If he is, Nick, we'll find him." *If I don't first,* Nick thought.

"Thanks for everything, Larry. You guys are the best. Tell Joe for me, okay?" Nick said.

"I will. He is briefing the brass right now. It's gonna be a long night for the whole squad." Nick nodded and gently pushed Maria in the direction of the parking lot.

"I have to be back here at the academy in only ten hours. Can't we just go to your house? Or a motel?" she asked.

"Your idea is completely logical. But no. Under today's stress, our resolve is going to be weak. It would be a mistake, honey."

She wrinkled her nose. Something he which recognized signaled disagreement. A "tell" she might want to work on as a detective.

"You know...you are wrong about one thing."

"What am I wrong about Maria?"

"My resolve is stronger than ever."

"Oh," he said, not knowing where else to go with it.

He opened the door to the Mercedes and drove the short distance to the college which hosted the academy and a number of permanent criminal justice and emergency responder curricula.

She got out, her rental Mustang key fob and purse returned by Joe Horner.

Maria walked over to the driver's side of the Mercedes and Nick lowered the window.

"Thank you for everything you did today. You saved me from rape, torture and probably murder. I will always be in your debt.

"You are missing out on the best night of your life by us going back to the farm. Just know it. The damn best,

Nick." She reached out and caressed his cheek and turned, walking back to the red Mustang.

The biggest message Nick got out of her words and demeanor was *Oh shit, this is a woman, not a girl. And she is one hell of a force to be reckoned with.*

He just wished he did not have to reckon with her.

Nick started the car and the two people in two cars drove to rural Polk County to where others they loved and who loved them waited anxiously.

He let out a long breath. His leg hurt like hell. He had accomplished his mission. And, he had released his newly appearing sister from her dangerous husband. Forever.

Nick had had to knock on doors and deliver bad news to families as both a deputy and as a detective. It was one of the worst jobs in law enforcement.

Tonight's was strangely easier. Of course he knew his sister was in deathly fear of the man she had "married" in some sort of ceremony sans any legal licensure.

But, at some point, she must have loved him. Loved the man her brother killed today. He wondered if it would make more sense in the morning. Or next month?

He decided it would probably be one of those things in life you just did not understand and never would. He accepted it. More or less. And drove on watching the red taillights of a red Mustang.

My bed at their home in St. Petersburg would feel really good tonight. Better than the cot in Polk County. Then, the cot was better than the floor.

I've slept under far worse conditions at a number of places around the world. But I've also shared a bivvy sack with Lola in the pouring rain in an open boat. The best night ever.

Nick quickly reviewed the bivvy sack. He remembered while the outside conditions had been deplorable, the company and the sense of the whole experience had been pretty damn wonderful. He put a large bag of frozen green peas he found in the freezer on his leg and tried to go to sleep. Rabby Burns said it best, the thing about the best laid plans of mice and men oft going astray.

4

Morning would come far too early for the ones who had to get up at dawn. But the usual security protocols had to be maintained, no matter how stressful the day had been.

Nick's cot was by the front door was where he had slept on the floor. Within feet of his sister still sleeping on the sofa.

Maria's cot was in clear sight at the rear door. Clear enough for him to see her wave at him before putting on her sleep tee shirt. Not after. For several seconds, hands on bare hips smiling. Smiling a serious and very grown-up smile.

Lord, I wish she would hurry up and get an apartment. And Lottie and Carly would move to Key West. And Erica, as wonderful as she too was, would move into her new old craftsman-style house several blocks from Lola and Nick.

Angie. She needed a whole new life. Hopefully nearby. A job. A place to live in peace and safety. A new start.

Lola. Finn. Nick. It was enough for day-to-day life. Erica would work there. Maria and Angie would visit on weekends, Maria's case load permitting. The other two? Who knew?

Normal—the old normal is what I want. I want to hear Lola softly breathing beside me every night. Not too much to ask, is it?

He drifted off sleeping still on high alert like in the Ranger days. It had been a long, trying day. And a damned painful night. But, he had been successful. Maria was safe. He was alive. One of the worst members of the Bekrić crime family was dead. The head of the snake was hiding under a bush somewhere and needed to be found. Many of his henchmen were in Pinellas County jail awaiting arraignment on multiple charges.

Nick drifted off, half waiting for the game cams to alert. They did not as the hours marched towards dawn and the country sky, unsullied by city lights, began to brighten.

Maria finished putting on her new golf shirt, trousers, and old trainers awoke him. Probably by design. The sounds, though not loud, caused Angie, nearby on the sofa to stir.

Erica came down the steps in one of Nick's old shirts, ready to send off Maria with a full stomach. Nick went to the bathroom while it was empty. The shower smelled like water, soap and something sweeter. Perfume? He washed his hands, brushed his teeth and walked out alone to pull on yesterday's clothes long enough to open the barn door and get Maria underway. He heard soft voices in the kitchen and walked in for some very necessary coffee.

It was pretty bold of her going to class today after being kidnapped from the end of class yesterday. She owed a debt of gratitude to the students who saw what was happening, drew all the right conclusions and reported it immediately.

And to Lola for programming Maria's phone to allow them to track it.

"Hi, all," Nick said as he poured a cup of just finishing coffee dripping into the pot.

"Hi, yourself. How do you feel?" Erica asked.

"Like I fought a bear and barely won."

"I wouldn't say 'barely.' Decisively comes more to mind, Nick," Maria beamed.

He nodded.

"At least I can drink coffee this morning. The bear can't," he replied.

"I cannot begin to tell you how relieved I feel without that animal stalking me," Angie said as she walked in from the living room.

"What's the agenda today, Nick?" Lola asked, also appearing and seeking coffee.

"I need to speak with Rob Gadsden and inquire about two things. The first is he was going to have somebody track down Ibro Bekrić and the others on the flight manifests coming into Tampa or St. Petersburg/Clearwater Airports from either O'Hare or Midway in the past week. We need the answer. We are not safe until the Chicago head of the Bekrić crime family is removed from the game.

"The second thing is to find out if FDLE is finished with our two primary sidearms," he said.

"Is 'removed from the game' as a euphemism for 'killed,' or do you mean it as just a broad expression?" Angie asked.

"More the latter, but I don't care which happens. If he resists arrest and dies, so be it," Nick said.

"Speaking of shooting, today is the day I get to shine on the academy range," Maria noted.

"Front sight, coordinate your breathing, press straight back," Lola advised.

"Listen to her, Maria. She's the best shot in our little family here," Nick said seriously.

"Better than you?" Angie asked.

"Yep. Better than me."

"Honey, among the Rangers, CID, sheriff, task force and our agency...how many firefights have you been in?" Lola asked, since he normally did not talk about his prior life.

"Lola, I truly do not know. I have tried to forget the ones overseas. There were a lot. More than I could reconstruct in my mind. I guess I remember the face-to-face ones. And the ones where I was wounded. You know about the ones since the agency was formed. You were generally there."

"I certainly remember you saving me against the Jamaican kingpin at our front door in St. Petersburg. I remember the one in Roatan—you do, too, Maria—and the bear. The bear was more sheer guts than accuracy though, since it was from inches away from his claws and teeth. I've counted seven scars on your torso. One looks like an IED, one like a knife. The rest are bullet holes."

"Like I say. I try to forget them. I am going to open the barn so Maria can get her undercover red-hot rod out," he said, walking over to his cot and picking up the AK laying on the floor.

"Right behind you!" Maria said.

"Me, too!" Angie added.

Lola picked up the Mini-14 and followed along to cover his six.

Maria off, Nick decided to walk the property and check the cameras and look for anything out of place. Angie followed. Lola went back to be the farmhouse defender. It was a job not yet rendered obsolete by yesterday's death and arrests.

"How's everything going, brother? You okay with killing your brother-in-law. Of sorts, that is."

"It was him or Maria and me. He didn't leave any other option. Maybe I could have relieved the crushed larynx with a pen or straw inserted as a breathing tube. Who knows?"

"So, you just watched him?" she asked.

"Partially. I had Maria tied to the bed naked. I needed to see if she had been raped or otherwise drugged, beaten or whatever. I had a probably dead homeowner somewhere. I didn't know if there was anyone else in the house. Good or bad."

"I'm glad he's dead. I am glad one of the two of us did it. I only wish it had been me. You have enough ghosts to worry your dreams, dearest."

He put his free arm around her shoulder and they walked silently, though Nick's vigilance did not decrease at all.

Nick waited until nine-thirty to call Rob.

"Good morning, how are you, Rob?"

"Busy, but I understand from my Tampa Bay crew you have been too. Took on a two hundred-sixty pounder bare-handed, did you? Wasn't the damn bear enough?"

"He had already killed a homeowner and had Maria tied to a bed. He was down to his skivvies when I arrived. There was not a lot of time to choose options."

"Why didn't you just shoot him? It would have been justified to save her life."

"I was in the doorway and he was exactly between Maria and me. I could not chance it hitting her," Nick said.

"Tough. The report I saw said the fight did not take too long."

"Well, you know my endurance is not so good anymore. I have to finish them quickly. I sure as hell can't run, Rob."

"Point taken. To answer your question, my Tampa office has your two pistols. All cleaned up nice, too!"

"Thanks. The pistols were actually question two. Question one had to do with your look at the Chicago to Tampa Bay manifests for name ending with a letter with an accent over it. Did you encounter Ibro Bekrić, perchance?"

"Give me a second. I am in my office in Tallahassee. It's on my desk somewhere."

"Bekrić, Ibro. Got him! Arrived two days ago apparently alone," Rob said.

"Please share the lists with Detective Joe Horner at SPPD. He has several in custody. But not Ibro. Was it Joe you got the report from?" Nick asked.

"No, his boss. But the boss speaks well of him."

"Me, too. He was a stalwart in my task force. I need to figure out whether Ibro is trying to escape now or is still determined to kill my sister. Or the other young women I am trying to protect for his Virginia relative, Luka Bekrić."

"Nick, this thing, like everything you seem to touch, has a life of its own. I am flying down to your area today. Maybe we can meet for a confab?"

"Absolutely. I will adjust my trip to pick up the two pistols at your Tampa regional office to coincide with your arrival. I take it you are coming over to St. Petersburg, too?"

"I am, after I stop in at the Tampa office. Want me to bring the guns to you in St. Pete?" Rob asked.

"Perfect. Listen, I could bring my sister down to let her talk about the Bekrić operation in Chicago. Would it help, since a lot of those guys are in custody?

"I suspect she will have to ID the guy I killed, since she was his wife by a non-licensed Bosnian wedding ceremony. She does not consider it binding though and has always kept the Wolf name."

"Yes. Do it. I am sure Joe and the guys at SPPD would like to have her identify the ones in custody with the names she knows them by. SPPD only has the names on their licenses, which could be from counterfeit IDs."

"Why don't we meet at SPPD Headquarters. Just ask for your friend Joe. Say about four. Maybe we can grab something to eat after. If there is any snag, I will let you know."

They broke the connection and Nick assembled his A-team for a talk.

He decided to take Lola's small van, do a TSCM on the new BMW and drive it to the meeting and back to Polk County. He doubted if Ibro had been part of any surveillance but did not particularly care if he recognized all of their vehicles at this point.

Nick spent some quality time with Finn, who had not suffered any lack of attention with the house full of women who adored him.

He really wanted Lola to go, but she told him what he knew already. She had to stay and protect the homestead. He did not mention swapping cars. He just used his set of keys to the small van. Knowing he was going to have to lie on his back, he tossed his Bug-out bag in the van and hung a suit, shirt, tie and put some dark socks and dress shoes in the back. He also remembered to take a pair of loaded magazines for the Shadow Systems CR 920 pistols and his inside-the-waistband holster.

He and Angie left. She was in a business suit and looked like a model. He was in jeans and a fishing shirt and looked like a flats guide. Which would change after he checked out the BMW and put on the suit. Then, they would look like twins modeling the executive look on any runway. New York, Miami, or Paris. Except one of the models would be limping.

Nick was slowly breaking his sister in on things like OPSEC and surveillance detection routes. He considered everyone needed to be aware of their surroundings, but she did particularly, since the most dangerous Chicago Bekrić of all was still lurking about, his location unknown.

Nick circled the block around the house. They entered by the alley, and he activated the power gate into the backyard and its parking. She stayed in the van as he checked the yard and the GTI and Beemer. Angie went into the house with him while he disarmed the alarm. He could tell from the alarm panel everything had been alright and did not need to clear the whole house.

Both grabbed some more clothes and she took the time for a long, hot shower.

She held the AK, ready to toss or slide it to him as he ran the bug scanner under and inside the BMW. He also did an underbody check on Lola's—now his—GTI. Both were clean.

They went inside and he put on the suit and the holster for his soon-to-be returned pistol. Time was beginning to be of the essence, so he did not go upstairs this trip.

It was only ten minutes to the St. Petersburg Police Headquarters so they had time to sit outside chatting.

"Where do you think Ibro Bekrić might be, Angie?" Nick asked.

"Since he probably thinks nobody knows he's here, I think he would have checked into a luxury hotel. He is rich as Croesus and conceited. He believes, as I do, his men won't give him up to the police. The guys I saw and who I assume are the ones in custody, are his inner sanctum of enforcers. He demands and gets the utmost loyalty and pays them well for it," Angie said. She looked lovingly at her long-lost brother. One so much like her she would have recognized him out of a crowd anywhere. One she had never seen in a suit.

"So we should look in the top resorts in the area? Hotels he could check into without advance reservations?" Nick asked.

"I think so, honey. It would fit."

"You and I will share this with both Joe Horner and with my statewide friend, Rob Gadsden in a few minutes."

They chatted until, looking at his Luminox watch, he realized they should go. Fashionably late would not cut it with this crowd.

He started the BMW, which thankfully did not explode. Angie came from behind the shed, where he had sent her, and got in beside him. He pressed the button on the keychain, and the gate opened. They pulled into the alley and watched it automatically close behind them as the rear of the car broke the beam on the mechanism.

He accelerated down the alley and not long later they were parking at SPPD's headquarters complex.

They asked for Detective Joe Horner at the front desk. Minutes later, Joe and Rob walked out and greeted them.

"You all are twins, right?" Rob asked.

"No, he's the older and better looking one," Angie answered.

"I believe he's the older, but might argue the latter part," Rob said as they walked down the hall to an interview room to chat.

"What I'd like to do is have a bit of a lineup where we have you name each of our bald and bulky suspects from behind a one-way window, Ms. Wolf," Joe said.

"After that and chatting about whatever Joe needs in further elaboration about them and the possible whereabouts of Ibro Bekrić. Then, we need to take you over to the morgue and have you positively identify the person we believe to be Adin Dedić, in your capacity as next of kin," Rob said. Clearly, Nick thought, the two had developed a plan for the afternoon.

He also noticed Rob was carrying a thick padded manila envelope which looked just like it may contain two upscale compact 9mm pistols. Shadow Systems ones, quite probably. He sure hoped so.

From a booth protecting her identity and words, Angie was able to positively identify the three Bekrić associates and comment on their particular use. She mentioned one was pure muscle. A knee capper. The other two were trusted gofers, also with violent capabilities. They had apparently come in with false IDs as the driver's licenses and credit card in their wallets and the names Angie gave differed. Both the SPPD and the FDLE men took careful notes. All had been armed, Joe later told them and had Illinois concealed pistol licenses. Which were not recognized by Florida and would add another charge to a growing list.

Back in the interview room, Joe and Rob asked Angie a variety of questions to fill in blanks in their case files. She obliged and recited her answers clearly and without hesitation. Nick sat back and listened proudly. And carefully. The more he knew about Ibro Bekrić's people and his organization in general, the better chance he had of bringing him to justice. Yes, the robust law enforcement agencies of the Sunshine State had been brought to bear against the crime boss, but Nick needed him neutralized right now. It was personal.

"Rob, please share what you all learned about the manifests from the flights these guys took in," Nick asked.

Rob responded in detail, to which Nick asked, "Since we now know Ibro Bekrić' came into Tampa International on Tuesday, arriving around four in the afternoon, we have to assume he took a taxi or a rental car to a hotel. He was not at the commandeered house where the standoff was, so let's assume hotel. He probably did not have time to rent a condo on the beach or anything. It had to be a place he could walk in and flash his credit card and have his luggage carried up. Angie says he is a conceited high life sort of a person.

"It strikes me, pressing the airport rental car agencies should be something we should do. I fear the taxi companies might be a needle in a haystack.

"He flew under his own name, so unless one of his henchmen, whose names and flights we already have, rented it we might be able to determine his transportation description. Then press for tracker information from the rental company.

"If there is none, we begin hitting top hotels in the area. The higher priced ones he might see advertised at the airport walking over to the car rental counters."

"I think it's a worthwhile approach. I understand there is a lot of interest in him for money laundering now in Chicago. They would like him back and are watching banks for him possibly transferring money out.

"Angie, does he have a wife and kids?" Rob finished.

"No, he's a big-time player. Not bad looking in a mature brutish sort of way and flashes a lot of green. So, if you are asking is he flexible to relocate, I'd say the answer is 'very.'"

"Good to know. I have a contact up there on the federal judicial side I have been talking with. We agreed to exchange mutually beneficial information," Rob said.

"Good luck on it being a two-way street," Joe said.

Rob shook his head sardonically.

"Instead of us fighting our way over to the airport at the height of rush hour, let me have some of my agents who are already nearby to do the groundwork on this. I'll make a call right now and get them on it," Rob said and excused himself to call.

The next stop was the morgue. Angie identified her kinda husband with no sign of emotion.

The four then drove in three cars over to 4th Street North and had a quick Tex-Mex dinner, missing only the *cerveza* because two were on duty. As a habit, Nick did not drink when armed, which he finally was with one of the two returned pistols both smelling lightly like Ballistol, his own preference for gun cleaning.

Lola's was in Angie's purse in the envelope. Not legal, but there anyway. These were dangerous times for her.

He knew Joe pretty well, but Rob only from a pure case standpoint. Several cases, actually.

In the conversation Rob said he was a widower and fifty. He had a late teen son getting ready for Florida State University. He loved his job, but the travel was getting a bit old.

His interest in Angie was subtle. But it was there, and it seemed to her brother, reciprocated.

Towards the end of the meal, Rob received a message from one of the Tampa agents assigned to track down a possible rental car in the name Bekrić.

He had found one. It was a silver Jeep Grand Cherokee and he gave the license plate number.

"The good news," Rob began, "is we have the car and description. The bad news is there is not a GPS tracker on it."

"Still, it's a great lead," Nick said, knowing exactly what he was going to do with it.

"He's probably in for the night, so we will have officers beginning to screen hotels at first light," Joe said.

"Call me, Joe, if you want some help from my folks," Rob offered.

They shook. Rob handed Angie one of his business cards "in case you think of something which would be helpful in locating Bekrić."

They parted and Nick and Angie got back in the BMW.

"What now?" Angie asked.

"How about a little sleuthing?" Nick asked, and she nodded with enthusiasm.

"Before we go. You have Lola's 9mm pistol in an envelope in your purse. It's for a dire emergency. If you need it, hold it in two hands, like this." He illustrated with his own very similar pistol. Keep your trigger finger straight out and off the trigger." Again, he illustrated. There is no safety. Just press the trigger to fire. Then, trigger finger out straight again, unless you need to shoot again. Got it?"

She nodded.

"Second, you said Bekrić would probably pick an expensive hotel. I doubt if he would use Tampa with his guys already in St. Petersburg. There are some really nice ones here. Let's try the waterfront one downtown first. It's where he might be pointed by the rental car company if he asked about St. Pete hotels.

"I don't think there is a gate in the parking area, but we'll find out very shortly," Nick said, putting the car in gear.

The ride to the hotel was brief. They lucked out. No gate and need to get a ticket to get out of the parking garage.

They went in and in four circles up to another floor found the Grand Cherokee. It was in a valet parking space.

"Even better! I never use valet, but we can sure take advantage of his laziness tonight."

They hatched a plan and went in to the front desk, still dressed formally and hand-in-hand.

"Oh, hi," Nick said.

"My wife and I just got back from dinner and we noticed something in the parking garage.

"There is a new-looking Jeep Grand Cherokee." He gave the tag number and parking space number.

"It's in the valet area. The left front tire is flat as a pancake. And the driver's door is open. You need to get the owner to check it and make sure something hasn't been taken from it."

The desk clerk, obviously impressed with Nick's

beautiful "wife," went into his computer, ostensibly a valet record base.

"Okay. I have it. I will call the owner and tell him."

"Thanks," Nick, the good Samaritan, said.

"Oh, darling! I forgot my birth control pills. The little container thingy is sitting right on the console. We have to go back to get it."

"Alright, my love. They are too important to leave," Nick said and Angie giggled.

They turned and left as the deck clerk dialed Bekrić's room.

Back in the garage, Nick hid on the side of the door. Angie was out of sight in the BMW. She had the gun out and the windows down, so she could hear any conversation between the door and the Grand Cherokee. Nick's phone was in her hand, Joe Horner's number on speed dial on the screen.

In several minutes the door opened. From behind, Nick saw a man with a shaved head. He was about six-three and weighed at least what Angie's husband, his cousin, did. He was wearing a Hawaiian shirt and shorts. He had flip-flops on. An immediate Florida man upon arrival.

Nick let him get about ten feet in front and raised his gun in a two-handed isosceles hold.

"Mr. Bekrić. Stop and slowly raise your hands. Don't make me shoot you, but I won't hesitate if you do not comply."

The man stopped his shoulders rising to almost envelope his wide neck in shock. He put his hands up and slowly turned around.

"You!"

"Yep. Me. The one who wants to shoot you so badly. So, please give me the tiniest of reasons."

Nick squinted a little and made his trigger finger twitch.

Bekrić actually cringed.

"Call Joe to send in the backup! Tell them Bekrić is has a *Magnum P.I.* shirt and shorts on and I have not shot him quite yet, but I think I may have to before they get here."

Angie smiled at her brother, though neither could see one another. She pressed the button. Joe Horner answered.

"We have Bekrić at gunpoint in the parking garage," and named the hotel and floor of the parking garage.

"He is dressed like a bald Magnum PI and is waiting to be saved by friendly police officers who don't want to kill him so badly," she said.

"Please ask Nick not to kill anybody else this week. We are on the way. I am ten minutes out, patrol will be sooner. I'll also call your new friend Rob," letting her know he noticed the chemistry also.

Within three minutes, Bekrić was cuffed from behind and patted down. In two more, Rob came rolling in, blue lights flashing in his grill. Five more minutes and Rob was on the scene. The entire floor of the parking garage was flashing blue.

Nick reached into his wallet and removed one of Guy Kellogg Bail Bond LLC cards and tucked it in the breast pocket of Bekrić's garish shirt.

"He's the legendary bail bondsman to the rich and famous. I think you will owe me for the introduction."

"The only thing I'll owe you is a slit throat, asshole," Bekrić said.

Nick grinned broadly at him.

"Did you guys hear him threaten me? How about you, Sis? Did you hear him, too?"

"I did. Ibro, you have developed such a potty mouth since I have known you!"

She gave him the identical grin her brother had. It was so strikingly the same Rob and Joe privately commented on it later.

"Rob? Joe? May I kick him in the balls?" Angie asked sweetly.

Several patrol officers snickered.

Rob and Joe looked at each other quizzically for a moment as if they were actually thinking about letting her do it.

Joe answered.

"Angie, my wife would kill me if I let you ruin those great high heels. A guy like this probably is wearing a cup because just looking at him makes people just want to kick him in the balls. Don't you guys think so, too?" he turned and asked the patrolmen. They all nodded vigorously.

The prisoner was assisted to the rear seat of one of the marked police interceptor SUVs and taken "downtown" for arrest charges and interview.

"You may be more feisty than your brother," Rob said to Angie, who just gave him a demure smile. One her brother certainly could not replicate.

"Okay, you ruined our night, but saved a lot of searching in the morning. What do you say we give this capture to SPPD for the records?" Rob asked Nick.

"Absolutely. They cuffed him. They own him. Until he bonds out with Guy Kellogg and skips. Then, I will own his ass when I bring him in bound and gagged in the trunk of the BMW." There was the grin again. On both of them. The two lawmen looked at each other and shook their heads.

"Night, guys. Angie and I have things to do and people to see," Nick said.

"He means he misses his harem back at the farm-house. Lola is watching Lottie, Carly and Maria. Oh! And Erica who is as gorgeous as daughter Lola," Angie added.

They got in the BMW and left St. Petersburg in their rearview mirror. It had been one hell of a two days.

5

The ride back was an ultimate bonding between a very tired sister and brother. They had worked together for the first time ever and brought their objective to a successful conclusion. It was satisfying. The kind of teamwork they both had dreamed about, but never thought could ever occur.

It appeared they could give up the farm and return to their respective homes. Of course Angie and Maria did not have homes yet.

Maria had prospects. She was two days from finishing the transitional academy and being sworn in as a Tampa detective.

Angie's path was not quite as clear. She had a savings account in Chicago, but otherwise no money, no job, and no home.

What she did have was the one thing she had wanted for over thirty years. She had her loving brother back. And, with his help, she would remedy the small things.

The job might take some thinking. The only real job

she had since dropping out of college at nineteen was as an exotic dancer. She was quite good at it, and at thirty-two, still had some headliner years left if she wanted to go back into the same endeavor,

Angie had also been adept at managing and training dancers in Chicago.

It might be a bit difficult to obtain references with one of her superiors dead and another one getting booked currently.

Since Lottie, the heiress, and Carly, her lifelong friend, were also dancers, maybe they could give some advice. She knew Nick, and particularly Lola, would not be ashamed of her if she continued to do what she knew.

The BMW was smooth and fast and she fell asleep in mid-thought. Nick finished the drive in silence.

"Lola. We are coming in. There's no need to open the garage and stand guard as we arrive. Angie and I caught up with Bekrić last night and called Joe Horner. He is in jail now. All of the Chicago mob who we could determine to be Tampa Bay are in custody. One, as you well know, is dead. I believe our threat condition just dropped to normal. We can clear out of the farmhouse and move home, baby."

"Did Bekrić go down hard?" Lola asked.

"Not really. I got the drop on him and my sister called the police.

"Angie cracked up the assembled police officers, Joe, and Rob when she sweetly asked if she could plant a high heel in his groin. They thought about it and decided probably not."

"She has your sense of humor. It's amazing after thirty years to see all the similarities."

"Even I see them. By the way, I am pretty sure she

was serious about the kick. See you in about fifteen minutes."

The women at the farmhouse had already gone to sleep when awakened by Nick's call to Lola. Lola had walked into the living room, the only occupant of which was Maria.

However, the other three joined them immediately.

Lola briefed them on Nick's call.

"Sounds like we can get on with our lives," Lottie commented, thinking of a new Florida home, as Carly did. Erica thought of the impending move to her new house. Maria just wondered how soon circumstances would require her moving away from Nick and Lola. And, how long she could delay it.

They went back to bed, as did Nick and Angie when they arrived. The only difference in sleeping arrangements was Erica insisting to take Nick's cot and let him sleep in "a real bed." Which importantly had the other raven-haired beauty in it.

Nick felt back home for the first time in over a week as his partner snuggled up to him and went to sleep. He could feel her warm breath lightly blowing the hairs on his chest.

Smiling, he thought "Yep. I'm home," and went to sleep. One other person stared at the ceiling for a long time on her cot near the rear door. She was up and heading towards the academy early the next day.

Later in the day, when Nick, Lola, and Erica were packing cots, guns, food, and everything but personal items, Angie met with the two other dancers.

"You guys have spent your career dancing. Just like me. I am at the point of wanting to relocate to Tampa Bay to be with Nick. I have no furniture, car, job, or very much money.

"Dancing, recruiting, training, or managing dancers is all I know.

"What are your thoughts? Get a dancing job and try to quickly work my way off the pole or stage?" Angie asked.

The other two thought a while. Finally, Lottie spoke.

"Carly and I have been scouring the Internet while the rest of you have been running to and fro. We have decided Key West is beautiful, but may be too limiting. It's a hundred miles down a narrow road from the rest of the world.

"There's island living right here in Tampa Bay. And lots more things to do. And we want to use some of that money to travel. At Key West, the nearest big airport is Miami. One hundred sixty miles away.

"I am going to get a financial manager for all this money. Maybe put it in a trust. Maybe invest some.

"We have an idea, since like you, dancing is all Carly and I know, I should buy or start a club. A real high-class joint. The best girls, drinks and surroundings. Maybe a high-class appetizer bar open at the beginning of rush hour. Pub food for lunch and during dinner.

"What do you think? We could get Nick to help lay out the security needs and maybe train the bouncers.

"We'd need help with experience in the business. You could be our first hire.

"This is just an idea, but one we have been talking over for a coupla days," Lottie said.

"I think it sounds exciting! I'd love to help you two put it together and run it while you are traveling," Angie said.

The last task was the bucket line to move the sandbags to a stack outside the house. It took a while and was as exhausting as it had originally been.

Nick and Erica did a walk through and he called the realtor. The realtor came over, accepted the keys and unexpectedly for Nick, a check from Lottie.

They formed a convoy led by Lola and her mother in the BMW, Lottie and Carly in the Mercedes, and Nick and Angie in the larger van. Finn was curled up in Angie's lap and slept the whole way.

Out of habit, Nick did a quick walk around when they arrived at the house on Central Avenue. Everything was fine.

"Lola, it looks just like a dancing pole in our bedroom. How on earth did it get there?" Nick asked.

She broke out in the most lascivious of the many lascivious smiles she had previously given him.

"It's a little surprise from the girls to you," she said.

"I am assuming only you will use it. I can imagine our little detective being the first to strip down and try it," he said seriously.

"Oh, not to worry. It will just be me. And Mom of course."

Nick looked at the woman with whom he could communicate wordlessly. He could not read her at all. He hoped she was kidding. Pretty much hoped.

His wise Cuban foster father told him once "Boy, you are better off to keep your mouth shut sometimes than to open it and prove how stupid you are. I live by it and believe it is why Marisa and I have had a wonderful marriage for thirty years so far."

Lola met his stare with a half-smile on her face. He let her win the stare down and did not say a word.

Maria came home that night shocked to find Tampa PD had switched to Sig 320 semiautomatics and she would be issued a compact model to carry upon being sworn in on Monday. Lola assured her the adjustment from her familiar Glock would be an easy one as she had done the same exact transition at FHP with no problem before she left the agency.

Lottie received a call from her Boca Raton realtor advising they had a bid for her father's home. The realtor advised it was a fair one. She could counter or just accept. She decided on the latter and sold the house furnished. It was a cash buyer, as many multi-million-dollar homebuyers are. The closing was fast and she and Carly were back in St. Petersburg by the end of the week.

Maria was sworn in at Tampa PD and issued her badge, unmarked car, and new pistol. She was assigned to a general response team instead of one focusing on specific crimes. It was felt exposing her to general detective work was a more efficient way to break her in to US, Florida, and Tampa law enforcement. Neither she nor anyone else disagreed with the approach.

Nick and Lola spent the next several days contacting their insurance and law clients and catching everything up. What had seemed months, actually was not.

Lottie, Carly, and Angie found a realtor who specialized in business sales from Sarasota up through the northern parts of Tampa Bay. There were no exotic dance clubs for sale. He took them to look at several restaurants. Carly's pre-law degree paid dividends as she asked the right questions about why the restaurants had come onto the market.

"Was this business mismanaged? Or, underfunded from the start?" she asked. She made it plain they could live with bad management, unpopular menu, or poor health department inspections.

"What we can't live with is bad traffic patterns or access, not enough parking, or insufficient hotels nearby for which a club might be a draw for bored business travelers.

"We are not looking to be 'boys night out' for drunk college kids on spring break. We will create a classy environment and need a neighborhood which will support it.

"If there are hookers walking down the main drag nearby, forget it," she told the realtor.

"They found a possible location just north of Sarasota. They saw it and arranged a second showing of the empty former restaurant at six-thirty. Nick, Lola, Erica, and Maria were all invited to comment.

"Nick remembered the building in several eatery iterations, none bad, but neither were any particularly good.

"The place we hit in Northern Virginia was set up okay from a security standpoint. The camera placement inside was good. There was a gap with none out back. A security issue when dancers come in from the back alley. More lighting was needed. I think a police alarm would be good in case there was an Antifa or similar rush in, or even a large fight beyond the capability of the bouncers. AEDs, fire extinguishers somewhat more than code requirements, first aid kit. Things like those items should be there and accessible," Nick said at first glance.

"We'd have to build a main stage and several smaller ones. Install poles. Maybe a wall back there"—Lottie pointed—"for dressing rooms and an office."

"I noticed, like in most places, the ladies' room was larger than the men's. There will be many more men wanting to get rid of some beer than non-dancer women for sure.

"I wonder if you could move the door to the ladies'

room and include the room in with the dressing room with only interior access. Then, make the men's room the ladies' room and add a larger men's room?" Erica suggested.

"I have a guy who does wall moves and renovations. Let's get him in here to give an estimate for these ideas before you put any money down," the realtor said.

The two primaries agreed.

The realtor promised to have his construction friend come in and bid on the items suggested and left them. A quick poll was conducted and Italian won.

Olive Garden was decided to be dependable Italian comfort food. None were Italian nor gourmets, so OG it was.

"How can I be a guest dancer?" Maria asked during dinner.

"I guess it would not be unheard of to have a mystery guest with a Mardi Gras mask," Carly said.

"Maybe you could have another one the following week?" Lola said to Carly's delight and her fiancé's chagrin.

"And another to cater to your more senior guests," Erica shocked everyone, including her daughter.

"Well, this is Sarasota. There are a lot of rich older guys driving around in Bentley convertibles, Porsches, and the like," Lottie noted.

Erica caught Nick in a slight eye-roll.

"This has been great, ladies. I think you professional dancers are onto something here. The non-professionals...I just don't know. You are all beautiful and fit enough, it's just...well, I don't know," he said, leaving his thought hanging in mid-air.

"I already have the check, Nick, so don't try to be your usual man of the house," Lottie said.

"I won't then. Thank you, ma'am." He rose and all rose with him since they were all going to sleep in the same place.

The next morning, Bail Bondsman to the Rich and Famous, Guy Kellogg called him from his regional headquarters atop a bank building overlooking the Sarasota waterfront.

"Thanks for the referral of this Bekrić fellow last night. The St. Pete office handled it after his first appearance up there. Apparently the judge thought he was a moderate flight risk, based on a hundred-thousand-dollar bail."

"I would agree with the judge's assessment. He is a mean-ass Bosnian crime lord with fingers in dancing clubs, human trafficking, probably money laundering through the clubs and a pedophile resort in Roatan," Nick noted, adding "I suspect the government prosecutors up in Chicago will negotiate him away because all we have him on down here is accessory to kidnapping."

"By pedophile resort do you mean the one where the congressman was killed?" Guy asked.

"The very one. I was there in front of the dishonorable congressman when he was shot. I was next on the agenda until a very nice Honduran detective sergeant put the shooter down."

"So, you figured you'd capture him, turn him over to the cops. Him being a big crime boss and all, he would skip and do a runner, and you would bring him back for a decent, but smaller than usual fee? Did I miss anything?" Guy asked.

"No, I believe you hit the high points."

"And you weren't going to call me and warn me about what a high risk dude this Bekrić is?"

"Oh, heavens no, Guy. I would never insult your

experience and intelligence to tell you something so obvious. You could smell this guy's risk quotient all the way from down in Sarasota."

"Well, yes. I did. I'll call you and Lola if Bekrić skips."

"I will be waiting for your call," Nick said as Kellogg hung up.

"Was that Guy?" Lola asked as she walked into the room with a tray upon which were three steaming cups of coffee. "What was he saying?"

"Sounds like he was busting Nick's chops," piped in Erica.

"Was he? About Bekrić?" Lola asked.

"Kinda. But it's a hundred-thousand-dollar bail bond. Which is a twenty-thousand-dollar fee for bringing him back," Nick said.

"You could get yourself a third of a new car," Lola said.

"Nope. I don't buy my cars with agency money. Besides the last time I bought a new car, I lost it immediately."

"No comment. Don't forget the big diamond we added on to the car deal, okay?"

"I do not recall hearing that," Nick responded in perfect court-speak.

Lola, who was not a major jewelry fan anyway, let it slide.

The three dancing entrepreneurs returned excited. With the cash sale of the two and a half million-dollar estate in Boca Raton, Lottie was able to write a check at closing for the restaurant and gave a check to the construction company to begin rehabbing the new dance club.

Maria came in later and advised she now was the

chief investigating officer of a chain of convenience store robberies in Tampa.

"Tell us about it," Lola prompted.

"It's a gang of about five or six late teens. They are Black, Latino, and White. Have the look of gangbangers. They carry decent weapons. Seems orchestrated.

"Car pulls up by front door, they pile out with pistols and short weapon. Sawed-off shotgun? Cheap submachine gun? Unknown. One stays at door, others hit store. One does the cashier robbery of the register, others go for beer," Maria said.

"Any shots fired so far?" Lola asked.

"Not yet. A couple of older customers roughed up."

"How about cameras? Anything?" Nick asked.

"Older independent stores with either non-operational cameras or none at all," Maria said.

"Customer witnesses help?" Nick asked, though experience already told him what the answer would be. He had had a perpetrator once described to him as a black/white sort of a guy with a black nickel-plated pistol.

"Witnesses have been...ugh, less than helpful," Maria said.

"As chief investigating officer, do you have a team working with you?" Lola asked.

"There is a holdup team for all the robberies recently. I am part of it and just heading the convenience store segment."

They just want to watch your logic and your actions as you break in. I'll bet there is a detective sergeant standing back running things with some seasoned detectives ready to swoop in when you need them Nick thought to himself. He was pretty certain Lola was thinking exactly the same thing.

"Do any of your fellow detectives wear vests when working armed robbery cases?" Nick asked.

"I have my thin one on under my shirt. I think they all do, too," she said.

"Do you have a long gun issued? If so, do you keep it immediately at hand when responding to a holdup in progress?" Lola asked.

"I do. It's in the trunk. Now you mention it, I will put it inside the car when I get a call."

"Remember, your pistol is what you use to fight your way to a rifle or shotgun," Nick said.

"Yes, dad."

"Just be real careful, honey. One against five or so armed idiots is a bad ratio. Even untrained, they can put up a heavy curtain of lead," Lola said.

"Lola knows the need to take care. Nobody patrols more alone than a trooper. Their backup is often far off. They have scary ass jobs, Maria," Nick added.

"Have you fired the Sig?" Lola asked.

"Just a quick fam course."

"Let's slip down to one of the indoor ranges with night hours. There are a couple of good ones just south of the Skyway Bridge. We can eat on the way back," Nick said, going to the supply cabinet and taking out one box of 9mm practice cartridges and one of carry hollow points and some earmuffs. "Lola and I need to practice with our new pistols and Erica needs to reacquaint herself with her agency revolver."

Lottie and Carly were already out to check the new property progress, so they left them texts saying the alarms were on at the house.

The next hour of shooting was beneficial for all. The two PIs liked the Shadow Systems 9mm's more each shot. The other two did well continuing their familiarity with their pistol and revolver, respectively.

Maria remembered Nick saying Lola was both the better shot and driver. Lola had replied Nick had far more firefight experience than she would ever have because of his long combat experience. She had privately told Maria later he had fought in some of the most inhospitable places on earth. Lola admitted he had to withhold some locations from her for non-disclosure agreement reasons.

Because of not believing Nick's boast about Lola, Maria subtly but closely compared their targets. Lola's were great, with small groups. Nick, who aimed and shot faster, had even smaller groups. He seemed to be master of the double tap or controlled pair strategy, his groups showing pairs of touching holes throughout the small circle of holes in the bullseye. His bullseyes were not sixteen holes, but eight pairs of holes clustered in the same space. Interesting, she thought. She would ask him about it privately one day.

The next day, she went to the criminalistics analysts area after roll call.

"Hi, I'm new. I'm Detective Maria Sosa," she said to another pretty Latina in the office of several.

"Hi, Maria. I am Anna Rodriguez. Nice to meet you. What can we do for you, Maria?"

"I've been assigned to investigate a series of convenience store holdups. They seem to primarily be in the Ybor City area and hitting independent stores. Most have Indian or Pakistani owner/operators.

"What I wondered is if one of your services was plotting them on a map with dates and times so I could detect a pattern?" Maria said.

"We sure do plotting. Let me take a quick look at our

latest robbery database," Anna said, sitting at her computer and tapping into a spreadsheet.

"Okay. I have five in the database. How many have you had?"

"Six, Anna. Let me give you the latest one yesterday afternoon."

She watched as Anna updated the database, then designed a format and saved it as "Ybor Convenience Stores" with the date range.

She printed it out and gave five copies to Maria.

"You are a miracle worker!" Maria said.

"Oh, no. This is an easy one. You should see how long case comparisons on cold cases can take! Give me your phone." Anna sent her a text with her information. Maria saved it in her Contacts, the new business card exchange.

"Thanks! Coffee sometime?" she said to Anna.

"You bet! I am always here. You should meet all the analysts. A couple are not in right now. Maybe on our coffee day." Maria smiled and left.

She dropped a copy of the annotated map off at her sergeant's office with a note and went to her car.

She started with the oldest holdup last week and re-interviewed the owner. He could not add any more information than that which she had inherited. She went in chronological order, oldest to newest. By lunchtime, she had a good picture in her notebook. She would type it up and add it to her case folder on the seat beside her.

Before she could get in the drive-up line, the radio crackled and she heard her call sign followed by "units in the area. An armed convenience store holdup in progress." The name of the store and address was given followed by "Handle Code-3."

She remembered her advice from her PI friends and pulled over and removed her M4 rifle from its case in the trunk. She put the tip of the barrel in the passenger floorboard, flipped on the blue LED lights in the grille and windshield and rear window and pulled out of the Wendy's. She knew where the store was. She had just been there.

Maria activated the siren and sped the mile to the scene, concentrating on vehicles approaching to see if any had groups of gangbangers and looked like they were running from the robbery.

She turned the siren off a couple of blocks from the store and slowed down. As she rounded the corner and the store came into sight, she saw several late teens with guns running from it. An older man stepped out, shaking his fist at them.

One turned and shot at him with a pistol from about forty feet. The man ran back into his store.

Maria stopped her car and stepped out, rifle in hand. She shouldered it and yelled, "Halt! Police!"

The shooter turned to her and aimed. He fired the same time as she did.

Her accuracy with the Armalite pattern carbine was greater than his. His bullet flew past her, albeit too close for comfort. Her .223 bullet hit him in the chest and he folded. The car, which she identified as an older Nissan Altima, powered off leaving the teen on the sidewalk. She saw four occupants, including the driver. She got back in her car and picked up the Motorola radio microphone.

She gave her call sign and said. "Officer involved shooting! One suspect down at Pack and Run store in Ybor. Need ambulance and sergeant now! I am going in to check for other victims."

Her sergeant was the next person on the radio. "Detective, back up is a minute away, including me. Wait for our arrival. Anything on the rest?"

"Yes, Sarge. Green old model Nissan Altima heading for downtown from this location. Occupied four times."

The radio dispatcher put out an All-Units with the car's description and direction of travel.

By this time, Maria was on scene. She parked her Taurus, blues still flashing and approached the man down with her gun in hand. She kicked his gun away but marked its location in her memory.

She knelt beside him and felt for a pulse. None. She heard what she knew to be an ambulance coming and let them deal with resuscitation. She took a medium evidence bag out of her slacks pocket and picked up the shooter's pistol with her pen in the end of the barrel and put it carefully into the bag and sealed, timed and signed it as her sergeant pulled up along with several patrol SUVs and the EMTs.

Maria looked at the face of the person she had shot.

"You okay?" the sergeant asked. His name was John Ross. She would shortly find out he had been one of Nick's task force detectives a couple years ago and a good friend.

"Yeah. I think this guy is dead. He shot at the owner who went back inside. I listened to you and have not checked on him yet to see if he was hit. He ran pretty quickly before this guy turned and shot at me. I shot him almost simultaneously. His gun is here in the evidence bag. I handled it with my pen in the barrel. There should be two casings on the sidewalk we'll need to protect."

Ross turned to an arriving detective.

"Take his pistol in the bag here and put evidence pyramids over two cartridge cases on the sidewalk.

"You! Jones. Go inside and check on the owner. This guy shot at him. He may be wounded. If not, please take his statement and those of any witnesses in the store.

"Maria, give me your sidearm. It's procedure in any officer shooting," Ross said.

"I used my rifle. It's in the front floorboard," she said, pointing to her Taurus almost up on the sidewalk. "My friend Nick Wolf taught me your pistol is what you use to fight to your rifle," she said automatically.

"Nick Wolf? The PI? With a limp?" he asked.

She nodded. "He's my friend and old boss at the task force he headed."

She stared at him, open-mouthed in surprise, but said nothing. The emotional impact of taking a life was sinking in. Ross looked at her and realized it. He would get her to the chaplain first, then a psychologist.

His thoughts were interrupted by the sound of multiple shots some blocks away. Maybe thirty shots.

Before he could react, the radio reported "Shots fired, police officers involved" and gave a nearby inter-section location.

He keyed the mic of a handheld and identified himself as responding.

"Maria, can you drive okay?" She nodded. "Follow me! I think our guys are in a firefight with your robbers."

He sprinted for his car and she got into hers. He took off, siren sounding and she followed behind him for the short ride.

The shooting had stopped as they arrived. The obvious score was Tampa PD four, Robbers zero. This time, there were no deaths, but several critical injuries and one minor. Officers approached and Ross supervised the scene and told Maria "moving weapons and putting them in evidence bags" is your job to supervise.

He did a quick triage and keyed his handheld for multiple ambulances to respond. He knew the one back at the convenience store would order a medical examiner.

This thing had grown big and newsworthy enough Ross called for a member of brass to respond and bring a public information officer, or PIO, to handle the media.

Detective Sergeant John Ross, promoted largely because of his contributions to the task force a couple of years ago, knew while only lunch time, today bode to be a long, long day. His new detective had done well, including recovering to assist at the second shooting scene. She would have to give a statement, as would initially arriving officers. These would go to a shooting review board. He was confident she would come out with a Deadly Force Justified finding.

Nick Wolf. Damn! Small world.

He did not have a rifle evidence bag in his car, so he handled Maria's newly issued and freshly used rifle with Nitrile gloves on as he put it in his trunk with an evidence tag.

"Maria, it would be premature for me to congratulate you yet. You still have to be interviewed and give a statement. And there will be a shooting board, which I feel will be a nonevent. But, I can say it looks like your convenience store robberies case was solved lock, stock, and barrel today. As soon as I can turn it over to one of my seasoned detectives, I will clear from this scene. I want you to follow me back to headquarters and we will put you with a chaplain and schedule a psychologist interview. It is standard practice. Is there anyone you need to call?"

"Yes, Sergeant, my friends Nick and Lola. I temporarily live with them since coming over from where we worked a case in my native Honduras. I was a detective sergeant with the Honduran National Police. Because of the case I was just kidnapped."

"Out of the academy in St. Petersburg? And Nick found you and had to kill the kidnapper bare-handed? That was you?" Ross interrupted.

"Yes. I thought they would have told you."

"I just came back to duty after vacation leave yesterday. I guess nobody had a chance to tell me.

"If Nick and Lola come over here, let me know. I would like to see him. I remember how worried all of us were when he was shot. Then, he recovered, went private and started getting famous. Him and his movie star partner!"

"Yes, my Nick and Lola all right!" she smiled proudly.

They left for headquarters and Maria called Lola on her cell phone. Lola said they both would be over to TPD headquarters immediately. She knew John Ross and congratulated Maria on landing such a top supervisor.

Lola told Nick what had happened and they drove over to Tampa to check on Maria's tumultuous first week on the job.

She came out and met them, accompanied by John Ross who greeted his two friends warmly.

"Why don't you guys get an early lunch or something? We have two things going on inside right now. A shooting review is being done. The statements of the arriving officers and some witnesses have just been provided, as well as Maria's own...also, we have all the holdup suspects except the one still in the hospital ready to be interviewed.

"Maria, your map with the robberies laid out in time and geographic order will be the basis for the interviews. I will conduct them with one of my senior detectives. I know it's your case, Maria, but I think in view of the shooting, you need to sit out the interviews.

"I have to go now, so I'll bet if you have questions about sitting out, these two folks can explain why.

"I will call or text as soon as I get results on the shooting review."

John shook hands with his two friends and hurried back into the building.

"How are you?" Lola asked.

"I think I'm okay," Maria said hesitatingly.

"Do they have you set up with a psychologist?" Nick asked.

"It's in the works. I just spoke with a Catholic police chaplain before you got here."

"Did the session help?" Lola asked.

"Maybe. I'm not as religious as I should be for a Latina," Maria admitted. "My mother was always disappointed in it, God rest her soul."

"Let's find a quiet booth at a restaurant and you tell us what happened," Nick said as they walked to the BMW. Maria noticed Lola slipped in behind the wheel.

"I have commandeered it," Lola said, noticing the confused look. "Nick loves my GTI, so we switched."

Maria turned to Nick for corroboration, but was met with an impassive look.

At a nearby café, Maria related the morning from the analysts to the radio call to the shooting to leaving the scene for the larger shootout blocks away.

"This could get a lot of publicity. You might want to mention to John you don't need publicity due to the thing with the Bosnians and being there when the congressman was shot," Nick said.

"I will. It would not be a good time for me to get a lot of media exposure. Nobody from the US government has asked me about the shooting in Roatan. Commissioner Reyes told me to try to avoid such an interview at all costs. He hid my name in the report he sent to Washington. Yours, too."

"Good advice. Have you heard from him?"

"Not since I've been here. I told him I was with you and had a job as detective with Tampa. No response yet. I imagine he's busy preparing to retire and leave Honduras."

"Do you know what country he will choose for his retirement?" Lola asked.

"I do not. He has played very close on it. Actually on all his private life. I suspect the chief prosecutor and the Honduran President know, but no one else," Maria said, adding, "I really miss him. He was not only a mentor, but almost like a father to me."

"I understand. I had one of those, too," Nick said.

"The Cuban gentleman who was your foster father?" Maria asked and he nodded.

"So. You two and I are likely unknown to the DC area branch of the Bekrić crime family?"

"The DC area ones, probably yes," Nick replied.

"But Lottie and Carly are known to them?" Maria asked.

"Yes," Nick said.

"And Angie is known to the Chicago branch?" Nick nodded affirmatively, adding, "but we don't know who is left to organize retribution against her with their head guy in jail with his team."

"I don't mean to sound ugly, and you know I love the two of you, but it looks like my greatest risk is being near Angie, Lottie, and Carly," Maria said.

"I am afraid I would assess your threat situation to be what you just voiced," Nick said.

"Sadly, both of you are correct. You need to stay away from Angie, particularly, but also the heiress and her buddy, to lower your threat profile. At some point, Lottie and Carly will move out. I think they have dropped the Key West idea with purchase of a club in Sarasota. So, they have been talking about Siesta Key or Longboat Key.

"There does not seem to be a timeline established yet though," Lola said.

"I think I need to find temporary lodging and a used car for personal use. I will drive my official car home each night. So, I have been thinking of a Miata or something cute and sporty.

"The good thing is starting in two weeks, I will be making more money than I have in my whole life," Maria said.

"Just know you are always welcome with us," Lola said.

"I know. And since I won't jeopardize my badge dancing at the new club, I will have to come over and practice on the pole in your bedroom."

"I will practice with you!" Lola said.

"I won't," Nick hastened to add.

"No, you will be the sole audience when all of us girls, including Erica, put on a full nude grand extravaganza for you!" Maria said. Nick looked at Lola who was smiling and bobbing her head. *Traitor!* he thought, all the time hoping his fiancé was just yanking his chain.

He just could not resist saying something, knowing whatever it was would be wrong.

"You, Lola, Lottie, and Carly are one thing, but my sister and future mother-in-law? I think that's a bit weird, don't you two?"

His first instinct had been right. He should have kept his damn mouth shut.

"I think you are too stuffy for your own good sometimes, Nick! Don't you, Lola?"

"We could help you find a good car," Nick said, moving on as speedily as he could.

"That would be good. Thanks. I met a woman my age today. She's an analyst. Cuban. I thought about getting her opinion on safe and reasonable apartments," Maria said.

"I think it's a great idea, honey. We can go around and look at them with you," Lola offered. Nick nodded energetically. He would have pedaled them around to Tampa car dealers on a rickshaw just to get off the subject of pole dancing extravaganzas.

Maria's phone rang. It was John Ross.

"I just got handed a note here in the interview room. The shooting panel met. You are cleared back to duty. I want you to make an appointment with one of our on-call psychologists. Check with HR to get the referral. Your carbine is still being checked. If you want another one until you get yours back, go to the armory and tell them I said it's okay.

"Now, I can officially tell you. You did a damn fine job under pressure and immediately helped me at the other shooting site. I'm proud to have you on my team, Maria. I'll see you in the morning."

Though not on speaker, Nick and Lola could hear the gist of the conversation and added their congratulations.

"We'll see you at home tonight," Nick said as they parted. "She's going to be a real asset to TPD."

"I believe so, too, Nick. And it looks like I may lose all my competition. Your sister does not count, of course."

"You don't have any competition. Never did. Never will. You are the one."

"And I have the BMW," she added as she pointed it towards the Howard Frankland Bridge over to St. Petersburg and home.

Between agency calls and processing bills, Erica had put a slow cooker of chili on and baked Southern-style cornbread with jalapeños. A simple green salad finished her menu plan.

Angie was with Lottie and Carly at the evolving club building and Maria was not home yet, so the three sat down to a quiet dinner.

"Erica, you make the best cornbread. It's spicy with the jalapeños and not sweet like the cake-tasting stuff in restaurants. Hot, buttery and good!" Nick said.

"I might have lived most of my life in Northern West Virginia, but remember my roots just east of Richmond," she explained.

They talked about soon they might just have Angie living with them.

"I'm going to have a spare bedroom and could always use a little money if Angie or Maria want to move in with me," she said. Nick raised his eyebrows and was deep in thought.

"He's thinking it would be a great opportunity, but may be too close. Walking distance," Lola said.

Nick nodded his head not anywhere near as surprised at Lola reading his mind as her mother was.

"Well, Nick, which would you rather be a couple blocks away?" Erica asked.

"Angie."

"If you are worried about the amorous little detective, remember what my mother used to say," Erica said.

"And what might that be, Erica?"

"Absence makes the heart grow fonder."

"And what does practicing exotic dancing on the pole in our bedroom do?" he asked.

"Nothing, I hope. I plan to use it, too. Lottie and Carly are going to give Maria and me lessons for the big show."

"You are kidding about this big show, right?" Erica just gave her a smile which explained exactly where her daughter had gotten her smoking version of it.

Remembering the most recent time he had thought better about continuing to speak and had not followed his own advice, Nick shut up.

Joe Horner called Nick the next morning.

"The justice guys up in Chicago are extraditing our Bosnian crime boss. Our state's attorney decided to not fight an accessory to kidnapping the Maria Sosa. The folks up in the Midwest have some heavy charges for him. Six felonies so far. His attorney up there agreed to it. My guess is he will either try to bribe witnesses or disappear."

"So, what's going to happen now? My buddy Guy Kellogg issued a bail. I suspect he spent last night in a luxury hotel," Nick said.

"He had us call a taxi for him. I, being a smart detective, noted which taxi company we called and obtained where they dropped him off. It was the hotel inside of Tampa International, Joe said.

"So, he's either going to run or already has," Nick said.

"Yeah. I am not sure when he violated his bail. Probably when he bought tickets to somewhere else?" Joe asked.

"I would think. I will call Kellogg and find out for sure. I suspect Bekrić is in the wind now. He did not have any false identity paperwork you released back to him, did he?"

"Negative, Nick. Just the usual driver's license and credit cards. We are all over this. I had two officers ready to take him to Tampa International to turn him over to a Con Air flight. It would take him to Oklahoma City, then use a smaller plane to deliver him to Chicago. With all the crime there, you'd think it would be a hub for them, but it isn't.

"My guys are checking now. He just checked out of the hotel. The counters are a quick walk. We will look pretty stupid if we are empty-handed for his extradition flight.

"Let's think about this for a second. He would probably like to head somewhere with no extradition treaty with the US. The Caribbean, Central and South America all do, though our relations with Cuba and Venezuela are strained so badly they would probably not honor an extradition.

"The rest are the usual suspects: Eastern Europe; the Middle East; Southeast Asia; and a lot of Africa. The first group includes his homeland of Bosnia. If I was him, I would either make the big trip home to Bosnia in disgrace or go to Mexico and buy my safety with the offshore funds he almost surely has. It would not shock me to learn he has some connections within the cartels. So, flights to Bosnia or Mexico are the first I'd check if I was you," Nick said.

"Good! I will let my guys know right away. And you for your bond enforcement when we find out," Joe said and hung up.

Yeah. Like I am going to Bosnia or the more dangerous Mexico for twenty grand. No damn way Nick thought and said the same to Lola, who had been listening in.

"The only way we should touch this is if he gets a car and disappears or comes here."

"Good point. Let Erica know when she gets in and I will call Angie now," Nick said.

"No worry about Mom. She is taking a couple days off to finish packing for her move from the beach to the cottage here."

"Right. Okay, let me call Angie."

He did and her response was "Will I ever get to a point where I don't have to look over my shoulder for a Bekrić?"

"I can't answer you for sure. I hope so and promise to do my best to guarantee it, honey."

"I know. I'm just whining. You just helped me lose over two hundred troublesome pounds," she said, referring to her husband.

"My guess is the detectives will find he got on a plane to Mexico. He likely has contacts who can make him disappear there," Nick said.

Logic, he soon found, while usually better than scientific wild-ass guesses, still was not always reality.

————

Ibro Bekrić was not en route to Bosnia, the last place in the world he wanted to go, or to Mexico. At least not for now. He went into the valet parking and watched for a time when all the attendants were sprinting for cars. He found the fob for a Lincoln of some sort and took it. He walked into the garage pulling his wheeled suitcase and smiled at everyone he saw. He saw a Lincoln SUV and pressed the Lock button on the fob. Nothing.

Ibro continued the next Lincoln was a sedan. He pressed the fob and was rewarded with its horn blowing. He opened the driver's door and popped the trunk and put his suitcase in it.

He left valet parking without having to pay, since the Lincoln's daily tariff was charged to someone's room.

Ibro avoided the Interstate into town and got onto Dale Mabry. He put on his sunglasses and a ball cap and maxed his Visa on every bank ATM he saw.

The withdrawals with the thousand of flash money he usually carried, gave him a good grubstake.

Luckily, the Lincoln was almost full of fuel. Ibro stopped at a supermarket and purchased four fifty-dollar gas cards to national chains.

Normally, he would have to go into a convenience store to pay cash or use his only credit card at the pump to refuel. This way he could refill his tank with a modicum of invisibility.

While still on Dale Mabry Highway, he decided to exploit his credit card to the extent possible. He would identify his location in this one area then stop using it.

At a Walmart, he bought a burner phone and activated it. He bought and loaded a reloadable Visa. He bought lots of food and drink not requiring heating. He bought an atlas. Then, he left fast in case one of the area police agencies already had his card in the system.

Ibro put his belongings in the Lincoln and studied the atlas for a moment before deciding his route.

It was a full day before the owner of the Lincoln tried to claim it. It took another hour to look for it, the keys and for everyone to agree it was stolen. An hour later, Joe Horner was apprised.

And Ibro Bekrić was in the wind by then.

6

Guy Kellogg called Nick and Lola.

"What do you know about the status of Ibro Bekrić?" he asked.

"I know the state made an extradition deal with the federal government to send him back to Chicago instead of Florida pursuing a pretty lame charge on him. Apparently he left the hotel before they could pick him up. It took a while to find the hotel and determine he had stolen a car from valet parking. A Lincoln, I believe it was.

"What were they going to do with him after they picked him up?" Guy asked.

"Take him to the airport and turn him over to Con Air for a two-legged trip back to Chicago to face a bunch of charges. Serious stuff. Especially relative to the more minor Accessory to Kidnapping charge Florida was going to lay on him," Nick said.

"So, this didn't happen relative to a case, such as the Grand Jury?"

"No. The state's attorney cut his deal beforehand."

"I think I have a good chance of saying the court changed the bail deal on me and can get them to return my bail money as a voided deal. What do you two think?" Guy Kellogg asked.

"It seems to me they switched the deal on you and eliminated your requirement to deliver him to trial by doing away with the trial," Nick said.

"Thanks. I am going to have my attorney petition the court along those lines. I want my hundred grand returned to me."

"Seems to me you have a reasonable claim. God knows where Bekrić is by now. Let us know how it turns out. We'll do the same from this end." Nick hung up.

"This whole Bekrić thing is unique. Kellogg is going to petition the court in Pinellas saying his bail was fulfilled when they decided to swap him. It seems to me he has a pretty good case."

"It does. Should we harden back up? After all, we don't know where Bekrić is or what's on his mind," Lola said.

"Well, you heard me call Angie. I suspect we need to stay hardened up. We should let Lottie, Carly, and Maria know for sure. I've already caught him once. I doubt he'd be stupid enough to come back for a second try. But, who knows?" Nick said.

Maria was the next to return. Nick and Lola brought her up to date.

"Well, like we spoke about at work today, my main liability is being near Angie, who's the real target."

"You are correct, but forgetting you were the captive whose kidnapping got his nephew or cousin or whatever Angie's husband was, killed. We don't know how these guys think. We do know they are very family-centric. Being there might make you a target," Lola said.

"But Nick killed the cousin. And captured Bekrić himself. Nick and Angie are the big targets.

"Maria, this is not worth arguing about. We are all targets, primary or secondary. If you'd feel more comfortable checking into a motel, go right ahead. Nobody will blame you," Lola said sternly, her lack of patience with the young detective showing for the first time and taking Maria aback. She immediately turned to Nick.

"Maria, Lola is exactly right. We are all targets. A bullet will not discriminate between a primary, secondary, or tertiary target. If it would make you more comfortable, get a room for a couple of days. Or maybe go help Erica move. She will be spending the night at the cottage, not the condo they found. You should be safe there," he said.

"Maybe I should stop thinking about myself and help you and Lola keep the rest, who are untrained, safe."

"Your choice," Nick said, already knowing she had just made up her mind.

Lottie and Carly did not require much updating because Angie already told them what was going on.

While the women had glasses of wine or beer, Nick went into the kitchen. They had replenished groceries today, and he fixed a plate of sandwiches, bowl of chips and pretzels, and a large bowl of fresh fruit.

"Dinner's ready," he announced and stepped clear of the door before they came in.

"Erica, it's Nick. Are you over at the cottage? I just fixed ham and some beef sandwiches, chips, and fruit. Why don't you take a break and come eat with us? Okay. See you in five minutes," he said and hung up. *Hung up. This is not a receiver phone with a cradle to hang it up on.*

It's a current generation smartphone with more capability than computers had fifteen years ago. I guess 'hung up' is a vestige of the past like saying 'ice box' or such.

He sat down to a shaved beef sandwich on multi-seeded bread. It had a sauce with a lot of horse radish and a little sour cream. He added pepper to taste and dropped his hand down by his CR920 when he heard the rear door open. As he thought, it was his future mother-in-law. She had worked hard lifting and packing all day and still was a knockout. There was his Lola in eighteen or twenty years. He smiled.

Lola, knowing exactly what he was thinking, blew him an almost imperceptible kiss. Nobody saw it. Except Maria who tried to hide a scowl behind a smile.

Nick got the GTI and BMW key fobs and went out to transfer his gear to the Volkswagen. He grinned to himself. The GTI was the same year as the BMW and had about the same mileage. He had always admired it and had considered getting one instead of the larger sedan. His choice had been based on the recent longer trips and occasional business need to carry passengers comfortably.

Nick would never admit to Lola he jumped at the trade. He did not have to because she probably already knew.

He was thinking some Abarth or Borla exhaust for the hot hatch when Joe Horner called his cell phone.

"Hey. I just received a tip our errant Bosnian may have been seen in the Central Avenue area. I know you either have a house or an office there and wanted to let you know," Joe said.

"Both actually. The office is downstairs and we live upstairs. Thanks. I will let everyone know and we'll be careful. Would you call me if your officers arrest him?"

"I will. Gotta go. I am heading over that way," Joe said. Nick gave him the address and told him to feel free to drop by.

Nick immediately went into the house. He put on an over-the-shirt tactical Kevlar vest and picked up the AK. Putting several mags and a flashlight in the outer vest pockets, he gathered the ladies.

"Joe Horner just called. He received a tip that someone meeting the description of Ibro Bekrić has been seen in the Central Avenue area.

"I'm going to go out and sit in the dark behind the rear shed. Lola, would you and Maria take the front inside, since I won't be able to see it?" he requested.

Lola got their Ruger carbine and handed an AK to Maria.

"Why don't the rest of you go upstairs?" she suggested.

As Nick was picking up a folding lawn chair to take with him, Lola was getting ready to set the alarm system on Stay. He nodded he was aware and went out the door. She locked it behind him.

Nick sat outside for an hour, glad for the bottle of water he had brought out, but mad with himself for forgetting bug spray.

During the first quarter of the second hour, he perked up. A car was slowly driving down the alley. It stopped.

It was an old sedan. Someone got out and was rattling the gate. Nick moved silently around the perimeter and stepped into the alley's gas light. He had the AK aimed from the shoulder.

"Something I can help you with? Or, should I just empty a 30 round mag right now?" he said to the kid, who had been unaware of his presence until right then.

The kid looked up. The car screeched off leaving him there. He went running after it, screaming both in terror and for his friend to stop so he could get in.

Nick began to chuckle. He was pretty sure if he went out to the alley, he would find a urine trail chasing the car, which had disappeared around the corner. He still heard the kid, who may have been nineteen, still screaming as he chased his disloyal friend who deserted him.

Nick heard the door. Lola was there, but not silhouetted, as she was savvy enough to douse the lights first.

"Everything okay?" she asked in a low voice. He walked over and let her share his mirth.

"Even without me there, he would have been pretty shocked if he had gotten in. A couple of steps would have turned on our motion detector flood lights," Nick chuckled.

"At least it was not Bekrić," Lola said.

"Bekrić was much cooler at gunpoint than this little shit was. I kinda think Bekrić has had guns pointed at him before."

Lola went back to bed and Nick to his lawn chair. The night passed without further excitement or humor.

The next morning, Nick transferred over to his bed to make up for being awake and uncomfortable all night. The bed was an option he had not always had available to him after being on watch all night in theater in the Rangers. He was asleep quickly.

Lola came in and gently awakened him around ten.

"Honey, I am going down to Sarasota and look at the progress on Lottie's club. You are safe. Detective Sosa left hours ago." She giggled, adding, "Maybe not too safe. Mom is downstairs working."

"Uh-huh. Whatever. Be safe. I love you," and he was

asleep again. She unnecessarily adjusted his covers, patted him on the butt and went downstairs.

"Nick is out for at least a few hours after last night. I will be on the phone if you need me, Mom," Lola said and picked up the keys for the BMW and left.

She headed south on I-275 towards the Sunshine Skyway Bridge. Before the anti-jump fences had been installed, it had been the number two suicide bridge in America, behind the Golden Gate. She had worked a number of them as one of the troopers always positioned nearby. Waiting.

Just before the Dick Misener approach bridge to the Skyway, a Lincoln flew past her. Her trooper sense clocked him north of 120 miles per hour. She had seen him coming and pulled far to the right side. The very thing she hoped for then appeared. An FHP cruiser. It was a black and tan, which is how they referred to the black and yellow marked units for some reason.

It was not standard fare. It was a two-door Challenger. And, not just a Challenger, but a wide-bodied Scat Pack of which the FHP had a couple. Four hundred eighty-five horsepower. She was sure he had been sitting out of even her sight when the Lincoln came by because he was still accelerating when he passed her. At this rate, he would catch the Lincoln in the short distance before the bridge. Not that he would use it, but the car would go one hundred seventy-four miles per hour. Significantly more than any Lincoln ever made.

Making sure another trooper was not coming to assist at speed behind her, Lola sped up. They were both in the left lane crossing the two-hundred-foot-high Sunshine Skyway Bridge. Lola knew from personal experience how narrow the lanes felt at speeds in excess of a hundred. The real test would be the long sweeping straightaway beyond the hump. As she crested the hump and looked ahead, she saw the trooper kick up his speed and brake right behind the Lincoln. *Was he going to do a Precision Immobilization Technique, or PIT maneuver? She did not have enough faith in the Jersey barriers separating the bridge from the drop into Tampa Bay herself. No! he was waiting for the causeway portion to end and to have land on both sides of the Interstate.*

He is hanging close to the tail of the Lincoln, which is back up to one-twenty or so again. He's backing off some. The Lincoln seems to be having problems and swerving.

The trooper is backing way down! It must be a tire overheated or something on the car being pursued.

Lola saw the car careen off the road just before the rest area and roll. She counted three complete revolutions before it stopped upside down, three intact tires and one blown out one still spinning.

She pulled in behind the trooper who had bailed out of his vehicle. She knew him and called, "Jack Holloway, it's Lola!"

He looked up and recognized her immediately and waved her on as they sprinted towards the car. They saw flames and knew they had to get the driver out as quickly as humanly possible.

Trooper Holloway tried the door. Jammed! He hit the window with a window breaker and it broke. They pulled the large pieces out of the frame.

The driver was unconscious and bloody. The trooper leaned in with a knife and began working on the seatbelt.

Lola could feel the heat and knew the fire was growing at a geometric pace.

There was no need to tell Jack, he felt it too.

"The guy is big and the window opening is going to be tight!" he yelled.

Lola ran around the other side and tried the passenger door. Locked.

She said, "Toss me your glass breaker!"

He did and she broke the side window and manually unlocked the door. It opened.

Lola went inside and grabbed the guy under the arms and started tugging. Jack Holloway ran around and assisted as they pulled the victim, who she recognized to be Ibro Bekrić, out of the car amid quickly growing flames.

As the two dragged him about eight feet, there was a dull "Poom" sound as an initial explosion occurred. They dragged Bekrić faster and the whole car raised off the ground in a loud, fiery explosion.

The concussion knocked both the trooper and the former trooper to the ground. On hands and knees, they dragged Bekrić further away.

"My mic is ruined. Will you check this guy while I call for an ambulance and fire to be sent from Manatee, since we are now in Manatee County."

"Yes, and tell them you have apprehended fugitive Ibro Bekrić."

"I know. My license plate reader picked up the Lincoln as stolen and associated with an armed and wanted fugitive."

He got up and looked himself over after being blown down by the explosion.

"You okay, Lola?" he asked.

"Yeah. I think so. Bekrić here has a pulse. I will call the St. Pete detective running the case against this guy and let him know where he is," Lola said. Lola moved him into the recovery position.

She put his left hand behind his head, lifted his right ankle and hip and rolled him towards her. She grasped him behind the right knee and brought it up. He was propped on his side, head laying on his hand, propped by his arm. If he were to throw up, he would not choke to death on it.

Trooper Holloway ran back.

"Fire and rescue are coming from Manatee as are a couple deputies to help with traffic until we get more troopers here. Nobody from FHP is real close, unfortunately," he said.

She kept checking for pulse and airway. As he gained consciousness, Bekrić started getting rambunctious.

"Toss me your cuffs. He's stirring and I am too sore right now to fight a two-fifty Bosnian thug."

She rolled him out of the recovery position, put a knee between his shoulder blades and cuffed him from behind.

"Stay lying face down. If you try to get up, I will kick you back down. If you try a second time, I will assume you are going to assault this trooper and shoot you dead. Do you understand me?" Lola asked with a sternness cultivated over a decade as a law enforcement officer.

Holloway grinned at her and snapped a cellphone picture.

"I see you have not rolled very far from the old FHP tree, Lola!"

"I was not trained. I was indoctrinated into being a new person, Jack."

"Hey, I read about the assassin and the bear in Ocala National Forest. You just became who all of us want to be if we ever grow up," Trooper Holloway said as a plethora of types of sirens got louder and the Manatee County authorities flew towards them at speed.

Lola remembered Joe Horner and called him.

"Joe, it's Lola. I am at the south end of the Skyway, southbound with the trooper who just caught one Ibro Bekrić. Your Bosnian is still needing some first aid. I suspect he will be transported to Manatee Memorial. His wounds do not seem to require a trauma center. I will let you know on the hospital shortly, okay?"

"How did you get involved?" he asked incredulously.

"I was driving to Sarasota when Lincoln passed me at one-twenty. I saw a trooper friend coming after him. Bekrić had a blow out and rolled three times. The trooper and I pulled him from his burning car just before it blew up. End of story," she said.

"You must have caught this 'be unbelievably there' thing from Nick," Joe said.

"Naw. I always had it. See you at the hospital probably."

The Manatee EMT's had arrived and were checking Bekrić.

"Where to," Holloway asked, nodding to the victim.

"Manatee Memorial, he does not appear to need trauma care."

Lola turned to them.

"Keep him cuffed and be very careful. He is a highly sought after crime boss out of Chicago. Considered armed and dangerous. He escaped just before a date with Con Air," Lola told them.

She knelt to her knees and whispered in Bekrić's ear.

"I know you are big on family honor and all that crap. But you *will* drop trying to get even with Lottie or any of us. You owe us now. Our family and your family are even. I pulled your unconscious ass out of a burning car just before it exploded. You'd be a crispy critter if I hadn't. Got it?"

He looked the beautiful woman in the eyes and nodded affirmatively. "You saved me. So, I will give you something else, pretty woman. Adin and Angie's little boy is alive. Not dead like she thinks. My uncle Ludo Bekrić is looking after him in Woodstock, outside of Chicago. Tell him Ibro says to give him to her now." She nodded and said, "Thank you. Good luck, Mr. Bekrić." He smiled back.

I kind of believe him. Probably. Possibly. We'll check it out. I mean...what did he have to lose? she thought. *They won't let him get away this time. Nick has a nephew! Lord, he will be so happy!*

"I will write your actions up as a good Samaritan," Lola heard Trooper Holloway in the background.

"Maybe they will give you a medal or something.

"Thanks, Jack. Forget the medal and just let me drive your car sometime," she responded and added, "I officially turned the prisoner over to you, if anything comes up about his bond, okay?" "Sure," he responded, knowing it was she who had started dragging Bekrić from the burning car first.

He pulled out his pad and gave her a receipt, though half in jest.

Lola called and woke Nick up on her way to give the good news to his sister.

She took Angie aside when she got to the club site and told her about the capture.

"You really think it's over?" Angie said.

"It depends on honor among thieves. I told him it had to stop. I told him what I had done while he was unconscious. I told him our two families were even now.

It was over. He nodded 'yes'. Can I believe him? No idea. But he's back in custody, and I don't think it matters since he will not escape custody this time."

"Lola, I'd like to believe him. He is mean as can be and crooked as hell. But I always thought he had some sort of sense of honor about him. I sure hope so. I don't have much faith in Chicago justice. Federal, state, or especially local. So, we'll have to see how guilty they find him. I do feel better though," Angie said.

"I guess you couldn't have left him in the car until after it exploded, right?" she added.

"Right. I am your brother's fiancé. He is the most honorable man I have ever met. Would you have me less so, Angie?" Lola asked.

"Of course not. I really don't know my brother. But I do believe you are right about his honor."

"Did you say 'fiancé'," Lottie asked.

"I did."

"Like a ring and all?" she asked Lola.

"I drove the ring down here."

"Was it his idea or yours?"

"Becoming engaged or the car versus a ring?" Lola asked.

"Both of course, silly!" Carly answered for her friend.

"Does this mean we have to stop flirting?"

"If you didn't flirt, I would wonder if I had chosen a fiancé who was not hot enough."

"Great point," Angie added. "And you girls know my job is to help Lola make sure things don't get carried too far."

"It's not the two of *us* you have to worry about," Lottie said.

"We know," Lola and Angie said in unison.

The three women led Lola on a second tour of the building showing how much had been done in several days.

"Given Angie's help in recruiting and hiring performers, we may be able to open in a month," Lottie said.

"How about codes and permits and all? Sarasota is high income and can be a bit hoity-toity," Lola asked.

"Got it covered. There was a famous club here for years. It looks like a lot of Sarasota old-timers miss it. We have all the paperwork approved," Carly, the soon-to-be manager, said.

"The other big news is we have found a house!" Lottie exclaimed.

"Oh? Where is it?" Lola asked.

"It's on the Gulf Intracoastal Waterway side of Anna Maria Island! It's four bedrooms, three baths and has a pool and a dock. It was renovated by the current owner and has hurricane shutters, new top of the line appliances and the bathrooms have been redone and updated. The roof is only four years old and the stucco was painted pink two years ago. It reminds us of a big flamingo!"

"It's really convenient for us, too, Lottie," Lola said.

"How's that? It is probably forty minutes from your place in St. Petersburg," Carly said.

"True, but we keep the boat at a high and dry marina right across the Intracoastal from where you will be living. The address is actually Anna Maria."

"No! We had no idea. I guess we won't be needing a boat now, huh?" Lottie said.

"Nope, and we won't be needing a pool!" Lola said.

"I didn't mention everything. A pool and a hot tub!" Lottie said.

"Even better! Nick may have to get a larger boat though...but maybe not. I'll see what the capacity of ours is. We've only had a max of three of us so far," Lottie said.

"The other news is the girls have asked me if I want to live in one of the spare bedrooms since I'll be working at the club recruiting and all," Angie said.

"Convenient! I know Nick will be excited about all of this. When can we see it?" Lola said.

Plans were made. Lola looked at Angie. She seemed happy over the rapid turn of events which so simplified her messed up life. There seemed to be something else though. Nick always told Lola her sense of perception was the best he had ever seen and was so invaluable in their cases. And the sense was accelerating like Holloway's four hundred eighty-five horsepower police car...really fast.

"What is it, Angie?" Lola asked.

"Oh, there is just one heartbreak I will never get over. It's a long story. I promise to share it with my brother and soon-to-be sister-in-law one day."

"Okay. Just know, we are always ready to listen and help," Lola said, just knowing in her heart it was about the little boy.

Angie nodded to her. Just like Nick did. It was almost eerie, Lola thought. It kind of made things easier for her to fathom Nick's sister, however.

"Do you want a lift back to the house, Angie? Or are you going to ride with Lottie in the Benz?"

She looked at the two, and Lottie said, "Why don't you go ahead with Lola? We will be here for a long time yet. Looking and dreaming!"

The reverse of the drive back was much more sedate

than the one over, although Lola was always a fast driver.

"We are on the way back. Crossing the Skyway shortly," Lola told her mom.

"How many for dinner? I like Nick's sandwiches, but it's time for some real knife and fork food," Erica said.

"Four of us, unless Maria shows up early."

"Good enough. See you in a half hour or so, Lola."

———

Erica fixed steaks, baked potatoes and a salad for dinner. She put three each in the oven for the still-missing Maria, Lottie, and Carly.

"I still have some things to do at the new house and will probably sleep there tonight," Erica said, excusing herself after dinner. She had driven over from the condo, so she drove her car the several blocks in the dark to the cottage.

"We have some quiet time, guys," Lola said as she put dishes in the dishwasher.

"Angie, please share the heartbreak thing with your brother and me. It's a perfect time."

"It will be tough, but I have to tell Nick sometimes. I got pregnant just after Adin and I went through the Eastern European ceremony without any sign of a marriage license.

"It was actually an easy pregnancy, and we had a beautiful baby boy.

"His name was Adin Nicholas Dedić, and he was the best baby anybody ever had.

"Adin Sr. was volatile. We had a horrible argument, and he left and took baby Nicky with him. Nickie was a couple of months old. He came back without my baby! The bastard told me he would show me who was boss and had thrown the baby into the river in a burlap bag full of bricks. Nobody would ever find him. I almost stabbed him that night. I had taken a butcher knife and put it under the pillow. I just could not bring myself to do it. What if he was lying? I'd never know where Nicky was then!

"That was two years ago. He would be just two years and three months old now. Now, I admit to myself he really did kill Nickie. Thank you, big Nicky for killing Adin. I only wish I could have done it with my bare hands like you did.

"Lola had not had a private time to tell Nick what Ibro had told her and watched as he stared at his sister with horror.

"Okay. I have something to share. Nick, I am so sorry I could not privately tell you first. Just listen and forgive me," Lola said.

"Angie, I told you I made peace with Ibro about his vendetta ending and reminded him I had dragged him out of a burning car just before it exploded.

"He looked me in the eye and told me he owed me. His gift was to tell you Nicky is alive. Ibro's uncle Ludo is keeping him in Woodstock, just outside Chicago. He said to tell Ludo to give Nicky to his mother and that he, Ibro said so."

Lola was watching the range of emotions her own Nick was experiencing. She had never seen him so struck by words. Angie was crying tears of relief and happiness.

Lola got up and went over and knelt beside Nick and hugged him.

"We have to go there. Tomorrow. All three of us. We

have to get my nephew back," he said. "Angie, what do you know about this Ludo?"

"Nothing. I never heard of him."

"I'll get on the computer and do a search. And get tickets and a rental car," Lola said. "Let me go over to the cottage and tell Mom first. She will have to come and take care of Finn," Lola said. "Boy oh boy. Finnie is going to love having a little Nick to look after!" she said and saw Angie laugh through her tears. Nick was doing a Nick thing which always fascinated her. His brain, amid high emotions and major new facts, was spinning as he planned and recalculated and amended. She was sure it was what made him such a good Ranger sergeant and leader in combat.

Lola got her flashlight and walked out to go to Erica's. Angie got up and sat next to Nick. He put his arm around his sister and held her closely as she sobbed into his shoulder.

"We'll get him back and everything will be fine. Don't you worry. They were sitting the same way when Lola returned and turned on her desk computer.

"Got him! Woodstock, Illinois. Sixty-seven. Wife is sixty-six. Married forty-seven years. No children. Member of the Woodstock Eastern Orthodox Church. Owns a tire store. Nothing about being a gangster. Not even a parking ticket," Lola said.

Ten minutes later, Lola told them they all had tickets out of Tampa International for Chicago at ten in the morning and a rental car waiting for them at the airport.

Maria arrived, then Lottie and Carly minutes after. They removed their dinners from the oven and Lola explained the news and the trip for tomorrow.

Angie walked in and said, "I won't be holding you to

the room on Anna Maria since I expect to have a toddler. It wouldn't be fair."

"Let us meet little Nicky. If he's as cute as big Nicky, you're still on!" Lottie said, causing everyone but big Nicky to laugh.

"What do you think we should do? Call Ludo first, or just show up?" Nick asked the general audience.

"Mom said we ought to give him the courtesy of calling him," Lola said.

"What if he does not want to give up my nephew and does a runner?" Nick asked.

"I've never seen you go after someone and not catch him, honey."

"What time is it in Chicago now?" Nick asked.

"Seven thirty," Angie said. "I think I should be the one to call him," she said.

Nick nodded but handed the phone to her where she was sitting next to him.

She went to get up, but he shook his head. After all, he was the Wolf patriarch all of a sudden.

"Mr. Ludo Bekrić? My name is Angie Wolf Dedić. I was Adin's wife and am Nicky's mother."

"How did you get my name?"

"From Ibro. He was here in Florida and said to call you and talk about my son."

"How about Adin? What's he got to say about this?"

"Adin was killed by the police after kidnapping a Tampa female detective. We made peace with Ibro. He said to call you and tell you so."

"Ibro is my nephew. He put up with Adin, but I don't think he liked him so much."

"Me either, Mr. Bekrić. Adin beat me a lot and stole our baby and told me he had killed little Nicky. I believed it until today when Ibro said Nicky was alive and fine with you and your wife in Woodstock."

"This was a bad situation," he said with a lingering Bosnian accent. "Which is why Ibro wanted my wife and me to keep baby. To protect him. Which we did and do."

"Thank you so much for protecting my precious little baby boy, Mr. Bekrić!"

"I was separated from my own brother for thirty years. We have now found each other. Nicky was named after my brother. We, and his fiancé, want to come visit with you, Mrs. Bekrić, and my precious baby."

"This is good. Boy is age where he needs young mother. Crawls fast and walking too. Good boy. Into everything though. This one has mind of his own!"

"We would like to come to see you and your wife and Nicky tomorrow."

"Is okay. Call this number when near."

"If you need to talk with Ibro, he is recovering at Manatee Memorial Hospital. Get a pencil and I will tell you the number," Angie said as Lola handed her a slip of paper with the number on it.

"Ibro shot by police?"

"No. He was in a car crash. Minor injuries. He might have even been released by now," Angie said. They terminated the call on a positive basis.

"I think your call went amazingly well, sis."

"Me, too, Nick. We'll see tomorrow though. What if he calls and reaches Ibro? And Ibro changed his mind?"

"I doubt he could have built a large criminal enterprise by being indecisive. If so, we will deal with it as things evolve," he responded.

They packed light bags for an early departure. Nick and Lola decided to go to a murder capital armed under authority of LEOSA, the Law Enforcement Officers Safety Act. Nick put his retirement detective sergeant badge and creds and proof of approved weapons requalification in his pocket. Lola left without retiring, but served the requisite ten years under an amendment to the act and received a proof of service card and maintained her qualifications.

They presented their unloaded 9mm pistols for inspection for placing them into one locked and checked bag. Both considered the red tape worth it to be armed in Chicago.

They picked up the checked bag upon arrival, checked for their weapons in private and picked up the SUV they had reserved.

Lola entered the address in nearby Woodstock into the Nav system and then subtly loaded both pistols and a spare magazine for each with their usual 124 grain +P cartridges.

Traffic was heavy and the drive took longer than they anticipated.

"It's going to be so difficult to not run to Nicky and fold him in my arms when I see him," Angie said, "but I will be a stranger to him. It would probably terrify the little guy."

"We will just take it calm, quiet and easy. Play it as it comes," Lola said.

When the NAV showed the ETA to be five minutes, Angie called Ludo Bekrić.

The neighborhood and their house both suggested Ludo had done well in the tire business. All hoped tires were all he trafficked.

As he pulled up, a tall, burly older man walked out the door. He had thinning hair, but not shaven. His face was also free of facial hair. He may have had a resemblance to the Bekrić clan, but it did not jump out for identification purposes.

More than anything else, he had a friendly, welcoming smile.

"This is bittersweet to Alice and me. A baby needs his mother and we never approved of how we got Nicholas. But we sure did the best we could to take care of him," was his introduction.

He looked at three very handsome people. Two were obviously brother and sister, one was, well, just a knockout.

Ludo extended his hand to Angie automatically after this assessment and said, "Angie, welcome to our home. You two also."

Angie took a chance and hugged him. It appeared to have been the right thing to do.

They walked in and saw a beautiful toddler hiding behind Ludo's wife Alice and shyly peeping at them.

Ludo held out both arms and softly said, "Come to *Deda*, boy. The little boy grinned a grin Lola recognized immediately and squealed. He ran to Ludo and jumped up into his arms. Ludo hugged him and pointed to Angie.

"Nicky, there is your *majka*. Your mama! Say hi to her."

The little boy looked at Angie hard. He smiled and said, "*Mama*?"

"Oh, yes, Nicky! I am your mama. May I hold you?"

He stuck out a lower lip and looked at her suspiciously.

"Sit by us on the sofa, Angie, while the others meet Alice," Ludo suggested.

They did. Nicky kept furtively staring at Angie. There was no sign of fear. More curiosity.

Nick and Lola helped take the pressure off the little one by meeting and chatting with Alice. She offered coffee and Nick immediately became her friend.

Lola could not take her eyes off the boy. She now knew what her Nick looked like as a toddler. The boy may grow to have his late and not lamented father's build, or not. But the face, the eyes, the hair. It would have been impossible not to recognize the little one as direct kin to the larger versions so captivated at him at this moment.

The conversations were abbreviated life stories. Ludo did not know Angie's, only she was a dancer at one of his nephew's clubs. Now, he learned how she got there and why. As an immigrant, he knew full well people had to accept what they were offered just to get by. He told how he worked installing tires on sixties cars for years until he was able to buy the shop. How he had turned down family business offers and illicit support. How Ibro was the only one who understood his uncle's stalwart opposition to crossing the line into illegality. It was the very reason Ibro saved little Nicky from his disturbed nephew and turned to his own uncle to keep the child safe.

Alice, who was of Irish descent, talked about the little boy. How sweet he was, his excellent health and his pervasive curiosity.

"We did not have children of our own, so we did not know what to expect. My friend down the street said during the 'terrible twos' little ones are curious and prone to tantrums. We only experienced the curiosity part. The closest thing to a tantrum is sticking his little lower lip out and stubbornly digging in," she said.

"He did it a few minutes ago. The lip and later the

grin are so characteristic of his namesake sitting across from him," Lola said. Nick beamed at the comparison.

He eased onto the floor, always difficult with his left leg. Both the Bekrićs noticed this.

He very softly said, "Nicky, will you come to see your uncle?" and smiled. The little boy looked interested but held back.

"Oh, come on. My name is Nick. Just like you. Come over here to see me."

Nicky slowly climbed down from where Ludo was holding him between himself and Angie.

In his stiff-legged toddler walk he slowly made his way over the six feet of separation. Nick held both arms out, as Ludo had.

Nicky squealed and rushed into them and was quickly enfolded in a soft bear hug. He turned and faced Ludo and his mother. Ludo nodded supportively. Angie smiled between happy tears. Even Lola, the shield maiden, had tears rolling down her cheeks.

Angie did a little wave and Nicky returned it and giggled. She eased onto the floor and crawled over on all fours as Lola captured it in video on her phone.

Angie positioned herself by her brother. After a while, Nicky wiggled his way over to her lap. After another short while, he was sleeping soundly on her chest, making her quite easily the happiest woman alive.

"Alice and I spoke of this last night. We will miss him so much. But he needs his mama. Someone younger with the energy to keep up with him. We decided, assuming it went like it has, it was the right thing to do."

"Ludo, you two are retired. I can only assume from your beautiful home and the neighborhood it's in you are financially well set. For the value of this home, you could get a similar one near us in Florida. You and Alice move down. Be his Deda every day. Leave the snow blowers here. Enjoy life and Nicky for always," Nick said.

Angie and Lola were nodding their agreement. Ludo looked at Alice, who smiled and shrugged.

"You give us all your numbers and addresses. We will talk about it. A lot. Now, while the little one is asleep, you should take him. Alice has his stuff and a car seat in the kitchen."

Ludo rose and took the sleeping Nicky and sat back down beside his wife. They made the perfect photo of loving grandparents. So perfect, Lola memorialized it in a photo for them and later, Nicky.

Nick edged over to the sofa and used it to climb to his feet.

"Nicholas, come over here. While the women load the car, let the men talk," Ludo said.

Nick took Alice's place as she got up and led Lola and Angie into the kitchen.

"Tell me about your leg."

"I was in the 75th Ranger Regiment. Combat all over. Bullet, knife, and IED wounds. But it took a pedophile with a .45 and a fourteen-year-old girl hostage to cripple me as a cop. I am lucky with the limp. One of the bullets clipped my femoral artery. A SWAT operator with a tourniquet saved me from bleeding out where I lay."

Ludo nodded.

"The people at the jail let Ibro talk with me. He said to tell you he forgives you for what you had to do with Adin. He was amazed a man with a limp could do such a thing against a beast like his nephew. He said he should have done it himself years ago.

"He also said take good care of the woman with the long black hair. She saved him from a burning car just before it exploded into little pieces."

"Ludo, I captured him. He later got away. But, I have a sense, and Lola does too, he is an honorable man. Despite his chosen professions. Thank him for the message.

"Tell him if anybody, ever, anywhere, tries to harm little Nicky, I will kill them with extreme prejudice. Or Lola will. The same goes for my sister. We have just reunited after parting when I was barely older than Nicky. Nobody will ever harm her again under my watch."

"Under different careers and different times, you and my nephew would have been friends. You are very much alike. Resolute and dangerous. But, with good hearts," Ludo said.

Nick nodded and mouthed "thank you."

"Nicholas, were you serious about Alice and me selling out and moving to Florida to be near little Nicky?"

"Ludo, I was. From the very depths of my heart. He needs to be with his family. But you and Alice are all the family he currently knows. Yes! Move down and stay his family. And ours," Nick said eye to eye, his hand on the older man's arm.

"Fly down soon. Stay with us. Lola, Angie, Nicky and I will take you and Alice around to see houses. To see neighborhoods. To eat and to go out in the boat if you like."

"And fish?" Ludo asked.

"I have no fishing buddy, so I hardly ever go. If you were down there, we could go to artificial reefs offshore, to the shallow sand flats, to Tampa Bay. You name it. Your arm will be tired cranking fish in!"

"This has appeal to me. We will come to visit in a few weeks and will take a look. And you and I will fish!" Ludo said.

Nick proffered his hand, and they shook on it.

They turned the car in and checked the Pelican case with the guns in it. The car seat was gate-checked and the cooler bag Alice had prepared with Nicky's food and drink was carried on. All of this was new for the three adults. Lola did her amazing Internet research and arranged for the little guy to have a bottle for takeoff and landing to avoid ear pressure pain as much as possible.

They arrived back at Tampa late. Nicky had behaved really well and only cried once.

Lola held him for the first time while Nick and Angie tried to figure out the baby car seat latches built into the BMW.

The toddler made all sorts of little happy talking noises which thrilled Lola in a way which shocked her. She had never thought about children one way or another.

Holding one, which she considered to be a Nick Mini-Me may have changed her perspective.

Maria, Lottie, Carly, and Erica were awaiting their arrival to meet the latest member of the family. Only Erica had experience with babies before, and a most resolute one at that.

Nicky remained asleep while each held and admired him.

They realized one grand omission. No baby bed. Angie elected to sleep in one of the new sleeping bags on the oriental rug in the living room office. They made a small pallet for Nicky and put him down on it. Finn immediately lay beside him protectively, after grooming the baby to his feline satisfaction.

Nick spoke with the rest of the group.

"From a message Ibro Bekrić sent by way of his uncle as well as his and Lola's understanding, I think the Chicago threat has been pretty much eliminated.

"What we don't know about is the Northern Virginia branch. They have their hands full. The ones caught in Honduras are in for some bad times. The ones remaining in Northern Virginia have to contend with the same federal prosecutors who are cooperating with the ones Ibro is dealing with in Chicago. Their situation is exacerbated by the assassination of the congressman, lowlife or not. What I am getting at is I think all the Bekrićs we know about have their hands full staying out of prison and those of us in this room are low on their list of concerns now.

"Let's return to our normal lives, except our norm has just changed for the better," Nick said, turning to the toddler sleeping on the floor with his head now resting on his yellow guard cat.

Everybody agreed and headed for their respective, now temporary, sleeping spots.

Nick walked Erica back due to the late hour and star and moonless sky.

"Angie is thrilled over finding her son alive and now having him. She must think it's some sort of miracle," Erica said.

"She does. She's going to need a lot of guidance. Of us, only you are the one with any experience on inter-preting what a baby needs at any given time," Nick said.

"I will watch Angie and help every way I can. I now

know what you looked like as a toddler. Exactly like little Nicky," she said.

"Just like I know how beautiful my future wife will be in twenty years," he said, lightly punching her on the upper arm.

"Keep that up and I'll bake you a cake or something."

"Deal!"

He preceded her into the cottage and cleared it before leaving. It is what protectors do.

Nick walked back, smiling to himself. This has been one eventful month. He had to end the lives of several people. Lola had killed also.

He had his sister back and a bonus who looked like it could be his own son. He was going to be the fun uncle. The best ever.

He had a new car. Or rather Lola's old car. But the deal had been a great tradeoff for her hand.

They had solved cases, though the largest longest one had not paid anywhere near what it cost the agency. They had mitigated threats.

The male dog-day cicadas were singing, or whatever noise they make with their tymbal organ. There was a warm breeze blowing. It was a great Florida night.

———————

Nick called Guy Kellogg the next morning.

"Hiya, Nick. What's up?" was his greeting.

"Just checking to see if you worked out a deal with the courts on Ibro Bekrić?"

"Not yet. But it's looking pretty good. I should know today."

"If not, Lola has a receipt and picture of her turning

custody of Bekrić over to a trooper before the ambulance arrived at his crash scene," Nick said.

"You guys have got it together. Thanks. I may need it quickly. Just in case," Kellogg said.

"I have to come down to Sarasota this morning anyway. I will drop the original written receipt off to you. I will text you the picture as soon as we hang up."

"Thanks, Nick. I appreciate it. If I have to use it, you will get the normal twenty percent."

"I'll see you somewhere around nine-thirty either way, Guy."

Angie and Nicky were still asleep. Finn was still on guard but rewarded with a favorite treat.

He checked in upstairs. There was a flurry of action. He asked Lottie if today would be a good day to see the building and the house on Anna Maria. She said it would. Nick promised to call a bit before arriving.

He left a note on the pillow for Lola and kissed her lightly on the lips. Downstairs, he kissed his sister on the forehead and his Mini-Me nephew on a chubby little cheek. Finn got an ear scratch, for which he did not deign to awaken and Nick disarmed the alarm and walked out the door.

Nick started the three-year-old GTI and decided once and for all it needed a catalytic converter-back exhaust system. He pressed the gate opener and went through it and it automatically closed behind him seconds later.

He was early for either Kellogg or the two women still in the shower, so he headed north on 4th Street North and got a café con leche, eggs and Cuban toast for breakfast.

Nick then went south on 4th to 22nd Avenue North,

then onto I-275 South over the Sunshine Skyway. He knew Kellogg got in fairly early, so he went there first.

He greeted the two bail enforcement agents who usually worked out of this, Kellogg's main office out of sixteen around the region.

"Hi. The boss in?" Nick asked and was directed to go back to Guy Kellogg's open-door office.

Nick stopped at the door and greeted the bondsman and was waved in. Kellogg was mad and launched right into the cause of his anger.

"The damn court! The judge says the bond period did not end until the trooper cuffed Bekrić!" he growled.

"Gotcha covered, Boss," Nick said, placing the trooper's receipt for accepting the prisoner from Lola Caldwell, Bail Enforcement Agent for Guy Kellogg Bail Bonds, LLC, and the photo of her cuffing Bekrić.

"It was actually Lola who put the cuffs on, as the photo shows. But, given this receipt, it doesn't really matter. The court screwed up and they are trying to worm out of it. But you win, Guy," Nick said.

Kellogg let out the big breath he had been holding with a hiss which sounded like a tire going flat very quickly.

He studied the handwritten receipt.

"If an investigator for the State's Attorney Office asked the trooper to verify this, would he?" Kellogg asked.

"I am pretty sure he would. He was pursuing Bekrić with Lola right behind. Bekrić rolled his stolen car. Lola actually pulled him out of the burning car and they two dragged him off just before it exploded. Lola borrowed the trooper's handcuffs as an expediency and had constructive custody. Otherwise, why would he have signed the receipt?"

"You just saved me one hundred thousand dollars they wanted me to forfeit. Okay, eighty with your fee."

"I would split the fee since Lola being there was happenstance. However, I was the one who tracked him down and detained him at gunpoint to begin."

"Doesn't matter, Nick. We've always been square with each other," Kellogg said, taking out a large blotter-type check book, then writing and handing a check to Nick.

Nick took it and shook hands. They chatted for a few minutes and parted amiably.

Nick went downstairs to the bank both Kellogg's firm and his own both used. He deposited the check in its entirety.

"When are y'all going to be at the club? I am in Sarasota now," Nick told Angie.

"We are in the car now and about ten or fifteen minutes away. Go ahead and start towards the club," his sister told him.

He arrived just after the three women and walked in.

"Great progress, ladies!"

"Thanks, we are pleased," the formerly elusive heiress said.

"When do the security guys come in for the survey and to prepare a bid for lights and cameras?" Nick asked.

"They don't have to do a survey. I told them we had an in-house security expert who would listen to their equipment recommendations and show them where he wanted them installed," Carly said in her capacity as manager.

"Have I seen this expert?" Nick asked.

"Did you shave this morning?" Carly smiled.

Nick rubbed his chin and winked at her.

"I am getting caught up from the two-pronged Bekrić affair and the aspect also involving you, Lottie, with the trust fraud. But this is close by, and I will be glad to meet with the security folks at any time," Nick said.

Carly made a call, and they said could send someone over later in the afternoon. Nick asked them to arrange a look at the Anna Maria house also, thinking alarms and motion detector spotlights there, too.

"Nick, I made some comments to you about my stepmother a while ago. Could we step into the office and continue the conversation? It will have to be pretty quiet."

He looked at her questioningly, and she just smiled as she led him in.

The reason for quiet was sleeping in a portable baby bed. Nicky was curled up and sleeping soundly. Nick leaned over and looked at his nephew with pride. Oh, the things he was going to teach that little boy!

They sat down.

"Is this about your feelings your stepmother was the hit-and-run driver in the accident where your real mother, Danya Abelman Giannotti, died?" he asked.

She nodded.

"The police never solved it," Lottie said.

"When was it again?" Nick asked.

"I was nineteen. She had been Dad's secretary for years. I think there was an attraction on his part and an obsession on her part. I am almost twenty-four, so it was a bit under five years ago," Lottie said.

"Let's get my partner on the line. Five years on a traffic fatality like this is a cold case. I don't want to waste your money if it's not solvable. Our ex-trooper would know better than I," he said as he hit the speed dial for Lola.

When she answered, Nick brought her up to date. She had some questions.

"Lottie, this was about five years ago. What was the jurisdiction?"

"It happened on a residential street in Arlington. Which was the department doing the investigation."

"Not the Virginia State Police, then?" Lola asked.

"No, definitely the Arlington Police."

"Do you have the accident report?"

"No, but I do have Mom's death certificate," Lottie said.

"Did she succumb on the scene or later?"

"Right there at the scene, Lola."

"Do you remember anything about the car which struck her? She was a pedestrian, if I remember," Lola said.

"She was walking. Nothing on the car."

"Is the death certificate here in your things here or at home in the condo you shared with Carly?"

"It's up there."

"Did you tell the police you thought it may have been Laverne who either did it or paid somebody to do it?"

"No, I was away at college and rooming on campus with Carly. It was already investigated, and a report written by the time I was notified. The police called me. Not my father—I mean uncle. He was a basket case," Lottie said.

"So, they never knew there was a suspect?" Lola asked.

"No, I guess not."

"I know you don't like your stepmother or now, step-aunt. But, not liking someone is far from enough to take a vehicular homicide case to court on.

"What clues fueled your suspicions?" Lola asked.

"How quickly she moved in on him. How possessive she was immediately. How much she hated me. Little digs about my mother."

"Back to the striking vehicle. Let me ask you again. Was there any description of the vehicle striking your mother?"

"I am not aware. I never saw the report. It may be there."

"Lottie, I know you want to rest your mind about how your mother died and who was driving the vehicle which hit her.

"We have almost nothing to work on here. The event occurred five years ago. It's going to be expensive because you and I will have to travel up to Virginia to investigate a cold case.

"I think, but I will have to verify it, as next of kin you are entitled to copy of the report. Probably from the Virginia State Police.

"Just remember, if the investigating officer did not have enough to draw a conclusion on the spot, it's unlikely his report will be terribly helpful, okay?" Lola said.

"I understand. I want us to do it anyway. We can stay at our condo. I have to deal with selling it anyway. Do you think we can have Carly sign remotely?"

"Yes, by having her signature attested to by a notary public."

"Will you and Nick take the case?" Lottie asked.

"Nick? What do you think? It's going to be a stretch solving it," Lola asked her partner over the phone.

"Your call, honey. I will go with whatever you want.

This is your expertise. I may have investigated five traffic cases in my career. Only one was vehicular homicide and I was on scene quickly and had good witnesses."

Lola thought for a minute. They had changed opinions about Lottie. Originally they thought her to be a nutcase. Now, they were seeing logic and maturity.

"Okay, Lottie. We will take it. You can do the agreement and retainer check with Nick at home tonight. Just don't be disappointed if we cannot solve five years later that which a good police department couldn't solve immediately."

"I understand, Lola. We will do the paperwork tonight. Will both of you go up with me?" Lottie asked.

"I doubt it. In our normal practice, Nick takes the fraud and crime cases and I take the traffic accident ones. We have, between our insurance companies and law firms, more of those than any other class of investigation. It's virtually a full-time job for me."

Little Nicky was stirring, and Nick picked him up.

"Did you hear all of this, buddy? Do you want your beautiful aunt Lola and me to teach you how to be a private investigator? I know a firm you could end up running if you play your cards right!"

Nicky grinned a very familiar grin and giggled. If his uncle had ever giggled, nobody currently walking around on this earth ever heard it. The uncle thought Nicky's was just fine though and proudly walked out to what would be the main area of the club, nephew in his arms babbling away.

"Lord, brother. As if you weren't appealing enough already, seeing you with your lookalike in your arms would melt any female who has even a glimmer of a heartbeat," Angie said.

"It's all the boy. Not me. He's a chick magnet."

"Yeah. You just keep telling yourself that, Big Nicky," Carly observed, almost to herself.

"The security guy for the pricing can come in an hour and a half. Would it work for you?" Carly continued, though this time in conversational tones.

"I think so. Not enough time to look at the new prospective property in Anna Maria, but there is a folding rifle I need to take a look at. If I like it, it should be handy to keep in the surveillance vans," Nick said.

He put Nicky down and the child ran smiling and stiff-legged to his mother. She was seated and hugged him a while, then he climbed down and went over to Carly and held his hands out. She picked him up and hugged him eliciting another set of giggles.

"Nope. The boy is not going to be spoiled at all. I do, however, think he's already a lady's man," Angie said.

Nick went over to the nearby gun store from whose branch in Tampa he bought the AK's what seemed like so long ago. They had just taken a deposit on one, but it had not been picked up. The Smith and Wesson 9mm pistol caliber folding carbine was about sixteen inches folded. The Picatinny rail on top could accommodate a variety of sights.

Nick liked it and ordered two as well as two Sig Romeo red dot sights to put on them. While 9mm was not like his .223, 7.62x39 AKs, or the .308, it was sped up by being fired in a 16" barrel versus a four-inch one. The resultant performance was similar to a .357 Magnum handgun, the caliber many professionals, including Nick, felt was the best one-shot stopper of any handgun, including larger ones of the Dirty Harry ilk.

He just paid for pickup in Sarasota. Among cases, Kellogg, and now the club where his sister would work, he and Lola would be in Sarasota more often than ever.

Nick, Lottie, and Carly met with the representative from the security company. They walked around and Nick pointed out locations for surveillance cameras, emergency lighting, and a Von Duprin emergency exit bar for the rear door. He pointed out where motion detector lights and more cameras should be placed outside.

The last thing was a panic system with several actuators near the stage and in the office. They would tie into the burglar alarm system and generate immediate police response by the Sarasota Sheriff's Office.

The rep took copious notes and made several diagrams. He promised a bid by end of business the following day.

"I want to pay you for this survey, Nick," Lottie offered.

"This is *pro bono*. A little pre-opening gift. I thought about champagne, but I believe this was better."

Nicky got changed and rode back in the GTI with his uncle. The three women worked until about eight and came home.

7

Nick walked in carrying the toddler, who was babbling away. Erica stopped what she was doing and reached out her arms for him. Finn came trotting in and took up position.

Lola looked up and smiled at her two favorite looka-like Nicks.

"What are your feelings about going up to Virginia and taking on a case which may be impossible to solve?" Nick asked her.

"Mixed, of course. I may have an asset though. A couple years ago, I met a Virginia trooper at a national conference for female state troopers," she began.

"There is such a thing?" Nick asked seriously.

"There is. We hung out some and became friends. We talk every month or two, so I called her today. Her name is Bethany Alton. She works the Northern Virginia troop. Her buddy is an Arlington Detective named Mary Lewis. Mary heads up Cold Cases for the PD.

"She is going to call Mary and give me an intro over

the phone. I figure I will try to get the accident report from the Virginia State Police, or maybe Mary will offer it to me. I'm hoping she will work with me instead of against me. You know how it is, once you drop out of the badge club, you become *persona non grata*."

"It would be great if you have an inside track. All we have to do is solve it and get a conviction for Lottie. Neither she nor we care who gets the credit," Nick said, and Lola agreed.

"I have been amazed at the business acumen both ladies have, Carly especially.

"She can move the renovation, installation of cameras and alarms and begin recruiting forward towards club opening without Lottie there. She's a virtual whirlwind once she gets rolling," Nick said.

"Amazing, huh?" Lola agreed.

"It's the old 'can't tell a book by its cover' thing," Erica added.

Meanwhile, Nicky had toddled over to his favorite place to sleep. It was on Finn's shoulder as they both lay in the round cat bed. It seemed the purring put the little guy sound asleep every time.

"What's for dinner?" Nick asked.

"Take out, the dish I do best," Lola replied. "I was thinking of Olive Garden and a couple of family-sized spaghettis with meat sauce and lasagnas. And two salads. We have red wine in the rack. I can see two bottles from here. The ones aged in whisky barrels.

"Mom, you have to stay and help us eat it.

"Nick? Is the baby seat still in the GTI?" Lola asked.

He nodded as he read an email.

"Good. Mom and Nicky can go with me."

"Be very careful. Three of the four most important people in the world will be in the GTI.

"And, by the way. Congratulations! I deposited a twenty-thousand-dollar check from Kellogg this morning. Your capturing and cuffing Ibro saved him a net of eighty thousand. He was very happy to write the check for us," he said.

"It almost makes up what we lost on the whole Elusive Heiress case with Lottie," Lola said.

"No, it more than makes it up. Our total costs after Attorney Campbell's retainer of five thousand were only six thousand. Sounds like we are fourteen thousand ahead," Nick said. Lola nodded.

"My favorite large numbers are in horsepower and miles per hour," she said.

"I think I hear the three exotic dancers outside now," Nick said. As Maria became more involved in Tampa cases, she seemed to be arriving after dinner and in time to go to bed more and more. Nick sincerely hoped the trend would continue when Lola and Lottie went out of town, especially with Erica spending every night at her new craftsman's cottage now the threats were diminished.

Lola, Erica, and Nicky passed them in the rear yard as they approached the GTI.

"Back with dinner soon. Italian!" Lola yelled to them as the GTI roared out onto the alley.

Over dinner, Lola and Lottie decided to leave for Northern Virginia in the morning. Instead of flying, Lola pressed for using the larger surveillance van, thinking there was a probability Laverne Giannotti would require some watching. As Nick and Lola had found out on their last Virginia trip, the van was comfortable and had the bonus capability of accommodating a cot in back for one to sleep while the other drove.

"Sorry you don't have the new Smith & Wesson folding 9mm carbines yet. The dealer was not sure when they would arrive. Probably weeks. However, I doubt Laverne will put up armed resistance," Nick surmised.

"Since you are putting the condo on the market, will one of you drive my Camaro back?" Carly asked.

"Sure," Lottie said.

Lola did a quick weather report and determined what type of clothes they needed to pack. It appeared sweaters and light jackets would be in order. They would put blue frozen packets in the small Yeti cooler and pick up water, drinks, and snacks along the way for the roughly nine-hundred-mile trip up to the top of Virginia.

Angie gave Nicky a bath in a plastic tub and the warm water put him to sleep after his big day at the club and riding home with his uncle, babbling in response to everything Nick said. It was a guy thing. Something Nick had begun to realize he missed after the past few weeks.

Lola and Lottie left early. They were in no particular rush. Laverne was set now. Nobody with a badge had tapped her on the shoulder in five years. Lottie was out of her hair, and she had the big house and sufficient assets by spousal legacy to take care of her the rest of her days.

From Lottie's time perspective, she knew Carly was the brains behind the startup club operation. Lottie was finding overseeing her millions took time and thought. She still had to find an investment adviser, appoint a successor trustee behind her once the judge took away Campbell's appointment as trustee and made her the trustee, and had to complete the purchase of the house on Anna Maria Island. Thank heavens she had Carly and totally trusted her. And Lola and Nick for that matter.

Lola was in more of a hurry than her driving companion. She was anxious for things to get back to normal, though Angie and Nicky represented a new normal. And not in a bad way. It showed her a side of her partner she had had no way of seeing before. She had known he was a good and honorable man since the very first meeting. So had her mother. But as tough a Ranger as he always would be, the kinder side came out so much when he was around his nephew. The toddler looked more like a son.

Lola was pretty pleased, too, how often the little guy came and climbed into her lap and looked her in the eye and studied her. She had never been around children. Nicky may be as close as she wanted. Or maybe not. Time would tell.

Lola loved observing people, good and bad. And the uncle and nephew were about as good as it gets, she thought.

She drove the five hours to Jacksonville and on to the Florida/Georgia line where they stopped for a rest break. Lottie took the wheel from there. They were an hour south of Petersburg, Virginia by dusk and, forgoing the cot in the rear of the van, stopped at a nice motel and got a double room. Lottie paid, which meant Lola would not have to save the receipt and expense it.

They would be in Northern Virginia by midday tomorrow. About ten, Lola planned on calling Detective Sergeant Mary Lewis of the Arlington Police Cold Case Squad. Waiting should leave her Virginia trooper friend Bethany Alton time to call Lewis and set her up for Lola's call.

Ludo Bekrić called Nick early in the evening.

"Nick, it's Ludo. Were you serious about Alice and me coming down and visiting with you? And looking for property? Oh! And the fishing!"

"Absolutely, Ludo. Lola, Angie, and I look forward to seeing both of you. And, well, I don't think I have to tell you how happy Nicky will be to see you both."

"What if we came in two weeks, for a week? I could send you the flight information by text," Ludo said.

"Perfect, Ludo. And we definitely won't forget the fishing."

They chatted a bit longer, mainly about Nicky. Something had been bothering Nick, and he wondered about waiting to ask face-to-face, but went ahead now.

"Ludo, we were talking about how Ibro was a good man, how he put Nicky with you to protect him. What we didn't get into was why he allowed his nephew and a bunch of thugs to come down here to kill Angie and maybe put the boy at risk."

"It is easy, Nick. It was Adin behind the trip down to harm Angie. He set it up and talked the other three into it. Ibro found out after they had left. Ibro came down to stop him. He told me he would have killed Adin if you had not gotten to him first. He always liked your sister. He had to leave her thinking Nicky was dead as long as she was around Adin. Adin did not know where Ibro had put the baby, but if he got too curious, he would have found himself dead inside some deserted warehouse or a field somewhere. Or maybe never found. Just dead."

"I see, Ludo. Thank you for telling me. I understand his motivations. Say hi to Alice. I would let you talk with Nicky but he has been asleep for several hours. He and I will call you back in the next day or so." Nick could almost feel the older man smile on the other end of the connection.

After the call, Nick went into the kitchen where Angie was talking with Maria, while the detective was finishing up her leftover Italian.

He told his sister what Ludo had said. She believed him without hesitation.

"Maria, are you still seeing the psychologist after the shooting?" Nick asked.

"No, he cut me free. Said I was okay. But there is big news!"

"What?"

"I heard from Commissioner Reyes. He has liquidated everything in Honduras and is moving to Islamorada. He already has a house there. In a month, we are all invited down for a visit."

"I know you were worried about not seeing him for a while. Good news for sure!" Nick said.

"The problem is I don't have any leave built up yet."

"Can you take a few days without pay?" Angie asked.

"Maybe. I hate to just disappear. I started off with a bang and want the momentum to continue and not miss anything."

"You can take some weekend time if you fly down. I once took a trip down by car.

"Islamorada is about halfway along the Keys. It's too long a drive for a weekend down and back. You could fly though and get back by Sunday night.

"It would be worth it," Nick said.

"Would all of you go?" She asked.

"I don't know. A lot depends on the case Lola is on up in Northern Virginia. She may not be done with it by then. Let's take a look at the situation in a couple of weeks," Nick said.

"I mentioned meeting and becoming friends with a Latina at TPD who's a crime analyst, didn't I?" Maria asked.

"You did," Nick said.

"Her roommate just moved out. Left her hanging for half the rent. $450 a month. She asked if I would like to move in, even if just for a while."

"Is it in a safe part of town?" Nick asked.

"Yes. She did an analysis before moving in. Limited calls for service. Few of them are for violent crime. One registered sex offender lives two blocks away, but I am not what he likes."

"Comforting."

"Would you come to see me there?"

"Why don't you bring the analyst over to visit us?" Nick asked.

"I guess I could. You'd like her. Lola, too."

"I have no doubt we would. Maybe we could pick her brain and learn something from her useful to the agency," Nick said. "Are you looking at moving soon?"

"Maybe this weekend if that's okay."

"Honey, it's not like you have a rental agreement with us. You are a friend who can come and go as she pleases."

"Would you miss me?"

"Of course. Lola would too. And Finn. And Angie, though she and Nicky are going to share a house with Lottie and Carly." Angie agreed.

"The one on Anna Maria Island?" Maria asked. Nick nodded.

"So, the whole family is breaking up?" Maria asked.

"No, it's more evolving with people changing, improving their lives. People being able to live normally without the threat of a bunch of thugs kicking in the door to do harm," Nick responded.

"Would it be okay if I go try the pole? Angie, if you are not doing anything, I could use some pointers," Maria said.

Nick just shrugged, and Angie got up to climb the stairs with Maria. She left Nicky sleeping downstairs under Nick's and Finn's watchful eyes.

————

After an early motel night, Lola and Lottie arose and stopped at a Cracker Barrel for a comfort food breakfast on the way north.

Lola called her referral contact at Arlington Police Cold Cases Unit.

"Detective Sergeant Lewis," she answered, all business.

"Good morning, my name is Lola Caldwell. Trooper Bethany Alton may have warned you I'd be calling."

"Yes! Beth called me a couple days ago. She's an old friend of both of ours."

"We go back about seven years now," Lola said. "I am working on a case where a woman was killed in a hit-and-run in Arlington five years ago. I am looking to give my client closure. If I close it, you are welcome to the credit for the cold case. I don't want any credit," Lola said.

"Okay. How can I help you?"

"The only thing I think I need is the accident report. I know I can request it online, but thought it would be faster through you, and I would get some insights and perspectives about the case."

"Lola, may I call you that? I don't know about

perspectives. I can pull the file and read it and give you a copy. It's a public record in Virginia. Without having seen it, I would guess it will be a toughie. If the investigating officer who was on the scene and spoke with people wrote his report without any clue as to who the driver was, I think the probability of closing it five years later is somewhere between slim and none."

"You are probably right. But I am going to give it my best. Traffic accident investigations were my bread and butter for a decade as a Florida trooper, so I will concentrate on what experience I have on it," Lola said.

"Give me what you have so I can find the report before we go any further," Mary Lewis said.

Lottie was driving, and Lola had the death certificate in hand. She gave the date, time and location of death from the certificate and the full name of the victim, Danya Abelman Giannotti.

"You want to hold, or I can call you back."

"Someone else is driving, so I can hold and take notes when you find it. We will be in the area about two o'clock and can come by and shake hands if it's convenient."

"Sure. Hold a few minutes."

Lottie drove on and they waited about seven minutes, then the detective sergeant came back on.

"Sorry about that! Took longer than I thought. It definitely is still an open, though cold case. I have the report on the screen and am printing a copy for both of us.

"The investigating officer was a patrolman named Rory Moore. He's still around, serving as a patrol supervisor now in the same district of all things.

"It says the suspect vehicle was a small, older SUV,

maybe a late 80s to 1990 Bronco II model. Possibly red in color," Mary Lewis said.

"Thanks. My client is the victim's daughter. She believes the driver may have been her stepmother. She had been the father's secretary for some years and married him about as soon after his wife died as she could."

"Well, this will be the first actual suspect in the case. Does she have any real basis for naming her stepmother?"

"Nothing which would justify a search warrant, I'm afraid," Lola said.

"I could always drop by and question the stepmother. I can just tell her the truth. I am the senior cold case investigator and this one has cycled back up to my desk. Which ought to make sense to her, though it is pure BS."

"You will find her interesting. I met her once under totally different circumstances. She is not a very pleasant person," Lola said.

"My favorite kind!" Lewis exclaimed and sounded like she really meant it.

"I have to ask you, since I am unfamiliar with private investigator laws, do Virginia and Florida have reciprocity?" Lewis asked.

"Yes, I just looked it up. Virginia has PI reciprocity with six states. Florida is number one on the list. The agreement dates back to the late 1990s," Lola responded.

"Have you physically participated in investigations with police agencies since you became a PI?"

"Yes, a number of times in Florida and even in Honduras, where we were sworn in for a major investigation," Lola said.

"Boy, they had a big one down there with the pedo

resort and the congressman being shot," Lewis commented.

"That was the one we participated in," Lola said.

"Wow! Bet there are some stories there!"

"Oh, yeah!"

"How about call first and then drop by when you get in town?" Lewis suggested.

"Will do. It should be around two," Lola said, and they ended the call.

"Did it go as you hoped?" Lottie asked.

"Yes. She didn't shut me down right out of the gate, which was a very real possibility. The mutual friend helped, I'm sure," Lola said.

"Should I go with you?" Lottie asked.

"Probably not the first visit. She may want to question you later. But you don't really have any actionable evidence. Let's let her get invested in the case first."

"Okay. If you will drop me at the condo, I will start packing. We are going to sell it furnished. Maybe except for our new super big television. So, it's just clothes and some gourmet cookware to be packed. I can arrange for it to be shipped to Anna Maria."

"Is the Anna Maria house a done deal?" Lola asked.

"It will be by the time I give the go-ahead to ship."

Lola dropped her off as well as her overnight bag. She headed to Arlington Police headquarters, calling Detective Sergeant Mary Lewis along the way.

Lola was careful to lock her pistol in the gun safe in the van before going into the police headquarters. She asked for Lewis at the front desk. Soon a medium-height, probably low fifties woman walked out smiling and extending her hand.

"Lola? I am Mary Lewis," the woman said, and they walked back to a room with one office and several cubicles with detectives working. Lola noticed the detectives were older and wondered if this was true of cold case units universally. This was not something she had been exposed to as a road trooper in Florida.

"Come on in and sit down, Lola. Coffee?" She pointed to a coffee maker sitting on a sideboard.

"Not sure I have ever turned down a coffee. Guess my partner, Nick, has influenced me into drinking too much coffee," she said to Mary Lewis.

"I looked you guys up on the Internet. You look like you should be your own television show! How can you work seriously with a partner who looks like Nick?"

"It helps we are engaged, and our office is a two-story house we bought together," Lola said, not sure if it was a sufficient answer to a question she had heard before.

"You guys have had some pretty dramatic cases. Yet, this one seems boring compared. What gives?"

"You are perceptive, Mary. You must be a detective sergeant or something" Lola smiled.

"If you read about the Honduras case and the connected matter the news call the Elusive Heiress case, this is the end product to those. The client is the woman who was an undercover at the resort in Honduras where the congressman was killed. You and I briefly mentioned it on our phone call. She is also the one we referred to as the elusive heiress."

"And she alleges her stepmother was the hit-and-run driver?" Mary asked.

"She does, based on, I believe, wanting it to be true and some other signs she feels she has had over the past five years. She is in town and willing to talk with you if you want. I will leave it to you to determine her credibility," Lola said.

"I think you want us to look into it first and me to talk with her after we determine it's worthwhile?" Mary asked.

"Probably the best way to go to keep you from wasting your time. I'd like to give her closure by determining who the driver was, stepmother or not," Lola said.

"Well, finding the driver would close a cold case, though not a very pressing one. Patrolman, now sergeant, Rory Moore, is a good cop. He's conscientious and thorough. If Rory could not find the driver when he was first on scene, I doubt we will be able to five years later."

"I do, too. But I promised Lottie Giannotti I would try. So, I will. One thing I wondered about is whether records exist to determine if the stepmother, Laverne, ever had a red Bronco II or something similar?" Lola said.

"We would have to have her maiden name to start the search," Mary said.

"I looked it up. It's Godwin. Laverne Helen Godwin," Lola answered.

"I have a detective outside who is a whiz at record searches. He's pretty far past chasing perps, but he can solve more crimes on his ass than most detectives can with shoe leather." She got up and took a slip of paper outside to an older, heavy-set man at a desk. He looked up and smiled. Lola tried to read his lips and thought he said "piece of cake." She hoped she was right.

"Mary, since the patrolman was not a detective working a case, do you think he kept notes from any house-to-house he may have done?" Lola asked.

"No, I doubt it. We can ask him." She picked up the phone to dispatch.

"It's Detective Sergeant Lewis in the cold case unit. Do you have a cell phone number for Sergeant Rory Moore? And is he working something right now?"

She nodded at several responses, then hung up.

"Rory is not on a call. She's going to get him to call me," Mary said.

They drank coffee and spoke for a few minutes and the phone rang.

Mary Lewis answered, and it was the sergeant.

"Rory, I am taking a look at an old hit-and-run homicide. You worked it five years ago. The vic was a woman named Danya Abelman Giannotti. Do you remember it?

"You do? Good! I know there was no suspect and not good eyewitnesses. Did you keep any sort of interview notes?

"Okay. Are you anywhere near HQ? Maybe dropping by and meeting my guest here would be helpful.

"Great. Thanks, Rory. We'll see you then.

"He's on the way. Will be here in five minutes," Mary said.

Rory tapped on the door a few minutes later.

"Rory, this is former Florida trooper Lola Caldwell. She and her partner, Nick Wolf, are PIs in Florida. You might want to do an Internet search on them. It reads like a television action series. She's also an old friend of Bethany Alton with VSP. I know you know Bethany."

Moore nodded, he did.

"Sergeant, I am investigating the hit-and-run on behalf of the victim's daughter. It's a real long shot, but she thinks her stepmother may have been the driver. Did the name Laverne Helen Godwin ever come up in your investigation?" Lola asked.

"As you might imagine, I am going totally on faint

recollection here," he began, "but the short answer is no. Not a single name came up. The vehicle description, as I remember, was a red or maroon small SUV. Maybe an older small Chevy, GMC, or Ford from the '80s. Maybe '90s."

"Rory, late eighties or early nineties Bronco II seems to come up," Mary said.

"Could be. I just don't remember where the description came from. Somebody said it on scene and disappeared. It was pretty hectic with the pretty lady knocked fifty feet from where she was struck and in somebody's front yard. I got there pretty fast, and it was a busy, messed up crime scene even before I arrived."

"Sounds like most of mine when I arrived as a trooper. It was a black or white Miata or F-250 driven by a man or woman or Sasquatch," Lola said, and he nodded and smiled.

"Yeah. About sums most of them up," he said.

The detective from outside tapped on the door. Mary waved him in.

"Sorry to interrupt, but I thought you might be talking about what you asked me to look up," he said.

"We are, Bill. What did you find out?" Mary asked.

"Laverne Godman did not own a red Bronco II. She did own, and apparently still does, own a maroon Geo or Chevrolet Tracker. It may be a little smaller than a Bronco II, but it's in the same category. It was first a Geo Tracker, then GM used the Chevrolet Tracker nameplate." He handed Mary a sheet of paper he printed off his computer. The sheet also had a representative photo of a Tracker.

"I wonder about how difficult it would be to get a search warrant..." the patrol sergeant spoke aloud.

"Pretty difficult based on the fact picture, I'd say,"

Mary Lewis said. Lola did not say anything. She wanted to do some research and snoop around.

"You know," Lola began, "I doubt Laverne would have the hit-and-run vehicle in the garage she shared with her husband. No amount of her cleaning would have removed all the evidence of the hit.

"So, I am betting if she still has it, she has it stored somewhere. I would think she would have hesitated to turn a perfectly operable car over to a junkyard. It surely would raise too many questions. The only other possibility would be to go to a bad part of town, leave it parked and unlocked with a key in the switch and simply not report it when it was stolen," the PI said.

All agreed with her logic.

"My bet is, if it was really the hit-and-run vehicle, she has it stashed away somewhere it will never be found during her lifetime," the cold case supervisor said.

Lola had been thinking the same thing and had some ideas she was going to hold close. If she located a likely place, she would probably do something illegal to verify its existence. Which still presented the justification of a search warrant issue.

She needed to reach Nick and have him log into their special lawyer and PI research site and do a deep dive on Laverne Godwin Giannotti. A real deep dive.

The other thing she wanted to do was to find some former employees of Giannotti's firm when Laverne was his secretary. Maybe Lottie could help with the names or location of firm records. Unless, more likely, Laverne had the records.

The meeting broke up with the cold case unit chief deciding to go visit Laverne and see what she had to say, or more importantly, how she reacted. She promised to keep the rest in the loop.

Lola called Nick with her request as soon as she got into the van. She drove straight to Lottie and Carly's condo and found Lottie had left in her friend's Camaro.

She called her and asked if she knew the names of any of her father's former employees. She knew several she said and would prepare a list, possibly with numbers and addresses as soon as she found a stopping place in her trip to meet with the condo sales rep and a moving company to ship the small amount of clothes and television and cookware to Florida.

"Let's get it all together in one place and see if it might fit in the van. If so, I will take it back for you and save you what could be thousands of dollars," Lola offered.

"If you do it, I will pay you what the freight would have cost," Lottie said.

"Nope. It would just be a favor to a friend. You are paying for us to investigate your mother's death."

"Thanks. I will get the list put together quickly. Some of them came over to the house after the funeral for both my mother, and later, my father. Or uncle. I have to get used to saying it. I promise you will find none could stand Laverne. Nobody."

"Nick and I sure didn't. Not at all," Lola admitted.

"Lola, I will postpone the appointment with the freight company until we see what we have and whether it will fit in the van. Carly, ever the great businesswoman, did some preemptive work with the realtor. I think all I have to do is approve a couple of things. We might get her on the phone and have a conference call. The realtor was a big fan of both of us as dancers."

"Good! Let him reduce his commission as a kind of tip to you all," Lola commented.

"We'll see. I will finish with him quick and bring you the list in person. Maybe an hour?" Lottie said.

"Sounds good. Bye," and the call ended.

Since the hit-and-run occurred during a daily walk Lottie's mother took, Lola knew the scene would be close because the condo was only blocks from the Giannotti home.

She decided to walk over and get her bearings while Nick was doing the online research. She took the accident report, because of the scene sketch Patrolman Rory Moore had drawn.

It took her less than five minutes to get to the scene. She knew exactly what had happened once she saw it.

Danya had walked down the suburban streets from her home, stopped at the pedestrian crossing and walked across to the park entrance at the end of the crossing. Anyone who had done any sort of surveillance would have picked this as the kill zone. It was perfect.

She took a couple of photos with her phone and walked back to the condo. Carly had trashed anything in the refrigerator which might spoil during her unknown period of absence. Consequently, there was nothing to eat or even drink except for a couple beers and sodas.

Lola called Nick and told him what she had found and how she thought the person—if the hit-and-run was homicide and not an accident—had chosen the only decent kill zone on the walk. The park had paths, but not for motorized vehicles. It might have been good for a stabbing or the like, but probably not. Not if today was any indication of the pedestrian traffic at the time of Danya's death. Also, such an attack would be upfront and personal. Something she would think Laverne would avoid. Again, assuming the current line of inquiry she was following.

She had started to write the street addresses of the houses along the route so Nick could research them and determine who the owners were and whether they lived there at the time of Danya's death. Then she stopped. Lola decided not to bother Nick with the added research. She would find out how long they lived there and what they might remember very quickly on her planned door-to-door interviews.

Her phone rang. It was Nick.

"I found out Laverne has a mother who died four years ago. The mother spent the year before in a nursing home, then hospice. I am sending you her address and a Google Earth photo of the house. You will notice it has a rear, unconnected garage.

"Laverne inherited the house. My guess is she had constructive possession from the time of Danya's death to now. Somebody has been paying the taxes on it.

"She is an only child. Not even any nieces or nephews. She's it.

"Since you tell me she still has the Tracker, as near as anyone can tell, the garage is a good candidate for being where in hell it is," Nick said.

"Yes! Why not leave the murder car on ice. After some period of time, maybe nobody would remember it and she could junk it. After all, how valuable would a thirty-plus-year-old tracker be anyway?" Lola said.

"I tried magnifying the garage door to look at its lock. It pixelated too much and I could not see whether it's a lock on a handle, which I did see, or has been replaced with a padlock. Either way, it should not be too difficult to breach with your pick lock set."

"Are you suggesting breaking and entering?" Lola asked.

"No. I am suggesting when you are sure Laverne is not going to come over and check the place, one might put the magnetic Aaron & Ashley Home Inspections sign on the van, place a ladder upside the house and walk around back. It would seem logical to neighbors for a house sitting vacant for five years to be inspected to be put on the market for sale," Nick said.

"It would, wouldn't it? Have I mentioned I figured out you are a good bad boy and not vice versa?"

"No you haven't. You are probably correct in your assessment however," Nick replied.

"The cold case detective is going to try to interview Laverne soon. I will casually find out when and go then. I wonder how far is the house from where Laverne lives?"

"Wonder not. Your fiancé already determined it is five miles.

"It seems to me the big issue is finding the Tracker. You cannot admit to breaking in. So, what will be your, or rather the detective's, justification to a judge for a search warrant?" Nick asked.

"No clue. I will figure it out when we find the car and have to justify a warrant," Lola said.

"I would avoid photos of the SUV in the garage you broke into. The biggest stroke of luck would be side windows in the garage you could have looked through and spot it from outside," Nick observed.

"Looking at the Google Earth photo, the backyard seems pretty private. Tall fence and all. I hope to leverage the privacy during my black bag job," Lola said.

Nick chuckled, knowing Lola had used the term "black bag job" tongue-in-cheek. This was as far from a black bag job as could be. When he had a warrant as a CID special agent and went in to plant bugs in a suspect's home or business, *that* was a black bag job.

"Just be careful, honey. I don't want to have to bail you out."

"I will, my love. As careful as you always are! Bye!"

She was gone before he could retort.

Lola called Detective Sergeant Mary Lewis.

"Hey, it's Lola. What's going on?"

"I slotted some time tomorrow in late morning to pay an unannounced visit to Laverne Giannotti."

"Excellent! I can't wait to find out how she reacts to reopening the case. I hope she gets real nervous, because if she is as cool as a cucumber, we may be out of suspects!"

"My thought, too, Lola. Sure you don't want to come?"

"I don't think it will help you if I am there. I fear she would remember me from a few weeks ago and it would send up even more red flags than your surprise visit already will."

"I guess you are right. I might take Bill, the detective who came up with the Tracker for us.

"Have you found anything?" Mary asked.

"Yes. A couple of things. I walked to the site of the hit-and-run today. It was right where there was a pedestrian walkway across from the entrance to a park. If it was planned, they picked the only kill zone in the area. She probably walked in the park every day. And this was the only place to run her down without going up on the sidewalk.

"Second, Laverne's mother has a house. Laverne still owns it. I don't know whether she leases it or it's vacant. It has an unattached rear garage per Google Earth.

Sounds like a great place to hide a car you don't want the world to see."

"Good stuff! Why don't you ride by while I am interviewing Laverne. We can meet somewhere afterwards and swap what we found out."

"Great! Is it okay if Lottie, Laverne's stepdaughter, comes? I am committed to her in the morning," Lola asked.

"Yeah, I think so. I will want to talk with her sometime anyway," Mary said.

———

Nick handled calls all day. He picked up two fraud cases from insurance company clients and three traffic accident cases. Two from law firms and one from a third insurance company. He really needed to get his partner home.

He wrapped up the day and Erica walked over to advise she was headed home. He had helped her move the rest of the way into the craftsman cottage several streets over yesterday. The next thing was to help with painting. The rest a handyman would address.

"It's kind of busy without our special girl, isn't it?" Erica noted.

"It is. She's a dynamo. I miss her. We are hardly ever apart," Nick said.

"A little separation is probably good for the soul. Besides, you will have Maria, Angie, and little Nicky to fill the time soon."

"You are right. I am hoping Maria moves in with a new acquaintance at the police department soon," Nick said.

"It would be a good thing for her to get really busy at

work all right. And her own place is part of growing up," Erica said.

"She had her own place in Honduras. Somewhere in the capital city. She's not the little girl she appears to be. She is only about two years younger than Angie and five or six younger than me."

"You are kidding! I placed her at Carly's age."

"And everyone places you at early thirties. I guess you can't tell a book by its cover."

"I think I will go home and bake you something for that! Cake or brownies?"

"Brownies, always, chewy please."

"Okay. Finn, I am out of here. You are in charge," Erica said as she walked out the front door.

Every time Nick looked at the door, he thought about the trafficker of little girls he and Lola had killed at their front door. It was one of the cases where he had no choice but to violate Rule 4. Know your target (he did) and what is behind it (he kind of did—a street and a house).

Nick knew the .357 Magnum bullet had penetrated the bad guy and gone across the street. He was relieved to see the sound of the shot bring the old man who lived there out of his door and onto his sidewalk to see what all the commotion was. Nick knew then he was fine. He never suggested the man search for the bullet. He would not find it anyway. SPPD crime scene investigators had looked and not located it.

He heard the rear door. Too early for Maria. Must be Carly, Angie, and his nephew.

The next sound was an excited squeal and "Unca Nick!" which was as close as Nicky could get to saying his uncle Nick.

He heard running footsteps and swept the little guy

up in his arms. None of the next minute or two of words were as clear as his call was, but they were delivered with excitement and enthusiasm.

Nicky looked around quizzically and said, "Lolo?"

"Aunt Lola is not here. She is on a trip. I hope she will be back to us in a day or two."

Nicky tilted his head and peered at his uncle as if the latter was totally crazy.

Not knowing anything better to do, Nick just gave him a hug which was reciprocated with a sticky kiss and a giggle.

Nick held Nicky with one hand and used the other to push up on his desk. Long periods of inactivity, whether in a car or even at his desk, caused his left leg to stiffen. Angie and Maria would have to vacate the workout room while he worked to loosen his legs with the stationary bike or the treadmill later in the evening.

Unfortunately he knew they would retreat to the master bedroom and its pole. *It may be worth just walking around the block*, he thought.

Nick heard his sister and Carly in the kitchen checking the refrigerator and freezer and agreeing on what they would make for dinner. He was more than glad to give up chef duties tonight for sure.

He spent the next half hour on the floor playing with Nicky. Either the boy was tired from a busy day or his uncle had turned boring, but Nicky was soon asleep on a fish motif throw pillow on the floor, curled up next to his favorite cat, who was now also asleep.

Lola called to report nothing new except she and Lottie were going to a Thai place for dinner. She asked what they were having in St. Petersburg and he said he actually did not have any idea. He shared Nicky looking around and calling out for "Lolo," which thrilled her.

Tomorrow would be a big day on the case. The cold case detective would pay a surprise visit on Laverne Giannotti and Lola and Lottie would, pretending to be home inspectors, break into the garage in hopes of finding a red or maroon Tracker mini-SUV.

If it was not there and Laverne did not admit to the homicide, they were back to nothing. She told Lottie so.

"I just know the bitch killed Mom. I feel it in my bones," Lottie said.

"Honey, if the garage doesn't pan out and if the detective doesn't get a strong guilty vibe from Laverne, I am not sure what more we can do," Lola told her.

Later in the evening, the two parted at their motel doors. Meanwhile, Nick had built up a palpable sweat working out. He could feel his leg loosening.

Nicky was in bed and Angie, Carly, and Maria were in his and Lola's bedroom as he had forecast. On the pole. Two teaching by example, one eager student watching then trying.

The door was open, and Nick tried to sneak to the bathroom for a quick shower. He was called in to see Maria's progress. He had never really seen Carly or his sister work out on the pole either. At least they were somewhat dressed if undergarments counted.

Maria seemed to have the hang of it. She certainly had the hang of the seductive looks and moves. Nick remembered Carly telling him and Lola how deeply Lottie got into her performance, zoning her audience out completely.

He clapped and said, "Nice job!" and quickly adjourned to the bathroom and showered.

When he came out, they were still in there working the pole. Angie was doing some moves he would have thought impossible. Her physical prowess greatly exceeded what he would have thought. He hurried downstairs to his desk.

Nick was thinking about the Tracker. If Laverne had sold it to a legitimate junk dealer, the certificate of title would have been canceled out. Apparently no such thing had occurred. Unless she sold it to a sketchy junk dealer or a car stripper, it would not still be held on Virginia's records as owned by her. Using information Lola passed to him, he ran a Carfax on it. No salvage, no flooding, nothing. Just owned by the owner of record. He was worried about Lola tomorrow. Not so much because she was more than bending the law, but because of the ramifications if she got caught. With Lottie as an accomplice.

He would be glad when the operation was safely completed.

———

The next day, Nick received a call the two folding Smith & Wesson 9mm carbines were ready for him to have his credentials processed through the authorities for purchase and to pick up. He did the paperwork and payment as soon as the store opened then went to their indoor range and installed both small red dot sights and sighted them in for twenty-five yards.

In Arlington, Virginia, Lola placed the Aaron and Ashley Home Inspection Service magnetic sign boards on both sides of the white surveillance van.

Lottie put on jeans and a tee shirt to match Lola and they drove to the location of Laverne's late mother's home.

They parked directly in front of the home and Lottie knocked on the front door and, getting no response, walked around with a clipboard and to all observers (of which she saw none) was taking copious notes. Meanwhile, Lola, with her clipboard, walked around back and directly to the garage.

It did not have an electric door opener. Nor did it have a hardened padlock on a hasp. It had the original old key lock in the middle of the twist handle, one unlocked, turned and lifted to manually open the single car-sized door.

Before doing anything with the lock, Lola walked around the side of the garage and looked for a window. There was one on either side. Both had not been cleaned for years, probably decades. Both appeared to have raggedy curtains drawn.

One of the ladders on the top of the truck was for more than disguise. It was a small folding step ladder secured to the two larger, heavy ladders which were for looks only.

She removed the small ladder, winked at Lottie and carried it around to the side of the garage. She opened it and climbed to be able to peer in the window. She had brought something else from the van. It was an emergency window breaker for submerged cars or rescuing children or pets some idiot left in a hot car while shopping.

Florida has a good Samaritan law which allowed citizens to break windows in an emergency without legal risk as long as they called 911 first.

She had scanned the area for people in the yard on the side of the window she was going to breach and at the windows of the house next door. She did not see anyone.

Lola tapped the window with the small orange hammer with the tungsten point and the corner broke out and fell inside. Gloves on, more to prevent finger-prints than for safety, she brushed away shards of glass which had fallen on the outside sill.

She reached in and jerked the rotten curtain down and dropped it inside.

Using her pencil-sized high lumen Streamlight, she looked inside.

There was a small vehicle covered with a canvas tarp. A faded reddish fender showed as well as very small spoked wheels with little snow tires.

Lola let out the breath she was holding. It had to be the Tracker!

She simply had to know for sure though. The garage was so small the vehicle was less than five feet from the window. She climbed down the ladder and went to the rear of the house.

There was a rusty rake laying on the ground. It looked like it had been propped against the house at some time, but a storm or something had blown it over.

She took the rake back to the garage and climbed the ladder again.

Lola fiddled with the lock on the window and forced it open. Putting as much of her body in behind the rake as she could, she reached out and snagged the canvas with the tines.

A quick jerk ripped most of the tarp off a late eighties to early nineties Chevy Tracker. She saw damage on the driver-side front. The headlight was broken out and the surrounding front of the fender was dented.

Lola walked back to the rear of the house and replaced the rake. She found half of a brick and carried it back. She tossed it in, looking for the world like a kid had broken the window out.

She folded the ladder and walked around the house to Lottie.

"Sally, we'll have to come back later with a taller ladder to check the roof. We've done all we can here for now," she said in a louder than normal voice.

Lola fastened the small ladder on the roof rack and locked it.

They got in and Lottie looked at her.

"Well?" Lottie asked.

Windows up and pulling away, Lola smiled and said, "Yep. The Tracker is in there! Even has damage in the driver-side front."

"We've got her now!" Lottie explained.

"We have to come up with a non-criminal story about how we know it's there, but yes. We have her!"

She texted Detective Sergeant Mary Lewis.

"Mary, are you still in the interview?"

"Yes, wrapping up. Will call you from car in five."

They headed in the general direction from which they came.

Five minutes later, the phone rang. Lola looked at the number.

"It's her!"

"It's Lola," she answered.

"What an unlikeable bitch!" were the first words out of the detective's mouth.

"Let me modify something there," Lola said. "It should be unlikeable *murdering* bitch."

"What do you know I don't?" Mary asked.

"We peeked in the window of Laverne's mother's garage. There's a red Chevy Tracker in there. It looks like it has sat there for years. It also has damage to the driver's side front."

"Dare I ask how you learned this?" the detective asked.

"We did not know if the house was vacant or rented. Nobody answered the door. I walked around the back to see if anyone was there. There was a garage with a broken-out window. I looked in and saw the vehicle. End of story," Lola said convincingly.

"And the window was broken out? New damage or old?" Mary asked.

"Could have been either. I was a trooper. This detective stuff is new to me."

"Yeah, right. Well, we should meet and exchange our findings. What street are you on?"

Lottie told her being a native. And she told Mary Lewis.

"There is a Dunkin' Donut place on your street. Pull in there and look for Bill and me in a gray Dodge Stratus."

"Will do. See you soon."

"Lola, she knows, doesn't she?" Lottie asked nervously.

"She knows we trespassed. She may suspect more, but unless she goes back and interviews neighbors and finds one who saw me, but who I did not see, it's all speculation," Lola said.

They met at the donut shop and had coffee and celebratory donuts and did the introductions.

"You first?" Lola asked.

"Classic TV bad cop, good cop. I was bad, Bill was somewhat good. I mean, he played the role of 'somewhat good'. He's one of the best interrogators, oops! Interviewers, I know.

"Laverne Giannotti is one of the rudest, most unlikeable people I have met in a long time. I expect it of gang bangers, drug dealers, and pimps. Middle-aged widows who live in an upscale neighborhood, not so much.

"I cut right to the chase, and she tightened up. She said she wanted a lawyer. I said, 'Fine, but you are not under arrest.'

"She said, 'Then get the hell out of my house!'

"Bill said to me, 'Sergeant, I feel we should arrest her for the vehicular homicide of Danya Giannotti. Let her spend some time in the tank with the whores and female addicts. They will soften her up.'"

"And Bill, you were the good cop?" Lola asked with a smile for clarification.

"I was," he said.

"She just froze after Bill's suggestion. So, we said, 'We'll be back with an arrest warrant' and left."

"Mary. We need to go back to the house and protect that Tracker. She might panic and try to burn the garage down or something," Lola said.

Mary put the plastic cap on her coffee and stood up. Bill did the same.

"You want to lead the way?" she asked, and Lola nodded.

Back at the house and all at the front door.

"I am going to knock and try to make contact with a renter. If he or she does not answer, I am going to walk around back and see if anyone is there. If there's a garage, I will check to see if they are in it working on a lawnmower or something," Mary said.

"Sounds like perfect police procedure, Sergeant," Lola said. Bill rolled his eyes.

Around back, Mary did a hammer-fisted police knock on the garage door.

"Police! Is anyone in there?" She tilted her head. "I thought I heard something."

She went around to the broken window.

Mary turned to the six foot three and two hundred plus pound Bill.

"Do I lift you up to look? Or do you lift me?" she asked rhetorically.

He clasped two beefy hands together, and she stepped in for a ride up to window height.

Lola handed her the powerful flashlight she had used.

"Well, look at that! A vehicle which closely matches the hit-an-run vehicle. And accident damage. This is enough for me to secure a warrant to open this garage and tow this vehicle so our specialists can have a really close look at it.

"Bill, take my keys and protect the scene in case the horrid woman decides to destroy the evidence which may put her in prison. I will hitch a ride with Lola and Lottie down to the judicial center. I will call while we are en route and pave the way for an immediate search warrant."

An hour and a half later, they were back with a warrant and a departmental flatbed wrecker to deliver the Tracker to the CSI team.

Three hours later, the CSI team had gone over the Tracker. The damage was suggestive of a pedestrian being struck. There were blood traces on the bumper and broken-out edges of the left headlight.

Mary Lewis thought ahead after the Tracker was located with damage and obtained a DNA swab from Lottie. Once she found out there were blood traces, she pushed hard to get the comparison made.

They got the results in the following day. The blood belonged to the mother of Lottie Giannotti. Tied with the prints on the wheel belonging to

Laverne Giannotti, they had cause for an arrest warrant.

She had Bill choose another detective and go pick her up. Knowing when, Lola and Lottie got there early and parked just out of sight.

When the two detectives brought Laverne out in handcuffs, Lottie watched without passion from behind the dark windows of the surveillance van. Lola captured it on the van system's video. They waited until Bill and the other detective, who they did not recognize, carefully assisted the stunned woman into the rear seat of an unmarked Taurus and drove away.

They sat for a minute.

"How do you feel?" Lola asked.

"I don't really know. I thought I was going to be happy. Now, I am relieved, of course, but not happy at all. I always disliked her because of how she treated me. Now, I hate her for what I know beyond the shadow of a doubt she did to my mother. Hate is not a very warming, pleasant emotion," Lottie said.

"No, it isn't. In many cases, we warn people they may find out more than they wanted to as a case develops. While it's probably not true here, the evidence and her arrest certainly delivers a gut-slamming conclusion to your suspicions, Lottie.

"My advice, which I realize you have not requested, is to not stress over it. It's a door which closed to allow you to enter another. And think how exciting the other doors will be! Wealth for yourself and maybe for charities, the club, new friends for life. Your prospects don't need to be clouded by negative thoughts.

"Laverne is a cold, horrible person and a murderer. To hell with her. Try to never think of her again. She's not worth the effort," Lola finished.

Lottie reached over and squeezed her friend's hand. Lola could see a tear forming. Sadness? Emotional release? Anger? Probably a bit of each, she thought as she started the truck.

"We'll call Mary Lewis tomorrow for a status report. You know, to see if she needs anything from either of us. I doubt she will. We kind of orchestrated this to go down as APD solving a cold case. No publicity needed or wanted.

"Are you happy with the agency's performance? Get your money's worth?" Lola asked.

"Oh, yes! You solved a case nobody but I thought you could. Maybe not even you! You found me when I didn't want to be found. You saved my life more times than we may ever know. You and Nick counseled me more as a friend or family member than as a client. I will love you guys forever."

"You are our friend first and client second, honey," Lola said as she headed back to the condo.

"How about a big celebratory dinner? I'm on an extravagant expense account, you know," Lola teased.

"Yes! I know just the place. I wish Nick and Carly were here to enjoy it with us. And you will be guaranteed of the expense being approved, though the amount will choke a horse!"

They both slept until almost ten the next morning and awoke with filled stomachs and throbbing headaches. The wine had been really good. Lola had to recover the van soon since they had needed to take an Uber back to the condo.

Lola's phone rang, and the trill sent stabbing pains all the way into her brain.

She tried to focus and had very little luck, so she just answered "Lola Caldwell."

"Well, I know that," her fiancé said.

"We had a celebratory dinner with lots of really expensive wine. Perhaps too much."

"Good for you. 'Celebratory dinner with lots of really expensive wine' sounds like you need to share good news with your partner in all things," Nick prompted.

"Yes. Sorry. Yesterday and the day before went a thousand miles per hour. The Tracker was in the garage, had proof of the hit-and-run, including DNA evidence compared with Lottie's. The only fingerprints on the steering wheel were Laverne's.

"She has been charged with vehicular homicide, leaving the scene of an accident, tampering with evidence, and everything else they can think of. The cold case detective told me the state's attorney thinks they have a tight case and are going to try for life. Hell, even thirty years would effectively be life," Lola said.

"So, you guys are coming home soon? Nicky misses Lolo. Both Nickys do."

"My boys damn well better miss me! I will let you know our schedule after speaking with the detective. For now, I need coffee and the most powerful OTC pain reliever in Lottie's cabinet."

"Okay. Let me know what you find out. Love you. Bye." And he was gone.

Coffee and Excedrin later, Lola spoke with Mary Lewis on a conference call with Lottie being identified as listening in.

"I just had a sit-down with the prosecutor. I kept you out and Lottie only as the one who brought it to our attention who our first and only suspect was. She does not think she will need her. There's always the defense attorney, though he does not have your name, Lottie? He may subpoena her, but I cannot see why.

"My advice is to get out of town and resume your lives. If anything changes, I will call you then. I will certainly advise you of the disposition of the case, which, as you know, won't be anytime soon," the detective said.

"Mary, thanks to you, Bill, and the rest of your team for the gracious reception and help. I suspect we will be heading back to Florida today," Lola said.

"Right, Detective. I am selling out up here and moving there permanently. My condo is on the market, my Virginia car is on a sales lot and I am ready to get on with my life," Lottie added.

They had already sequestered the things to be moved to Florida in a corner of the living room. They cleared out the refrigerator and freezer, and foods in the cabinets and bathroom medicine cabinet items.

"Think this will fit in the back of the van?" Lottie asked.

"I do. Especially if neither of us is going to sleep on the cot back there."

They loaded house items in the van and Lottie's clothes, dance costumes (which took up virtually no room at all), shoes, and cosmetics in Carly's Camaro.

Since there was no particular rush, they left at four p.m. and stopped near Fredericksburg for the night as Nick and Lola had. This time, Lottie insisted on the best of the hotel choices near I-95.

"What's the use of being rich if you can't live like it?" she asked. Lola agreed heartily.

They pulled into St. Petersburg two days later just at dusk.

8

Everyone was there waiting, except for Maria who was still working a case over in Tampa. Nicky and Finn were the first to welcome Lola and Lottie as Nick was on a call.

Lola squatted down and hugged both as Finn rubbed his face all over her, claiming her in case anyone had forgotten she was all his. Nicky kept squealing "Lolo! Lolo!" as she hugged him.

Nick got off the phone and got in the first hug, followed by Erica.

"Congratulations, you two, on a case well-solved!" Nick said. "Another one in the history books. Lottie, have you heard from the attorney who is pleading to remove Campbell as the trustee and insert you?" he asked.

"Not yet. I will call him in the morning. I would think it would be a simple thing to do, what with Campbell heading to prison and all," she said.

"It is. I just sometimes think lawyers and judges have slower watches than the rest of us mortal beings,"

Nick said as Lottie picked up the toddler for a sloppy kiss and a tight hug."

"I believe his hug has gotten stronger while we have been gone," she said, handing him back to Angie.

"I am hoping he has his father's strength, but Nick's and my physique type. His father was built like a brute," Angie said. "Of course it didn't do him much good against Nick," she added.

"Carly, what's new on the club front?" Lottie asked.

"Lots. We have security in, painting done, a new big-ass bright neon sign you can see from the other side of the state being installed tomorrow. The last of the booths and stages will be completed by the end of the coming week.

"I think we are ready to start interviewing help!"

"Nick and Lola," Lottie said. "Do you think we need to do background checks on the dancers? And. can you do them?"

"Yes," Nick said. "I think it's important to see if there are any drug arrests in their history. You really don't want drugs to spread in the dressing room or anywhere. Background checks on the bouncers are equally important. Looking for brawling, battery, arrests."

"I wonder if the Bosnians did any of that on us and the bouncers?" Carly mused.

"I doubt it. They were crooks. You aren't. I think their bouncers came from the ranks of their protection racket anyway," Lola said. And Lottie and Carly nodded their agreement.

"Carly, anything on the house on Anna Maria?" Lottie asked.

"You betcha! The realtor said the owner is going to do a counter to your offer, but he does not think it will be too bad. My business Spidey sense says you should take it. The asking prices were in keeping with the neighborhood comps. And there is not a lot on the market there to begin with."

"I think our goals tomorrow should be to meet with him, call the attorney trying to get the trustee changed, and trade in the big Mercedes for something small and sexy."

"Sounds like you need a trooper's experience on the last part. I used to love to chase small and sexy cars. Only problem for me is they were driven by hot women or older guys with a paunch."

"Doesn't matter. Look what you ended up with," Angie said slightly defensively.

"I did far better than I deserve."

"Do you mean I can have the BMW back?" Nick asked.

"Of course not, silly man. It's my engagement car."

"By the way. You have a new engagement folding carbine, too," Nick added, producing the new Smith & Wesson for her to examine. "It fits in the small gun safe in both vans where we keep the short shotguns."

"Broken in, of course?" she asked.

"Yes, partially. You should finish the process with about three boxes of fifty each for familiarization anyway."

"Maybe tomorrow. These are pretty neat!" she said, placing it folded in the non-gun looking case which came with it.

"Do you have time to go with me?" she asked.

"I do."

"Good! Keep practicing saying those two words."

"I will. They have become a mantra to me. I walk through the house singing them like a cantor." Lola nodded approvingly then grinned one of her deliciously lascivious grins as Nick adopted a bass voice and walked away singing, "I do! I do!"

Both were at their desks early the next morning. Nick briefed Lola on the current state of the agency as she prepared expenses and the total bill for Lottie.

"You have four auto accident investigations, as I mentioned earlier. None seem terribly difficult, but we won't know for sure until you start digging into them," he said.

"My fraud cases look pretty straight-forward. This week is starting to make me feel we are getting back to normal," he said.

"Careful with predictions. We've found it doesn't take much to reinvent our normal to a new normal," Lola said.

"Let's go to the range. On the way, we can drop the GTI off for a modification to the exhaust system."

"Why?" Lola asked, surprised.

"Sportier tone and pick up a few horsepower."

"You know how Finn rubs his face on people and things he's claiming?" she asked.

Nick nodded, knowing exactly where she was going with this.

"So, you think this is my somewhat feline way of saying I want to put my mark on it?"

She just looked at him with a Mona Lisa smile and said nothing at all.

They dropped the GTI for the day and went back in the other direction for her to acclimate to the new little folding carbine. Dependability and shootability notwithstanding, Nick often liked guns because of looks and historical significance. Lola went with utility. She found this one highly useful in its design, with its seven-teen-round magazine in the grip and two twenty-three round mags in the butt. Sixty-three readily available rounds in a handy short range deterrent met a lot of qualifications for her.

After the shooting, they had a Tex-Mex meal and rode over to the site of the new club. It was pretty much complete except for staffing. Carly had posted some ads and gotten five applicants to interview tomorrow. She only had one bouncer applicant.

"If you are going to re-run your ad, make sure it does not look male-specific. Some really good bodyguards are women. I would think they could be great bouncers, too.

"Maybe make the big bruiser the doorman initially and a tough ex-military or ex-police female inside. I have seen hundred and twenty-pound female deputies put a come-along hold on giants and frog-walk them out of a bar or traffic confrontation many times," Nick said. "A lot of times, a female can de-escalate a situation and no hands-on will be required," he added.

"Wow! Our experience is the Eastern European outlook. Women dance, three hundred pounders break legs."

Lottie walked up and was listening with interest.

"Carly, I am a physically challenged guy who isn't really so tough. I just was forced to kill two of Ibro's big bruisers, one bare-handed. Size does not make someone invincible. Only scary looking," he said.

"Nick, what if we were specific? Something like 'professionally trained female security/bouncer needed for dance club and bar,'" she said.

He shrugged and nodded. Carly wrote down the suggested language and sat at the office phone to place an amended advertisement.

"You left out the giant bodyguard and bouncer for

the trafficking kingpin. The one who ran me off I-4 and totaled your first van. I am not sure of his ethnicity, but he surely fit the description of the two Bosnians," Lola said, adding, "Our Nick is far tougher than he admits and has proven it more times than he would ever admit."

"I'm just a doting uncle. I don't drive a two-ton four-wheel drive raised pickup and don't have a Rottweiler. I have a VW and a cat."

Lola and Angie rolled their eyes. Angie knew how strong and mean her late husband had been. She had been on the receiving end of it too many times. Lottie knew the bruiser who had held Lola and Maria and a squad of Honduran SWAT at bay. She knew he had, at the very least, broken limbs and burned down buildings during his protection racket enforcement. Maria had told her about Nick taking him down with one very precise shot to the head. She agreed with the others. He was a guy who didn't need to prove himself to anyone.

"Okay! Re-worded ad placed. They will get it in tomorrow. So, it will probably be a couple days before anybody calls on it and comes in for an interview."

They had time for a convoy to Anna Maria to do a final walk-through at the new house. Lottie's new car would have to wait until tomorrow.

Nick and Lola were off in different directions the next day.

Nick began the legwork on his latest fraud case. It was a civil case from one of their primary law firm clients.

A plaintiff was suing his firm's defendant, alleging they sold him an automobile that had been flooded in a recent storm surge. He was demanding the price of the car be paid him plus triple damages, and he would keep the car.

Lola's case was an automobile accident where a plaintiff alleged the insurance company client's insured had struck her deliberately inflicting damage on her vehicle and causing her a very difficult to defend against whiplash injury.

They had spoken at length about both cases before beginning them.

The red flag on the first one was the plaintiff wishing for monetary payment *and* to retain the allegedly flooded car. Money? Yes. However, keeping a car that, if the allegations were true, would be totaled. Normally, the insurance company would take possession of a flooded car and scrap it. Why keep a totaled car? Both PIs agreed something was definitely awry here.

In Lola's case, an initial question was why the plaintiff had not reported the accident to the police? Was it because, without a police report, their position would be more difficult to disprove?

They both left at eight thirty in the morning.

Nick fired up the GTI and sat smiling for a moment listening to the throaty burble of the new exhaust. Lola pulled up beside him before leaving through their rear gate and just sat there looking at him and at her former hot hatch. He looked at her and winked.

She shook her head and plainly mouthed, "Boys will be boys," and pulled off.

She had made an appointment with the insurance company's insured. She wanted to catch her off-kilter.

She sat down with the woman, a Ms. Lamond, after introducing herself and explaining, "Yes, I really am a private investigator. No, we don't all wear snap-brim fedoras and smoke cigars," to the older woman's aston-ishment.

"If you don't mind, I will record our conversation so I can listen more closely than I could if taking notes," she advised Ms. Lamond.

"Tell me in your own words exactly when, where, and what happened," Lola said.

"It was last week, and I was going to Publix to buy some bread and cereal. I usually go on Tuesday, but this time I went on Wednesday. It was so crowded, what with all the snowbirds down here now. I had to wait to even get a cart. Some rude woman grabbed the one I was waiting for." *Oh, boy. This is going to be a long, disjointed one,* Lola thought as she gently pushed the woman back to the serious part of the story.

"Okay. I took my bags—I had two because I don't like my bread squashed by other things in the bag—and walked out to the car. Someone had parked too close, and I had to put the groceries in the trunk because I could not open the passenger door. Do you need to see the car?"

"We will look at the car once you finish your story. So, you put your two bags in the trunk and then what happened?" Lola asked.

"I backed out and somebody blew their horn real loud. It was quite rude."

"Was this the person who claimed you struck them?" Lola asked.

"No. It was somebody else." Ms. Lamond stopped and seemed to be concentrating on the rude horn blower.

"So, they went past or waited. What happened when you finally backed out?"

"I headed towards the entrance of course! What a silly question."

Lola patiently smiled and said, "It's important to have the whole story in your words."

"Well, I had gotten almost to the far entrance and someone backed into me with a crash!" the woman said.

"Did they hit really hard?" Lola asked.

"Yes, I thought the car might blow up!"

"Did the crash cause either of your airbags to activate in your face?"

"Huh?"

"The protective airbags which open to protect you in a crash. There is one in the center of your steering wheel."

"Of course there is no bag on my steering wheel!" the woman said indignantly. Lola let it pass and told her to tell what happened then.

"The woman in the Jeep thing jumped out and ran around to me and motioned for me to roll my window down." Ms. Lamond stopped again.

"Did you?"

"I was afraid. She was really mad. Then, a man ran around my car from behind, screaming I crashed into her.

"I saw it all! I'll testify!" he said.

"Ms. Lamond. Who again was the man claiming to be at fault? The other woman, or you?"

"Well, her of course. Then, he said, 'Call the police! They'll put her in jail!'"

"I said, 'Oh, no! The woman said, 'No, we can handle this among ourselves. Lady, let me copy your insurance card and driver's license.'"

"So, I did."

"Then, what?" Lola asked.

"She drove away."

"How about the man?"

"I don't know. I never saw him again. It seems like she should have gotten his information, too. He was a witness," Ms. Lamont said, evidencing some logic for the first time.

"I suspect he was her accomplice, Ms. Lamond. Not just a stranger. It was a set-up accident most likely. Did you happen to get the car and home information for the woman? Or the man who claimed to be a witness? No?

"When did you get the demand letter from the woman who struck you?"

"The next day."

"You were right to immediately take it to your insurance agent. I represent his company. The letter will be evidence.

"Here is what we need to do. We need to go out so I can look at your car and take some pictures of it. Then I need to ask you to ride with me to Publix and show me exactly where this happened. I will need to see the very spot. Okay?" Lola asked.

She also questioned the lady again on descriptions of the driver and witness and got very vague descriptions. When asked if she could identify the two in person, she answered positively.

Ms. Lamond looked at her watch.

"When will we be back? I have lunch with the girls before our bridge. Today is bridge day, you know."

"We will be back very soon. I won't let you miss your lunch and bridge," Lola said and added, "Bring your keys and purse. I will have to look inside the car and you will have to lock your house. Okay?"

"Well, I guess it is," the lady responded with what seemed like her normal hesitation.

Her car was a five-year-old Ford Fusion. Lola copied the VIN and license number, which was easier than asking Ms. Lamond for her registration.

There was a scratch or two on the front bumper. Nothing more. The woman committing what Lola was sure to be a fraud was good. She managed to hit hard enough to get attention but soft enough to not inflate the airbags.

Lola showed Ms. Lamond the place where the airbags resided on the hub of her steering wheel, much to the lady's amazement. Lola walked around the car and saw no other signs of recent damage. Both bumpers and one fender showed old minor damage from what Lola was sure indicated inexpert driving on Ms. Lamond's part.

"Okay! Hop into my little van here, and we'll take a quick run over to the supermarket and you can show me where all of this happened."

Ms. Lamond looked at her watch and said, "Are you sure we'll have time?"

"When is your lunch?"

"Twelve o'clock."

"Where do you have to go for it?"

"It's three doors down from my house."

"I see. Well, we have an hour, so I am sure I will have you back with at least forty-five minutes to spare."

They went to the supermarket and Ms. Lamond showed her a location on the outer perimeter of the parking lot. Lola scanned the area and had an idea.

She got out and made a big X on the spot with a piece of chalk.

"We're done. Let's get you home in time for lunch and bridge."

On the way, she gently explained the efficacy of notifying the police about accidents, particularly if the other party does not want to share his or her insurance or driver's license. She was not sure Ms. Lamond got it but felt at least she had done the right thing in explaining it.

Lola dropped the lady off, amazed that someone not ten years older than bikini-wearing Erica could be so damned naïve. She returned to Publix to take some photos and talk to someone at the tire store across the four-lane highway from where the alleged accident had occurred.

She explained to the tire store owner she was investigating a popular fraud against a senior citizen involving a fake accident with a fake witness. Lola pointed out where it occurred and when and asked if he would pull his video feed.

He did, and as she suspected, it showed a blue vehicle back into Ms. Lamond's car. The female driver jumped out and ran up to the Lamond vehicle, gesticulating wildly. A man appeared from a parked vehicle and approached them. After a minute or two, the striking vehicle driver and the false "witness" both got back into their vehicles and left going in the same direction.

Lola pointed out this was a variation of the "swoop and squat" false wreck scam, and the false witness is a regular actor in the process.

He agreed to release the tape. She made a phone call to the Florida Bureau of Insurance Fraud and spoke to a special agent. After he heard the scam story and the evidence, he suggested that the tire store owner stop his camera system (so it would not automatically record over the evidence) and leave the film in the camera for him to pick up as evidence in the fraud case he was opening.

His office was just across the Howard Frankland Bridge from where they were, and he agreed to drive over and meet with Lola and pick up the videotape.

When he arrived, she gave him a description of the two suspects, a verbal summary of her investigation so far and a copy of the demand letter.

His viewing of the tape solidified the case. He recognized the pair from past cases. They had either gotten off on a technicality or had been found guilty and simply fined.

He was convinced the video evidence would bring their fraud career to a screeching halt.

"I'd like to speak with this Lamond person," he said.

Lola chuckled.

"I will be glad to go along and introduce you. She's a bit of an odd duck. I suspect she would not be stable under cross-examination." Lola suggested the interview visit to Ms. Lamond take place in three hours, mentioning the all-important lunch and bridge game now in progress. He agreed to meet her at Ms. Lamond's house at four o'clock in the afternoon. This gave him time to secure an arrest warrant for the husband and wife team, which worked out of Tampa.

They met back at Ms. Lamond's house at four and she introduced the special agent for the Bureau of Insurance Fraud. Lola stayed there for the interview.

She was home by six and typing up her report to the insurance company. It said the Florida Bureau of Insurance Fraud would arrest the two suspects the following day.

"Excellent work, Lola. Let me know when the arrests

are made. I will notify our client, Ms. Lamond, and close our case. Based on the projected things happening, go ahead and submit your bill to me. I'll be watching for it."

One down, three to go, she thought.

Nick's day was productive also. He put a small tool kit from the surveillance van into the VW GTI. Unsure what sort of surroundings were at the location of the man who claimed his newly bought used car was flooded were, he did not want the man to see the surveillance van. It may have to be used for its primary purpose later in the investigation.

He went to the house. Actually, it was a manufactured home in ill repair in a neighborhood where it fit comfortably among its peers.

Nick knocked on the door and a man with a pot belly and wife beater undershirt answered.

"Hi. My name is Nick Wolf. I am here to inspect the vehicle you bought from Good Used Cars over on US 19."

The man scowled at him.

"You a mechanic?" he asked defensively.

"No. I am an investigator for the law firm which represents the dealer."

"So you are like a private eye?"

"Yes."

"Then, how about get the hell off my property?"

"Sure. But we will get a subpoena to inspect the vehicle in the lawsuit?" Nick said.

"What lawsuit?"

"The one you threatened to get the price of the car, triple damages, and still keep the car. All based on your unproven claim the vehicle has been flooded."

"So, you people think I'm lying."

"We don't know enough about the vehicle to draw a conclusion. Which is why I am here."

"Leave! Or I will kick your limping ass out!" the man growled.

"If I leave without inspecting the car, you will not get anything. Nothing. If you sue, we will get a subpoena and I will come back. And I will bring a mechanic and we will take the car apart. You can put it back together your damn self." Nick turned to go.

The man grabbed him by the shoulder. Nick spun around, grabbed the man's wrist, and twisted it into a police come-along hold. The man screamed out in pain.

"You sound like a little girl. You just committed battery. I have every right to break your arm right now. As a matter of fact, it would give my limping ass a lot of pleasure."

Nick applied more pressure on the wrist, twisting it back to a very unnatural angle and the man howled again.

"Okay. Okay. Inspect the damn car!"

"Thank you. Get the keys, please."

Nick retrieved his notebook and a pen from the GTI. He checked for the seventeen-digit Vehicle Identification Number (or VIN) inside the driver's side of the windshield, the driver-side doorjamb, and the engine. They all matched and coincided with the numbers on the Carfax report he had pulled. That report also did not reflect any flooding or salvage having been added to the two-owner title.

He then opened the car and sniffed. No musty smell. A lot of cigarette smoke, but it was insufficient to mask flooding. He checked seat tracks, the glove compartment, floor carpet for condition commensurate with the age and wear on the rest of the car and for stains from flooding. None. Nick popped the edge of the inside door molding loose and looked inside for mud or water. Again, none.

He checked the headlight covers and the taillights for signs of water and did not find any.

Taking the keys, he started the car. It started promptly. He tried interior lights, radio, turn signals. None of the wiring which enabled these items was apparently soaked and rusted to the failure point.

Nick checked inside and out for signs of rusting. The only sign was expected. There was a scratch on the left rear fender and the bare metal had a line of brown rust in it.

Doing his homework before arriving, he had checked with the National Motor Vehicle Title Information System or NMVTIS. It had no reports of title washing on this car. Title washing is when a car declared totaled or stolen was retitled in another state. This one was Florida through and through.

None of his research had indicated a salvage title on the car. It could have been sold as a parts car with one, but not sold as a family car like this one was, unless previous damages had been noted and repairs made.

"Okay, I'm done. Somebody will get back to you on your claim."

The man reached for Nick again, and the PI stepped back.

"Did you really think I was kidding about breaking your damn arm?" Nick asked. The man stepped back and said nothing as Nick tossed the small tool case onto the front seat and got in behind the wheel.

"Have a nice day," he said, adding numerous epithets to it as he drove away. Not a single one indicating whether he cared if the man had a nice day.

Nick went home and immediately began his report to the law firm. His assignment had been to determine whether the car had been flooded, so the firm could recommend a legal response to the claimant he just had the displeasure of meeting.

The guy being a jerk had absolutely nothing to do with the case, so he made no mention and just stuck to the research sources he had used prior to going and the inspections he conducted while there. He described starting and running the car to test lights, radio and other items whose malfunction may suggest rusted wires.

Nick wrote his conclusion succinctly. "Based on my research and standard flooded vehicles inspection protocols, it is my opinion said vehicle has not been flooded and the claim is either misinterpretation by the new owner or likely, out and out fraud."

He emailed it to his firm contact and immediately called him and advised the report was in his inbox and Nick stood ready to discuss it at the firm's convenience.

Nick then asked Erica to bill the firm at their agreed-upon rate for the case number assigned by the law firm.

Unless something else cropped up, this case was closed and billed.

Lola's case was finished, but she wanted to wait for the two fraudsters to be arrested by the Bureau of Insurance Fraud agents before submitting her final report to the insurance company and the accompanying bill.

Now, for both, it was on to the next cases and some indication of normality in their lives.

The more momentous events for the next several days involved Lottie and Carly.

They closed on the house on Anna Maria Island and set a grand opening date for their club, though full staffing was not yet achieved. Lottie traded the big Mercedes on a much smaller sporty one.

The key point of these things to Nick and Lola was three and a half fewer people living at their house. Unfortunately, the half was little Nicky, who they would miss immensely.

Maria was working long hours and had not said more about moving in with the criminal analyst.

To celebrate everyone's good fortune, Nick planned a boating day for Sunday. Maria was iffy, but Nick bet she would find a way to show up. Erica jumped at the opportunity to keep the toddler for the day at her house.

The new house on Anna Maria was directly across from the marina where Nick kept the boat. Lola put together a virtual gourmet boating lunch which she stored in the large Yeti cooler on the boat along with bottled water, beer and some small wine bottles.

They idled out of the marina with Lola still practicing boat handling. Nick was not at all surprised at her prowess. If it had a steering wheel and went fast, she could drive it.

She planed off just long enough to beat traffic as they crossed the Gulf Intracoastal Waterway, then sneaked across a shoal of skinny water to the channel which paralleled the island near the docks with their boat lifts. Lola turned left at the channel and idled towards where she saw the four women standing on the pier waving.

Nick looked at the micro-bikinied group and was glad they did not meet at the marina. The dockhand would have had a blood vessel burst by now at the sight.

Nick was proud of how lovely and fit his sister was, but not interested in the others. All he had to do was look at the raven-haired beauty in her own bikini driving his—no, their—boat so confidently.

She came into the dock, bumping the throttle between forward and neutral to moderate the speed against a strong tide. Lola approached at forty-five degrees. As the bow was getting ready to kiss the bumper on Lottie's dock, she turned the wheel left. This pointed the propeller inward. She bumped the throttle in reverse, then back into neutral. The small thrust of reverse sucked the stern in, and she nestled the boat gently parallel to the dock. She looked at Nick for a sign of approval and was more than amply rewarded by the way he looked at her.

"Hi, guys," Nick greeted the four ladies. They tossed small bags with SPF tubes and towels and sun hats into the boat and Nick placed them in the side console door and the cooler seat in front of the console.

"So, where are we going, captain?" Maria asked.

"I thought we'd nip out into the Gulf and run down the Longboat Key to Longboat Pass. We can anchor and picnic and swim, though the current is strong in the pass. I will toss some floats out on hundred-foot lines to hang on to if the water is running fast."

"Not the little key you talk so much about?" Angie asked.

"It's ruined by too many people and too much noise on weekends. I don't like other people's music blaring," he said.

"We are running the risk of encountering the same at Longboat Pass, but Nick doesn't care about the Pass, so it won't ruin his harmony," Lola said.

"I guess I have a very tender karma," Nick admitted, knowing he did not at all in reality.

"Our choice is to head south on the ICW and idle

along with the madding crowd, or sneak around the end of Anna Maria, go through Passage Key Pass into the Gulf, hang a left and run down on the outside. It depends on the wind and waves. This is only a twenty-foot center console, and we have a load in it."

"Load? I beg your pardon!" Carly said.

"I misspoke. We have more pulchritude than the boat deserves."

"Much better phraseology," she said.

"Do we need tops on the outside?" Maria asked. Nick shrugged and looked at Lola.

"Assuming we decide the water is right to run all the way down on the Gulf side, we should be fine any way you want to be," she said.

Once they got out of the pass and into the Gulf, the decisions were made. Nick concentrated on his piloting.

About three miles down the length of northern Longboat Key, he spotted several creatures in their path. He immediately slowed down to idle.

"Look! Dolphins! Or are they porpoises?" Carly asked, turning to Nick. He was driving so he ought to know, she thought.

"I think they are bottle-nosed dolphins, but I am not sure. Porpoises are smaller and have more blunt faces. Dolphins can go all the way up to Orcas and have more pointed snouts."

"I thought Orcas were whales!" Angie said.

"Nope, sis. Dolphins."

"Nick, can we swim with them?" Lola asked.

"We can try. Is everyone a strong swimmer? If not, I'd like you to wear a PFD or personal flotation device." They nodded that they were strong swimmers. Nick was not so sure.

He pulled a coil of a hundred feet of 3/8" nylon line out of a compartment.

"Lola, would you hand me two of the preserver cushions?" he asked.

He tied the two cushion's handholds to the end of the line and played it out behind the boat, which had turned one hundred eighty degrees in the current. He tied the free end of the line securely to a cleat. Killing the engine, he told them to slip into the water gently so as not to scare the dolphins...*and not to excite any sharks, also*, he thought without saying.

"Stay next to the line, so you can grab a hold of it if you get tired or have a cramp or something. You can always use it to pull yourself hand over hand back to the boat.

"Stay still and let them come to you. Try to send out friendly vibes. These are very smart creatures and sensitive to the feelings they pick up from you," he said.

"Nick, you sound like you have done this before," Angie said.

He nodded affirmatively.

Four women in the Gulf gently treaded water next to the lifeline and waited. One larger dolphin came in first with hesitation. He passed next to Maria and actually brushed against her. He circled around and the others swam near, including a very young one which Carly named "Nicky."

The interaction lasted four or five minutes until the pod or school decided to continue northward.

Nick helped the four back aboard. They were excited, but more tired than they expected.

"Honey, will you start the boat? Don't put it in gear. Just get ready to once I have the line and cushions back in," Nick said.

"Which 'honey?' You have four here," Angie asked.

"Any honey."

Angie brushed past him and turned the key on the Suzuki outboard and it immediately came to life. She sat watching as he pulled in the hundred feel, coiling it as it came aboard. He threw a loop around the hank of line and untied the bowline knot holding the life preserver cushions.

"Angie, why don't you be copilot? I could use a nap in the sun," Lola said, stretching out on the cushions in the bow.

Angie looked at her brother for concurrence and he reached over and hooked the Velcro wristband for the engine emergency kill switch to her left wrist and sat on the copilot chair.

"Look around three hundred sixty degrees. Make sure you are clear and bump it into forward by pushing the throttle. Once in gear, push it hard enough to make the bow rise and the boat plane off. Then, set the speed at about twenty-eight cruise, or whatever you want," Nick said.

"Can I go fast?" she asked.

"Oh, Lord, Lola. I've got another one!" he said but nodded.

"Everybody get ready for blast off!" Angie said. And then she did.

Even with six people aboard, the boat popped up on plane and took off as she pushed the throttle all the way. Forty miles per hour felt much faster in two-foot waves and the whole group, minus Nick, were screaming with excitement as the boat occasionally left the water and went airborne for a few seconds before landing.

Angie ran wide open for five minutes before realizing how much concentration it took and the filling-loosening jars the hull made when it landed at speed. She took it back down to cruising speed and the bumping settled somewhat. Nick showed her how to moderate the bumping by adjusting the trim to keep more of the hull up.

Nick looked behind for traffic periodically and at the tell-tale spout of water coming from the side of the engine indicating the water-cooling system was working as it should.

They approached what Nick knew was Longboat Pass in thirty minutes.

"Y'all be discreet. We will stick our noses in and check it out, but I am seeing a lot of boats in there," Nick said.

Angie sat down, her torso demurely below the side deck of the boat.

It looked like a boater's convention inside the Pass.

"Hold your appetites for another half hour? I have another idea back where we came from," Nick said.

"Anyone else want to drive back up the Gulf?" he asked.

"Me!" Maria said and stepped up to the wheel. She had been watching Angie and planed off just as Nick's sister had.

Forgoing speed, she set the boat on about thirty miles per hour and pointed northward.

As she drove, she told Nick about the cases she was working and asked about his. He told her about the man who claimed his new used car had been sold flooded. She listened, but this case was boring compared to the ones they had in Roatan. Even hers in Tampa. But she was driving a boat in paradise next to the person she adored, so he could have recited the periodic table to her, and she would have been thrilled.

Lola was so unworried about the young Latina she dozed off happily. Besides, she had Angie, a veritable mama bear to watch out for Nick.

After thirty-five minutes, Nick pointed ahead for Maria.

"We are coming to the end of Longboat Key. The tip is Anna Maria. To the right is the pass we came through.

"The Key we were going to and was too crowded is directly ahead. Stay outside and let's see how crowded the Gulf side is," he suggested.

She dropped the speed and ran slowly about a hundred yards off the Key, after he guided her over a point of very shallow water.

"Here is a stretch with a couple hundred yards of privacy. Slow to walking speed. I am going forward to get the anchor. Listen for me and you and I will get us anchored up, okay?" She bobbed her head and smiled broadly.

There was a good two-and-a-half-foot surf heading in towards the beach. Nick knew his seven-pound Fortress anchor with its ten-foot chain rode and ample line would hold the twenty-foot boat. Or a thirty-five-footer.

"Okay, Maria, turn left at idle speed and face out."

She did, and he dropped the anchor gently off the bow in five feet of water.

"Now, bump the throttle backwards into reverse. Back up until I say the anchor is set."

She did perfectly.

"Got it! Neutral and turn key off to the left."

She turned the Suzuki off and gave him a hug.

He patted her on the back and said, "Let's feed this crew, Maria!"

She let go and opened the Yeti behind where they were sitting.

Lola had fixed plastic bowls with fruit, miscellaneous cheeses, plastic bags with a variety of crackers, Nova salmon, cream cheese, and capers.

"Okay, you guys. Head forward and choose your beverage from the cooler in front of the console. Carly, you have to get off the cooler first," Nick said to the sun-drowsy crew.

The meal was good. The drinks cold. The day warm. All was as it should be.

"I could not have imagined living like this growing up outside of Tegucigalpa," Maria said, balancing salmon and capers on a cream cheese cracker.

"Did you have the standard family unit?" Nick asked.

"You mean, mom, dad, brother, or sister?" she responded.

"Something like that."

"I had a great mom and dad and no brothers or sisters. Mom and Dad died when I was ten, so my *Tia* raised me."

"What was she like, Maria?" Lola asked.

"An angel from heaven. I look and am more like her, she says, than my mother."

"Was she married?" Angie asked.

"Once. My country has had a lot of violence and political upheaval over the years. Her husband was killed before I ever met him. They lived far away, so I had to move to be with her when my parents died."

"Is she still alive?" Nick asked.

"Oh, yes. She is about Erica's age. And, beautiful too. To me, at least."

"Have you considered getting her to move here to be with you?" he asked.

"It would be my number two dream for life." He dared not ask her what number one was.

"You should pursue it. Does she speak fluent English?" he asked.

"Oh, yes. She is an English teacher."

"My mother was a teacher. Did you know?" Lola asked.

"No, I did not. I am sure they would adore each other.

"My aunt has been very...uh, thrifty. Thrifty is the word. With her savings, the sale of her house. And my salary. We could both live just fine. I will try to make this happen. With all the excitement and new job, I have not had time to focus on it. Now, I will. I miss her a lot. She would love you two for all you have done for me."

"You should. She was like a mother to you. It would be great if you could be together now," Lola said.

"As your captain, I would like to announce it is way past time for sunscreen. There are parts showing which do not always show in the daylight. Dancing maybe. Those parts seem to be getting burned. Chop, chop, ladies!" Nick said, handing Lola some sunscreen as the others reached for theirs.

"My Indian blood is my salvation when it comes to resisting sunburn," she said. "And something I am very proud of."

"I am also," Maria said. "I am part Lenca. We are the indigenous people of the northern highlands of Honduras."

"Seems to me we are sisters, then," Lola said and hugged her.

"Looks like they are too busy to help. Back please, brother," Angie said, handing Nick the sunscreen.

Soon, he was looking at the growing dark clouds. It happened all of a sudden. *Gee, you'd think it was Florida or something,* he thought to himself.

"Hey, guys, we have to get ready to run. It looks like a storm which was not on the forecast is going to hit."

Everyone looked up and saw why Nick sounded so serious. They started dressing and packing. They learned very quickly how to drive fast, outrunning a storm.

By the time he got them to Lottie's dock, it was dark and thundering.

"Honey, you hop off here and I'll pick you up by car," he said to Lola and motored off before she could protest. As he knew she would.

Nick knew the tide was high and took a chance running on full plane across the shallows instead of following Anna Maria almost down to the bridge and parallel into the marina channel. He felt a couple of bumps as the motor's skeg hit the hard sand bottom, but the boat kept going.

He called the marina on VHF channel eight and told them he was coming in and to have the lift truck ready. They advised with the onset of a probable electric storm he would have to dock and tie up. They would put the boat in high and dry storage later. It made sense, and he came into the channel much faster than normal. He docked, tied up, put the containers of food in a canvas bag, and walked as fast as he could, in view of his disability, to the GTI.

As he got in, the sky opened up to rain, thunder and bright jagged lightning. He had just made it in the nick of time.

He left the marina and drove over the bridge he had just taken the boat past and turned onto Lottie's street. Lola and Angie ran out and got into the car and they started the drive home.

Angie called Erica and checked on Nicky who was asleep in Erica's lap at the time.

"Take your time. He has been fed, bathed, had a story read to him and is out for the count. He's just the sweetest little guy in the world," Erica told her over the GTI's speaker system.

"Do we have food left in the boat?" Lola asked so sleepy she could hardly talk.

"No, just drinks. They will be okay. The remaining food is in a bag in the hatch. I just brought it all from the marina. It was raining too damn hard to stop and evaluate it," Nick said.

"Good idea, brother!" Angie said from the back seat. Lola was dozing in the front.

"What a great day," Angie said. "Thanks for it. I think I needed it more than I knew."

"We all did, Angie. It has been one helluva couple weeks. At least we don't have to worry about the Bosnians anymore," Nick said.

9

The phone rang around ten the next morning. It was Ludo Bekrić.

"Ludo! How are you? Alice well?" Nick answered as the caller ID flashed.

"We are good. You still serious about us coming to visit little Nicky and you all, of course?"

"We are. We'd all love to see you," Nick responded.

"We wondered about in a week? Enough notice for you?" the older man said.

"A week would be fine. We have our normal case-load. Nothing particularly demanding, so some fishing time would be easy to plan."

"I am liking the sound of your words, Nick. Then we will go ahead with the travel agent and text you the flights."

"Great! Don't worry about hotels. You two stay here with us. We have room."

"All good. Watch for text," Ludo said, then rang off.

Lola heard the conversation from her desk.

"You know, Nick, I really like them. They are so

unlike the rest of the Bekrić bunch. What a difference when you choose an honest job and throw all of your efforts into it," she commented.

"Since Angie and little Nicky are back and forth between here and living with Lottie and Carly, we should get her to come here. We need to put them in the spare bedroom since Maria is still in the workout room and move Angie back in with her.

"What would you think of one of those mother-in-law cabins out back for Angie and Nicky? Instead of living with Lottie?" Nick asked.

"Could we help her finance a small home like Mom got around the corner?" Lola asked.

"Probably not. Real estate prices are over the top in St. Pete. Your mother lucked into a sweetheart deal we'd never find."

"You're probably right. We can ask Angie. I imagine childcare options are much better here than on Anna Maria," she said.

"I didn't think about childcare. I'm not sure I want my nephew growing up in a strip club. As the Wolf patriarch, of course."

"I believe your sister is just as stubborn as you and might tell you where to shove your patriarchal self," Lola said.

"She better not. My partner would punch her out!"

"Yep. Your partner might, if she told you to shove it. Actually, I am pretty convinced she would."

"Good. Now we have settled it, let's sit down with her soon. We have to tell her Ludo and Alice are coming anyway. This whole rigmarole of family meetings is way beyond my experience level, so I am just winging it."

Angie was excited for Nicky to see his *Deda*, as he called Ludo. She liked the man, but just his name and bulk reminded her of so much she wished to forget. She knew she could overcome it. For Nicky's sake, if not for her own.

In the ensuing week, Nick and Lola managed to clear all current cases. The several new ones were not particularly time sensitive. Nick got some of his seldom-used fishing gear cleaned and ready. He generally fished with artificial baits but decided on live bait for his trips with Ludo. He would pick up some shrimp at a bait shop on the way to the high-and-dry marina and castnet for whitebait such as scaled sardines, also called pilchards, or ones called greenies or threadfin herring, or finally, LY's or Gulf Menhaden.

The ones he ended up with and tended to have the best success with were the first ones, the pilchards.

The Bekrić's were scheduled to arrive at one in the afternoon on Tuesday. Angie and Nicky rode with Nick in the BMW to Tampa Airport to pick them up. Nick parked in short-term parking so Nicky could be waiting at the arrivals gate in the main concourse to greet his "grandparents." He was pretty clear with "Deda" and "Alice," and still called Nick "Unca Nick" and Lola "Lolo," with which both were perfectly satisfied.

Nick was holding his nephew who was scanning the incoming passengers. He spotted his Deda and started yelling for him before Nick or Angie located him in the crowd. Nick set him down and he took off to greet the couple. All together finally and hugs exchanged, they went to baggage and collected several bags apiece. Neither had traveled much, and packing was somewhat new for them.

Ludo insisted on sitting in the back next to Nicky's car seat and talking with him. Alice sat on the other side. Angie twisted around to watch the heartwarming interplay among the three people in the back. Keeping them in Nicky's life was something Nick highly endorsed. She saw why now.

"So, Nick. When are we going fishing?" Ludo asked when Nicky finally calmed down a bit.

"We can go tomorrow morning if you are not too jet lagged," Nick said.

Ludo's ear-to-ear grin was all the answer Nick needed.

"You know the day I can't wait for?" Nick asked.

"No, when?"

"The day you, Nicky, and I go fishing together. Can you imagine it?"

"I hope I live to see the day, Nick!"

"You will. It will come sooner than either of us can imagine. My foster father took me fishing beginning at age five. Nicky is getting there fast."

"Where is Lola?" Alice asked.

"She had to testify in one of the cases she solved. It was a couple who committed fraud on a senior citizen. Lola caught them dead to rights. She called just before you arrived. Both the husband and wife were found guilty and will be sentenced later. For now, they are cooling their heels in jail. They were not able to post bail."

"Were the criminals older people, too?" Alice asked.

"I understand both were in their thirties and their past arrest record will provide a term in prison. I suspect they will be out before too many years though. Neither ever hurt anyone physically and both are bright. They will know how to act and keep their heads down in jail and later in prison."

Nick told them about the bridge they were on, the Howard Frankland, being featured on Fox's show *Cops* with a high-speed pursuit and the two bank robbers jumping off the bridge.

"Did they die jumping? It seems so tall," Alice asked.

"No, they jumped just before land, so maybe fifteen feet or so. One guy was arrested by the Coast Guard who told him about the sharks in the area. The other one made it six miles at night, moving from concrete piling to piling. He was arrested in his boxer shorts on the other end."

"I bet he was embarrassed."

"I heard he was mainly exhausted and thirsty," Nick said.

"Lola's mother works with us in the home office every day and lives nearby. She is there now, fixing dinner in her daughter's absence. I think you will like Erica a lot.

"We also have a young female detective with us temporarily. We worked with her in Honduras and helped her relocate here. Her name is Maria. She saved my life in Roatan, Honduras."

"Tell us the story, Nick. Was this the case Luka is messed up in?" Ludo said.

"I am afraid it is, Ludo." He went on to tell the executive summary version, leaving out killing one of the Bosnians who had Lola at gunpoint. For all he knew, it could have been another relative of his house guest.

"Luka is as smart as Ibro. The problem is he does not have the sense of honor Ibro has. He is just a thug made good. In prison, he will be a big boss, after he kills some convict competition."

"Ludo, will Ibro do the same thing when he gets to prison?" Nick asked.

"The important thing is *if* he gets to prison. Chicago is a pretty crooked place. Always has been. The last couple of mayors have taken it even further downhill. Defunding the police, DAs put in by out-of-state money men to destabilize for political reasons.

"Ibro might be able to buy himself off, no matter the level of who tries him. Luka may have DC connections, but I don't think he has put away the kind of money Ibro has. Shit walks, but money talks."

"Is there anyone left in the family who might come after my sister and little Nicky?" Nick asked.

"I don't think so. The top two are scrambling to cover their own asses. The people left below them are going to be disappearing to the winds. None of them can buy justice."

The next morning's words were happy ones. They were all about fish. Saltwater fish, specifically.

"I would like to target specific fish for specific reasons, Ludo. Let me explain and tell me if you have another idea. It's your trip, my friend!" Nick said.

"First, we will stop and buy some fresh shrimp for bait. Then, once we get out of the marina channel, I will make a fool of myself throwing a twelve-foot cast net to catch bait fish.

"Second, the types of fish I suggest we target. I know a couple places we should be able to get a mess of mangrove snappers. These little guys' fillets are sweet and make wonderful fish tacos. Then, water permitting, we can run offshore and go to an artificial reef to look for grouper. To me, these are two are some of the tastiest fish I've caught."

Nick could see the older man's face radiate excitement and knew his plan, if well executed, would be a success.

The next morning, Nick's first stop was Dunkin Donuts for coffee for his big Thermos, and donuts for breakfast and maybe lunch. The second was a bait shop where he bought a couple dozen shrimp for his shrimp bucket.

They were at the marina on a second cup of coffee each when the light was first peeking through dawn's sky. As planned, he let the Sea Craft drift outside the marina's channel and threw the cast net. While it did not billow a guide-like perfect circle, it was good enough to fill the boat's live well with whitebait. A mile later, they were drifting outside the ICW channel and casting spinning gear for Mangrove snappers. It took a half hour for the catch to heat up, but soon they were pulling the small fish in with some rapidity. The smile on the former tire store owner's face was priceless. An hour later, the smile got even larger as Ludo hooked his first black grouper. The fight was on, not that the fish ran so much. Instead, he dug in and fought the reel.

Several hours later found them heading back with a reasonable haul of fish and no donuts left.

Ludo put both hands on Nick's shoulders at the dock and said, "Thank you, my son. I have never had a better day on the water or anywhere else."

"Move down here, Ludo. I believe there may be a few fish still out there for us," Nick said, and Ludo talked about realtors all the way back to St. Petersburg.

Both men began cleaning fish in the backyard. Nick did the fine filleting of the taco fillings, and Ludo proved an experienced cleaner of the larger groupers.

"These are not our Great Lakes fish, but they clean exactly the same." He beamed.

Erica walked out and gave him the card of a realtor she knew. He called and made an appointment for Nick, Angie, Nicky, Alice, and himself to meet with her late in the afternoon.

"After we have fully digested these fish tacos," he said.

While Ludo cleaned up, Nick and Lola went out and got everything necessary for a premier fish taco lunch.

The lunch was excellent. They decided fresh fish should be on the menu for dinner, especially fresh black grouper fillets.

Lola suggested some fresh shrimp to boil and peel for shrimp cocktails. They needed shrimp and more horseradish for the ketchup, horseradish, and lemon dipping sauce. Nick got in the GTI, really enjoying the sound of the new exhaust, and went to the store.

While Nick was gone, Lola, Erica, the Bekrić's, and Angie talked and played with Nicky.

All of a sudden, the back door was kicked open by a large young man with the requisite shaved head and attempts at a mustache and goatee.

Ludo recognized him by his appearance, not because he knew him well. It was Adin's younger brother, Samir. Standing there looking as crazy as his mother. A metal pipe in hand.

Ludo moved fast for a man well past his prime and his open hands struck Samir just inside both shoulders and knocked him against the doorframe. But his hands were apart and left an opening for a counterattack, which came in the form of the pipe swung hard against his jaw, knocking Ludo cold.

Samir, for that was exactly who he was, pulled a medium size pocket pistol and swung it around the room, pointing at everyone.

Lola was eyeing her desk in the other room, where her pistol was. But she knew she would die in the attempt to get it.

Samir pointed the gun at her.

"Get chairs. Bring them in here for the show. You come back with a weapon and the kid dies in front of your eyes. This, I promise."

He turned to Angie. "You, bitch. Strip. Pull one of these chairs and put it right here. Put another facing it. No, further back. The person in it has to see what is going to happen and I need space to do it!" he said.

Lola walked back in dragging two chairs.

"You, raise your shirt up and turn all the way around so I can see you did not get a gun or knife while you were gone!" Lola complied.

"You, two," he said, pointing to Angie in her panties and Lola, who looked like she was contemplating murder at his most violent. "Prop the old man up in the chair. Old lady and MILF, sit beside him."

He threw two rolls of duct tape to Angie and Lola.

"Tie everybody's hands in front where I can see them and ankles to the legs of their chair. When you are done, sister-in-law dearest, tie the bitch with the long black hair over there next to the MILF. I will tie you."

He picked up one of the cast-off rolls of tape. Ludo groaned.

"Samir, Ibro will kill you. He stopped the retribution. You will die," Ludo told him.

Samir, so engrossed with looking at Angie, ignored him. He tied her hands to the back of the chair and her ankles to the legs of the chair.

"You, bitch. I have plans Adin gave me if he could not do them. Pleasure myself with you, inflict pain all over your beautiful body, then kill you. All while your brother, who should be back soon, watches!"

It took Nick longer to pick up the items than he planned. The store was crowded with seasonal snowbirds.

He found the rear door ajar and walked in.

The first thing he saw was Lola duct taped to a kitchen chair. Her mouth was taped too.

She was using her head and eyes to warn him. It was too late.

Something slammed into Nick's head. He felt dizzying pain and saw stars for a second. Then the lights went out. He did not even feel hitting the black and white tiled floor.

He came to later. He had no idea how much later. He was also duct taped to a chair. Hands in front and both ankles to the front legs.

Nick could not focus. He heard a male voice yelling and blinked his eyes, reducing the figure in front of him from two people to one person.

That person was his sister, stripped to her panties. She had duct tape over her mouth and her hands and ankles were bound to the chair with it. Nick glanced around, still not fully focused. Lola, Erica, Alice, and Ludo were similarly gagged and bound. Nicky was free, but cowering, terrified in a corner with Finn.

The big bruiser, whose back was partially blocking Angie from Nick's view, turned around.

He looked like a young Adin Dedić. His words confirmed it.

"Aha! The brother who looks like the harlot has woken up! Samir told me if he died, to come here and rape and torture, then murder this woman in front of her brother.

"And that is just what I'm gonna do."

The younger Dedić had not taken duct taping 101, so he taped everyone in front. It worked for the rest. He was soon to be shocked.

Nick raised his taped hands directly above his head,

locked his elbows so they would end up against his ribs and brought the clasped hands down as hard as he could between his knees.

The tape ripped off, freeing his hands. Nick summoned all the fury he was feeling and stood, ankles still taped to the front legs of the chair.

"This is my family. Those I love. You die now!" he roared. As he shuffled forward, the roar became a growl like the wild creature he was emotionally morphing into.

Nick was eight feet away from Dedić. Dedić pulled a small Beretta from his pocket and fired twice as the ex-Ranger shuffled towards him.

Both rounds hit him, but Nick's adrenaline and focus tuned the hits out.

He crashed into Dedić, knocking him into Angie. She let out a muffled scream as Nick rolled Dedić off her and onto the floor, Nick on top pounding him in the jaw with his fists.

Dedić tried to push the lighter man off. Nick just raised a bit, slid back and thrust both knees straight down on the big man's solar plexus. Samir Dedić's eyes went round and not the usual more almond-shaped. He had a crazy stare. Eerie, crazy. His breath came from his mouth, and he sounded like a train, blowing air in and out.

Dedić grasped Nick around the neck and got a head butt to the nose. Nick flattened the nose completely, blood squirting everywhere. He rolled to the side and brought his heaviest ever uppercut into the man's groin. He felt a testicle virtually disappear, squashed like an overripe peach, then moved back up Dedić's body and continued beating him to death.

Nick did not even hear the door open as Maria

returned from work. She drew her pistol and held it at high ready as she assessed what was happening before her eyes. She holstered and bent and pulled Nick off Dedić, whose identity she figured out immediately notwithstanding the blood and destroyed face. He looked so much like a version of the man who had kidnapped, tied her spread-eagled naked and was ready to do things to her she could not imagine before Nick stopped him.

Maria saw the blood of two bullet wounds as she pulled Nick off and he fell to the side, still taped to the chair. The room was quiet, everyone more or less conscious but having their mouths taped. Only little Nicky was crying as he hugged Finn.

She saw a Beretta Cheetah pocket pistol on the floor near Dedić and picked it up, her pen in the muzzle to preserve prints. She was on full cop autopilot now.

Maria looked at Nick. She rolled him to a recovery position and saw neither bullet had exited. Okay. Two less wounds. No exits. She moved over to feel Dedić's pulse. There was a pulse, but she felt it weaken as she held two fingers against it.

She took her phone and put it on video and scanned the crime scene. Two down, toddler and cat in the corner, adults tied to chairs, one naked. She knew Angie had been destined for what Nick saved her from.

Nick. Always there. Thank you, Mother Mary for Nick.

Maria pulled her Spyderco folding knife out and cut Angie free and handed her the knife with the admonition to not use it on the big man lying beside her chair but to release the others.

Ludo looked like he had a large bruise coloring on the side of his face.

Maria dialed 911 and gave the address.

"This is Tampa Police Detective Maria Sosa. I just came upon a home invasion at this location. I need several ambulances and your Detective Joe Horner. Right now! Detective Horner is familiar with the case here. STAT on the ambulances!"

The dispatcher asked several stock questions. "No time. Have to secure scene. No, the attacker is no longer a threat" and killed the call.

One patrol car arrived minutes later, then two ambulances followed by Joe Horner.

Angie was now dressed. Joe started his preliminary questions with her and Lola and immediately got a sense of what had happened. A home invasion with rape, torture, and murder as its stated goal. Ripping Angie's clothes off would add sexual assault. Having the cute little boy there added child endangerment.

He watched as two sets of Fire Rescue paramedics worked on the attacker and his own friend, Nick.

Nick's wounds did not look life threatening. He also had a head wound they were trying to stanch blood flow on. The head wound could be the more serious injury. Nick had grinned at him once, then slipped into unconsciousness. Joe knew this was normal and also that the paramedics would attempt to stabilize him against the shock which always followed injuries Nick had sustained.

Joe could not make a call on the status of the big guy. He had been identified as the younger brother of the one Nick had killed a couple miles away. Some damn family! He would learn in the interviews for his report the good member of the family was the older man also being treated for head trauma.

Sunstar ambulances arrived and transported Nick and Dedić to the Bayfront Health's trauma center. He knew where he could find both Lola and Angie and freed them to go to be with Nick. He would go check on his friend later. He had a pretty complete picture of what happened, but the standard statements of all involved had to be taken. As to the attacker, Joe would not bet on him surviving long enough to be questioned.

The young Tampa detective had done well as first on scene. He was not sure any seasoned detective could have done better.

Joe and two of his detectives finished the interviews at the house in several hours. He picked up three black coffees and an assortment of creamers and sweeteners on the way to the hospital, knowing at best, hospital coffee sucked.

He figured the two women would need the java. He knew he sure did.

Joe flashed his badge unnecessarily at the ER desk and was escorted back to ICU by a nurse who knew him on a first-name basis.

The two women were sitting by a bed which had Nick on it, festooned with wires and tubes.

"Joe, they are coming out anytime to take him to surgery. He was stabilized, so they decided to wait for a certain surgeon who was on the way and has a lot of gunshot experience," Lola said.

Maria walked in and Joe gave her his unopened coffee.

"Nice job back there, Detective," he said to Maria.

"Thanks. Rote just kicked in," she said, having heard what Lola said from the hall.

"Since I already think I know what went down, your three interviews will not take long. They do have to be separate though," he said. Maria volunteered to go first.

She told him what she had seen and emailed him the video of the scene.

"So Maria, this was the brother of the one who kidnapped you?" Joe verified.

She nodded and then told him her observations and what she did, leaving out having to pull Nick off Samir Dedić before he killed him. No need to mess up a heroic deed with details.

He interviewed Angie next. She, unlike Maria, had been there when Samir Dedić arrived and his relative Ludo had tried to stop him and received a pipe upside the head for his efforts. The same one in Joe's evidence bag with Ludo's and Nick's blood on it.

Lola was a cop. He knew hers would be succinct. Joe was amazed to find she and the younger Maria had approximately the same number of years wearing a badge.

He walked her back to find Nick had already been taken to the operating theater.

All three women waited until Nick was back in a recovery area and the surgeon had promised he would be all right.

———————

Early the next morning, Ludo got Angie to direct and accompany him in his newly rented car. He told her he wanted to speak privately to only her and Nick.

They found Nick awake and in one of those stupid hospital gowns.

"You know, brother, if you go ditty-bopping down the hall in the open-back gown, you are going to moon everybody in the hall?"

"No need to be jealous, sis. You have the Wolf butt,

too," he said, his speech and consciousness a little improved over when she has seen him last night, but she knew he was being loaded with sedatives and painkillers. .32 or not, two bullet wounds had to hurt.

Ludo walked over and put his hand on Nick's good shoulder.

"In the short time I know you, you are family to me. Like your sister is. I want to talk to you two only.

"I have to ask you for forgiveness. I don't have a speech, so please just bear with me, okay?" Ludo said, and brother and sister nodded, his accent stronger with his current stress and emotion.

"Samir Dedić, as he told us, is Adin's little brother. He is little in age only. He is a brute like your late husband," he said, turning to Angie.

"I still marvel you killed these two pieces of garbage with your bare hands, Nick. You are wiry and have a limp. It must be training and determination. I knew at my age and lack of fighting experience, I had no chance. But I had to do it. Maybe I could hold him off until you got back, I thought. But I got knocked out, too.

"Anyway, I did not think Samir be someone to worry about. I seldom talk with anyone but Ibro. Ibro put out the word to lay off. I don't know whether Samir got the message, and if he did, he was not smart enough to know Ibro's word is law. Even to his older brother Luka on the East Coast.

"I think something went haywire in their branch of the family. Their mother was a court-determined para-noid schizophrenic. She is bat shit crazy, Nick and Angie. Adin showed a lot of her issues. I believe Samir had even more of them. I am shocked more than you can know about him being able to build a plan and come here to follow through on it."

"Angie, did you know of him at all?" Nick asked.

"Adin never mentioned him, but he kept family matters close and spoke little about them, she said.

"I knew If Samir did come, Nick, one of us had to kill him immediately," Ludo said, his tone making the former Ranger's blood run cold. He did not have to look at his sister. He could literally feel her tighten up in the chair next to him.

"It was so happy. I was in the family I would have chosen instead of the one luck gave me. I thought it was so distant a possibility that I didn't want to ruin the time for everyone as they were smiling. It was a mistake on my part. A horrible mistake.

"I am so sorry. You two could have died. Nicky too, even if by a wayward bullet. The others, too. I will thank God for you every night for the rest of my life, Nick. Thank him you are a gentle, kind man who has a powerful beast hidden within. A killer you can summon when needed."

"I will, too, Ludo. I thank God for finding my brother. Now, I will add for him being who and what he is. For what he can do. Breaking the bindings on your wrists, dragging the chair strapped to your feet. And beating the animal into submission to save me. And to save the others from seeing what was going to happen to me. Something which would have scarred precious baby Nicky for life," Angie said. She leaned over the bed against the shoulder without the bullet wound and sobbed into his hospital gown, soaking it. Ludo put his big, gnarled hands on her shoulder, unable to hold back his own tears.

Nick managed to hug his sister with his good arm and clasp Ludo's hand on Angie's shoulder. If ever a moment bound three people for life, this was their moment.

There was a tap at the door. It opened and Lola, Alice, Erica, and Maria slipped quietly in, feeling the emotion even before they saw it. Erica was holding Nicky, who was dressed up to visit his uncle, though he did not quite understand why.

"Everything okay?" Lola asked softly.

"Everything is perfect," Nick responded. "I was just waiting for the rest of my family. Now, you are here. I could not be better. Angie and Ludo are the same. I know.

"*Mi familia*," he uttered as he slipped off, having lost the fight with the sedatives being pumped into him intravenously.

"I just spoke with the doctor. He said Nick suffered a mid-level concussion from being knocked out with a piece of pipe. The surgeon removed two .32 auto bullets. One was in his shoulder. The other was in the muscle to the side of his six-pack. He said, due much to Nick's physical condition, the new wounds should heal quickly. They want to watch him for a day and may release him tomorrow afternoon," Lola said.

"What is the condition of the animal who attacked us?" Angie asked. "We have been referring to him in the present and past tenses, not knowing."

"The update on Samir did not come from the doctor directly. Detective Joe Horner gave it to Maria officially, cop to cop. Maria?"

"He apparently is somewhere in the middle between present and past tense. He is in a non-medically induced coma. A Nick-induced coma. His nose is flattened. If he recovers, he will have to have plastic surgery to ever breathe out of it again.

"Most of the seven occipital bones around his eye sockets are broken from blows by Nick's fists. These are very thick, tough bones to break with punches.

"He has trauma to the throat and larynx. How it will heal is unknown as yet.

"He has three broken ribs and one testicle is crushed beyond repair. The docs won't give a prognosis. But Joe does not feel optimistic he will ever interview Samir.

"Not much more to report except the state's attorney is treating it all as justified defense of multiple lives including a child's," Maria reported.

"Ludo, are there any more in the family or even extended family who will want to avenge Samir?"

"No one can be positive. I will say however, nobody liked him or Adin very much. Their crazy mother alienated everybody. There are no more males in the branch. The rest know to listen to Ibro when he says the revenge is over for good. The mother would try if she could, but she had a stroke and is unlikely to be mobile enough. I hear her mental condition is getting worse and worse and soon she will need to be put in some sort of crazy hospital," Ludo said.

"We better all let Nick sleep. The sooner he rests and shows good signs, the sooner he'll be home for the big gala show we have been rehearsing," Erica said.

Each bent over and kissed the sleeping ex-Ranger on the forehead, including Nicky. Even the tough old man who used to be able to stack large truck tires in a pile well over his head with no effort.

Maria missed and hit his lips with hers.

"Give me a second. I will see you shortly," Lola said.

After Erica closed the door to the private room, Lola buried her face in the already damp material on Nick's right shoulder. She let out hours of suppressed emotions all at once, her frame shaking.

After a minute, Nick said in a clear voice, "That's enough, honey. I didn't die, you know!"

She lightly punched him in the shoulder. He flinched.

"Wrong shoulder?" she asked.

"Wrong shoulder. But I love you anyway."

IF YOU LIKE THIS, YOU MAY ALSO ENJOY: TALON

BY BRENT TOWNS

Brace yourself for a roller coaster ride of hardcore action and military strategy in this pulse-pounding adventure straight out of a pulp fiction novel.

When the British government approaches the Global Corporation about stemming the flow of human trafficking across the globe, Hank Jones turns to Mary Thurston to form a team right for the job. The end result is a motley crew of outcasts, dismissed by the world but armed with exceptional talent and indomitable spirit.

Led by disgraced German Intelligence officer Anja Meyer and SAS reject Jacob Hawk, the team is autonomous, utilizing the full force of the Global Corporation and its resources as they trek across different continents in pursuit of their elusive foe —a worldwide phenomenon known as Medusa. Armed with the extensive resources of the Global Corporation, their operation spans across continents, defying danger at every turn.

In this thrilling blend of war, action, and adventure, read along as hardened soldiers face off against a ruthless enemy, discover unconventional methods, seek personal redemption, and experience a relentless pursuit of justice. Talon isn't just military pulp fiction— it's a gritty, high-stakes war against the dark underbelly of society.

So gear up, soldier, and join Anja, Jacob, and the team everyone fears on an audacious crusade by ordering your copy today. Let the action begin!

AVAILABLE NOW

ABOUT THE AUTHOR

G. Wayne Tilman is a full-time author. He is retired from the Federal Bureau of Investigation, and prior to the FBI, he was a Marine, bank security director, deputy sheriff, investigator, and security contractor.

Wayne holds baccalaureate and master's degrees from the University of Richmond and has been an adjunct faculty member there and several other universities. He holds the internationally recognized Certified Protection Professional board certification, generally accepted as the highest in the security profession. He also earned a US Coast Guard 50 Ton Inspected Vessel Master Captain's license.

Wayne writes espionage thrillers, mysteries, and westerns. His impetus to write in those genres comes from both personal experience and heritage—having a direct ancestor who was one of the first sheriffs in America, another forebearer who singlehandedly captured the real Desperado of song fame, and a mother who served as a counter intelligence agent.